A. C. Roberts

THE SUN, THE MOON AND HARRY

By the Same Author:

While Herding Cats, published 2010

A. C. ROBERTS

THE SUN, THE MOON AND HARRY

A Novel

Tudor Clark Publishing

First published in Great Britain, 2016

COPYRIGHT © 2016 by Robert A Clark

The moral right of the author has been asserted

This publication is a work of fiction.
All characters and events in this book are the product of the author's imagination. Any resemblance of characters in this story
to real persons, living or dead, is purely coincidental.

All rights reserved.
No part of this book may be used, transmitted, stored in a retrieval system or reproduced in any form or by any means whatsoever without written permission from the publisher/author, except in the case of brief quotations embodied in critical articles or reviews.

Tudor Clark Publishing
Granville
56 Goldthorn Road
Wolverhampton
Staffs
ISBN 978-1-326-83107-3

For Catherine
The girl I met on November 19th,
1965

Foreword

The Mid-Sixties in Britain

So much has been written, portrayed and said about the 1960s that we can sometimes be lulled into believing that we know what it was like to live through them, even if we didn't – 'if you can remember the sixties you probably weren't there', as the saying goes. However, that decade, which is credited for giving birth to so much of what we take for granted in our modern lives, was a very different time from now. The generation that led the charge into the 'swinging sixties' and the so-called 'permissive society' had grown up with the genuine austerity of post-war Britain in the late 1940s and 1950s – not to be confused with the austerity of modern political rhetoric. The sixties brought many changes for the better, both socially and materially, but it was still a very different world from the one we live in today.

Our story begins in 1965 – when the 'swinging sixties' were well under way – with two students meeting at a college hop. In those days the school leaving age was fifteen, when many youngsters chose to leave school and start work or go into some sort of vocational training. A relatively small proportion of school children took GCE 'O' levels, and even fewer took 'A' levels. A little over ten percent of eighteen-year-olds went on to higher education, and only around a half of those went to universities, the remainder attending colleges of advanced technology, polytechnics, teacher-training colleges, art schools and other specialist institutions. University and college students were, in many ways, an educational elite and were treated as such, having full tuition fees paid by the government, and the majority receiving very generous maintenance grants to see them through their courses, although these were means tested. On the other hand, life was unimaginably unsophisticated by today's standards. There were no computers and no internet; no social media; no mobile phones and thus no texts or emails; no video recorders, DVD machines or game boxes – if you wanted to see a film, you went to the pictures; there were just two, and eventually three, black and white television channels; central heating was still regarded as something of a luxury, as were foreign holidays and home freezers – microwave ovens, automatic washing machines, dishwashers and tumble dryers were all a long way off in the future; and many households had neither a car nor a telephone. If people wanted to communicate other than by speaking to each other face to face, they either wrote a letter or made a telephone call, which would often involve queuing up to use a public call box. Long-distance calls were expensive and only normally made after 6.00 pm when cheaper call charges were in force.

Social and moral attitudes were undoubtedly beginning to change in the sixties, but there was still a significant hangover from more austere times. The age of majority was still twenty-one. Below that age you were legally an 'infant' or minor – unable to vote; unable get married without parental consent; and unable to make a contract which could be enforced against you. The death penalty for murder was only abolished in 1965. Abortion was illegal, as were homosexual acts between men – even consenting adults. The contraceptive pill, which had been introduced in the UK in 1961 for married women, was only made available on prescription for unmarried women in 1974. The welfare benefits that single mothers enjoy today were not available, nor was there the general social acceptance of single parenthood. There was a widely perceived social and moral stigma attached to conceiving out of wedlock, and any unmarried woman or girl who found herself pregnant without the promise of marriage, the support of her family, or financial independence, had very few options open to her. Adoption was the reluctant choice of most young women in this situation, being preferable to the alternative of an illegal, back-street abortion – that is, if you knew how to find a practitioner, could afford the fee and were willing to take the significant risks involved. For those who were married and found themselves ill-suited or profoundly unhappy, divorce was expensive and only available to those who could prove one of the three matrimonial 'offences' – adultery, cruelty or desertion – on the part of their spouse. The concept of 'irretrievable breakdown of marriage' was not introduced until 1969. Employment protection laws and equal opportunities legislation, including laws against sex and racial discrimination were only introduced during the 1970s.

Today we live in a world of credit in which many people believe they have the right to possess things which they do not have the money to buy. The sage words of Mr Micawber are meaningless to them. In 1965, the availability of credit was extremely limited by today's standards. Adults in gainful employment might have access to hire purchase – the so-called 'never-never' – but otherwise you could only get what you had the money to pay for (although the corner shop might let some regular customers buy groceries 'on tick'). There were no credit cards – Barclays Bank introduced the first Barclaycard in 1966 – and no cash machines. Many working people still did not have bank accounts and were paid in cash. Those with bank accounts who needed cash went to their own branch, wrote a cheque and queued up to cash the cheque over the counter – provided that their accounts were in funds. The days of modern consumerism were only just about to begin.

So this is the world that our dramatis personae find themselves in when our story begins in November, 1965. They knew nothing different of course but, compared with today, it was another country.

There's the sun, the moon and Harry
Harry makes me smile
There is sad and there is happy
It will be happy this time
There's tomorrow now and Harry
It's a brand new song
Harry is my love
Harry is the one

Catherine Howe

Part One

YOUTH

Chapter 1
November 1965

'I'm Henry... Henry Irving; people call me Harry. What's your name?'

These were the first words she ever heard him speak. They were dancing together after he had approached her through the cavorting, Friday night throng. The student band belted out a crude cover of a Chuck Berry hit.

'Amy Anderton.'

They had to shout to be heard above the distorted blare of over-amplified pop music.

Amy was just nineteen years old. She had agreed to go to the student hop with her friend, Ginger, who was on the lookout for a boyfriend. Amy already had a boyfriend back home but she was happy enough to give her college room-mate a helping hand in her search for a 'feller', and anyway, she was at a loose end that Friday evening and quite fancied getting dolled up and having a bit of a bop at the university Students' Union. Girls didn't go to dances by themselves, and boys would normally go girl hunting in pairs. And that's how it was that night when Harry's friend, Phil, asked Ginger to dance and Harry homed in on Amy.

They danced until there was a break in the music, when Harry asked Amy if she wanted to go to the bar for a drink. She wanted to. She had seen the sign from Ginger indicating that she was happy with Phil, and so there was nothing to stand in her way – no need to make an excuse to go to the ladies' room. They walked side by side towards the bar which had been set up in a room adjacent to the student refectory where the dance was taking place. He was tall and slim. She wanted to look at him. She hadn't been able to keep her eyes off him while they were dancing, so taken was she with his looks: his thick, straight, floppy brown hair, his dark eyes and broad smile. She liked the way he was dressed too: slim fitting, polo-neck sweater under a black cord jacket. He asked her what she wanted to drink. She asked for a half of bitter. Harry liked that. He smiled and ordered the drinks. They went and found a seat.

'So, Amy Anderton, tell me about yourself. What are you studying?'

She liked his voice: clear, deep and accentless.

'Oh, I'm at the teachers' training college in town… doing science. I'm in my first year.' Amy spoke with a slight northern accent, which Harry found rather charming. 'What do you do?'

'First year classics: Latin and Ancient Greek. Don't laugh, I know it's not everyone's idea of fun. I just happened to be quite good at it at school.'

'That's a bit posh isn't it? I thought they only did classics at Oxford and Cambridge.'

'Well they do it here at Wessex too. And I suppose I am a tiny bit posh really. Is that a problem?' He said this with one of his broad engaging smiles. Amy just smiled back and thought: not in your case.

They sat and talked, completely at ease with each other. Harry found Amy quite enchanting. She was an attractive slim girl with dark shoulder-length hair, arranged in classic mid-sixties style with a deep fringe. She wore a printed dress, cut above the knee, which showed off her nice, American tan legs. But it was her face that beguiled Harry: her bright eyes, her full lips and her delicate nose which she could wiggle slightly like Samantha in *Bewitched*. They were oblivious to the passing of time, the coming and going of Friday night student revellers, and the thundering bass from the pop group in the adjoining room. They asked each other all the usual questions, but there were lots of jokes too and unforced laughter. After about an hour they returned to the dance floor where they danced for a while, holding each other gently in the slower numbers. Then they decided to adjourn to the Union coffee bar where it was quieter and they would find it easier to talk.

During the conversation, and apropos nothing at all, Harry suddenly said, 'By the way, what do you think of The Saxons?' Amy was taken aback.

'Erm... I don't know. I don't know much about them really, only the story of King Alfred and the cakes... and King Canute, of course, but wasn't he a Viking?'

'No... I mean yes, King Canute was a Viking, but I meant the group, the student band. They're called The Saxons. What else would they be called at Wessex University!'

Amy laughed. 'Oh I see... the group. I didn't know they were The Saxons. I see. Well, I hadn't really thought. They're all right I suppose. A bit too noisy but they're okay. Good to dance to.'

'Yes, well they're a bit crude... a bit unsophisticated, but they're the only pop group in the university and I've been trying to join them since Freshers' Week. They won't have me. They say they've been together for two years and are happy as they are, want to stick to being a foursome, but I think they're just a bit snotty about being third years and don't want anything to do with a mere fresher. They've had a couple of try-outs for record companies so they've got potential. No luck yet though. They could do with me: an extra guitar to fill things out a bit, plus some harmony vocals.'

'You play the guitar then?' Amy asked, not desperately interested in the direction the conversation had suddenly taken.

'Yes, I had my own group in the sixth form at school. We were called The Hawks... sometimes Harry and The Hawks.'

Just at that moment a stout young man with thinning hair and a rather unfortunate wispy moustache appeared on the scene. He glared at Harry, completely ignoring Amy, and snarled, 'Where the bloody hell have you been, Irving, and what in God's name are you doing here? You were supposed to meet me outside the Union entrance at eleven. It's now twenty past. My parents are waiting... they're furious.'

This was Hedley Stevens, a first year law student who lived in the same digs as Harry. His parents had come down from London to see some well known actor Harry had never heard of who was appearing in a production of *Twelfth Night* at the on-campus Wessex Theatre. After the show, they were due to take their precious son home to Maida Vale for the weekend. It so happened that Harry had arranged to meet an old school friend in London that Saturday morning and so, when Hedley offered him a free lift up to the capital on Friday evening together with a free night's bed and breakfast at the Stevens' residence, thus saving him a tidy sum in transport and lodging costs, he felt compelled to accept, notwithstanding his dislike for the pompous overbearing Hedley. He could go and stay the night with the Stevens and just hop on a tube the next day to get to the planned mid-morning meeting with his friend, Jon Geary, at the Salisbury pub near Leicester Square. It was Phil who had suggested going together to the Friday night dance at the Students' Union as a way of whiling away the time before Harry's late evening dash to London. Harry had packed a toothbrush in the inside pocket of his corduroy jacket in preparation for the trip.

'Christ, I completely forgot. I'm sorry, Hedley, I'll come right away. This is Amy, by the way.'

Hedley acknowledged Amy with the curtest of nods.

'Come on then, Irving, get moving,' ordered Hedley, 'I've told you, my folks are waiting. My father's in a foul mood because of you, and I've had a devil of a job finding you. It's just as well I ran into Phil in the refectory. He said he thought I'd find you here.'

'Yes... right.' Harry turned to Amy as he reluctantly got to his feet.

'Look, Amy, I'm ever so sorry to leave you like this but I've arranged to go to London with Hedley tonight. This is Hedley, by the way. I'm going to have to dash. Will you be all right getting home? I suppose your friend will be tied up with Phil.'

'I'll be okay,' Amy said, trying with only partial success to put on a brave face and hide her disappointment, not to mention her annoyance, at this unexpected turn of events. 'I'll catch a bus. They run until midnight at weekends.'

Harry stood for a moment looking nervously at Amy and shifting uneasily from foot to foot. Then he said, 'Right, well it's been nice meeting you, Amy. Er... see you around then. Bye.'

Amy said, 'Yes, see you around,' and then watched as Harry turned and walked away with Hedley Stevens towards the coffee bar door. As they walked, Harry looking glum with his shoulders hunched, she could see Hedley continuously berating him, and then the pair passed through the door and out of sight. She sat for a few minutes and drank the remains of a cup of coffee Harry had bought for her. Then she decided there was nothing for it but to make her way back to the college hostel in town where she shared a room with Ginger. However, she needed first to find Ginger and let her know what she was going to do, and so she returned to the student refectory where the dance was still in full swing and found Ginger and Phil on the dance floor. She explained what had happened and said she was off to catch a bus. When Phil heard this, he insisted that he give both Amy and Ginger a lift home in his old Morris Minor. Amy looked quizzically at Ginger, who nodded her agreement to the plan. Amy gratefully accepted Phil's offer.

The girls' hostel was located on a small college campus on the outskirts of the city centre. The college was an all women's Roman Catholic academy, home to some five hundred young women who were training to be teachers, and which consequently had strict rules concerning the admittance of males to its residential quarters: as a general rule, no men were allowed over the threshold of a hostel after seven in the evening. It was run by nuns and gloried in the name of The College of the Immaculate Conception. When Phil and the girls arrived outside the hostel, Amy thought it politic to retreat quickly to her room and wait for Ginger there, thus allowing Ginger time to say goodbye to Phil in whichever way she wanted and, if things had gone well, make arrangements for a future encounter. The room the two girls shared was spacious but sparsely furnished. There were two single divan beds, each pushed up against a wall on opposite sides of the room, a large wardrobe, a couple of chests of drawers, one ancient easy chair and two cheap student writing desks which doubled up as dressing tables. In one corner, the room boasted the luxury of a washbasin and mirror, but all other ablutions had to be performed in the communal bathroom along the corridor. The girls had put up posters on the walls, and the starkness of the room was softened considerably by the presence of their books and other possessions, which included a Dansette record player. Amy started to get ready for bed while she waited for Ginger. Twenty minutes later, her friend appeared.

Ginger was a slight attractive girl from Coventry. She had been named not for the colour of her hair but after her mother's favourite Hollywood star, Ginger Rogers. In fact her hair, which was cut short in an urchin style, was definitely brown. She was wearing a knee length dress and flat shoes. Amy wanted to know how Ginger had got on with Phil. After all, the quest for a boyfriend for Ginger had been the purpose of both girls' visit to the university that evening. Ginger had already worked her way through two boyfriends – Bryan and Bobby – in the nine weeks Amy had known her, and was now on the lookout for a third; perhaps Phil would fit the bill. Ginger told Amy that she had liked Phil, who seemed to be 'a nice boy', but that she didn't really fancy him physically, even though he was 'quite presentable'. They had got on pretty well and she had enjoyed the evening, but the deciding factor in Phil's favour was that he had a car, albeit a rather old unsexy Morris Minor, and, in the light of this, she had decided he would 'do for now'. They had arranged to meet the following evening: Phil would pick her up and take her to the pictures to see *Doctor Zhivago*.

'Did he kiss you goodnight?' Amy asked.

'Yes we had a bit of a snog in the front of his car... but no tongues. He tried but I didn't fancy any of that.

Amy laughed. 'Next time, maybe?'

'Ugh... No thanks. Anyway, tell me what happened to you. You seemed to be getting on like a house on fire with your tall Romeo. I could see you couldn't keep your eyes off him. What would Guy say if he'd seen you, eh?' Guy was Amy's longstanding boyfriend back home in Newark.

'Guy needn't worry, nothing happened. I suppose it could have done. I felt like I'd been swept off my feet. I've never felt like that before... ever. And then the rotten sod suddenly announced he had to dash off to London... at half past eleven at night! Some repulsive little man, a fellow student I think, turned up in a lousy temper and dragged him away. Said his parents were waiting to drive them both to London.' Amy looked forlorn.

'What's he called, your feller?'

'Henry Irving... Harry for short. And he's hardly my feller.'

'Henry Irving! Now there's a name to conjure with. He's that famous Victorian actor. There's a statue of him in Charing Cross Road in London, right by the Portrait Gallery. You must have seen it.'

'No. I've never heard of him.'

'Oh, I suppose you wouldn't have, doing science and all that, but he was the most famous Shakespearian actor of his day.' Ginger's main subject was English Literature.

'Oh well, I guess it doesn't really matter what he's called. He's gone... and anyway, I'm committed to Guy, even if he is a bit boring.'

'I could always try and fix something up for you through Phil. I'm seeing him tomorrow and I can ask him to ask Henry Irving to get in touch with you when he's back from The Smoke. Or you could give me a note for Phil to pass on to him with your address on it.'

'No, I don't think that would be a good idea, really. You know what my plan is for the future and I'm sticking to it. I don't want someone popping up out of the blue and throwing a spanner in the works. Guy is my escape route from the poverty I grew up with and I don't need some handsome dreamer, studying classics of all things, to come along and ruin things... I mean, classics for God's sake, how pointless is that?'

'Having a bit of a fling with Henry Irving needn't ruin anything. Guy's a long way away in Nottinghamshire. This is your chance for a bit of fun... real fun. I can tell how much you fancy him. We could go out as a foursome now and again: me and Phil, and you and Henry Irving.'

'No, Ginger, it'd just be too dangerous.'

'Why, for goodness sake?'

Amy looked at Ginger with a fierce yet knowing look in her eyes, and as a tear rolled down her cheek said, 'It would... it just would.'

* * * *

Harry had phoned Phil at their digs from London, and arranged to meet him for lunch the following Monday in the Bassett Arms, an old pub near the university's main campus. Phil was already there when Harry arrived at the appointed time. He was sitting at a table in the corner of the public bar smoking a cigarette with a pint of beer in front of him, absorbed in solving the *Daily Telegraph* cryptic crossword. Philip Semark was a wiry young man of average height.

He was far from handsome, in fact on a bad day he bore an uncanny resemblance to Mr. Punch, but his redeeming features were his thick dark brown hair, which was always immaculately fashioned into a perfect Beatles' mop top, a rather disarming smile and his impeccable dress sense: a significant private income allowed him to indulge his liking for the latest men's fashions. He was older than Harry, having spent a couple of years working in the family business before going to university to read History. Semark & Company was a successful firm of wine importers based in Kent. Harry greeted his friend before going to the bar and ordering a pint of bitter and a pork pie, after which he sat down at Phil's table. They exchanged pleasantries for a while and then Harry broached the subject of the previous Friday evening.

'So, Phil, how did you get on with your girlie on Friday? Amy said her name was Ginger. Was she okay?'

'She was pretty nice, really. Needed tarting up a bit, of course, but I found her quite attractive, despite those awful flat shoes she was wearing. And I liked her more the longer I talked to her. She's funny…very funny, and I like that. Yes, she's quite a poppet really, although I will have to work on her dress sense… perhaps buy her a few new clothes, if things work out.'

'Did you get anywhere with her?'

'Not very far. We had a big snog in the back of the car when I dropped her off at her hostel. I'll tell you something, she's a fab French kisser. And I managed to get my hand on her tits for a while. Outside only, mind you. Probably as much as I could expect when we'd only just met, and anyway, her friend Amy was waiting inside for her, so I didn't have long.'

Harry seized the opportunity to talk about Amy. 'Amy got home safely, then? I was quite worried about her. Did you see her?'

'Gave her a lift home with Ginger. She very considerately went straight inside when we got back to the hostel, so I could take my leave of Ginger in appropriate fashion.'

Before Harry could pursue matters, Phil launched into a blow by blow account of his Saturday night date with Ginger, prattling on for a frustratingly long time and giving precise and probably over-embellished details of how much progress he had made in his sexual advances towards Ginger on the back seat of the Morris Minor, although when it came down to it, he only seemed to have got as far as 'upstairs inside' – that is if he was to be believed at all. Eventually the story ended and Harry determined that he would now keep the conversation focused firmly on Amy.

'Um... did Ginger have anything to say about me and Amy?'

'Not really. She seemed quite amused by your name when Amy told her what it was,' Phil took a long drag on his cigarette and exhaled. 'She says you're named after some sort of famous actor or something.'

'Is that all?' Harry looked downcast. 'Didn't she say whether Amy fancied me, or wanted to see me again, or at least wanted me to get in touch?'

'Nope.'

'Bugger... Bugger, bugger, bugger!'

'Look, Harry,' Phil put his hand on Harry's shoulder, 'I didn't want to tell you this, and I didn't really think you'd be that bothered anyway, but Ginger told me that Amy had said she didn't want to see you again. Apparently she's got a boyfriend up north somewhere who she's been going out with for yonks. Apparently Ginger offered to pass on a message to you, via yours truly, but Amy said no. So that's that... or so it would seem.'

'Damnation!' Harry was visibly upset.

'Cheer up, old sport,' Phil said, trying his best to look sympathetic. 'In any case, you've been telling me ever since we've known each other – which is only a couple of months, I know – but you've been telling me, over and over, that the last thing on earth you want is to get tied up with some bird; that your top priorities in life are to get laid and make it as a rock singer… and not necessarily in that order. So I don't quite see your problem.'

'Well, it would have been pretty damn nice to have got laid by Amy.'

'I'm sure it would. She's a bit of a cracker, no doubt about it, but she's already got a bloke, and anyway there are plenty more fish in the sea… five hundred of them down at the Immaculate Contraception or whatever it's called.'

There was a long pause.

'Oh well, I'm sure you're right,' Harry said at last. 'There's that chirpy little Scouse girl in Languages who seems to like flirting with me. Maybe I'll try and see where I can get with her later in the week. And I'm going to have another crack at joining The Saxons.'

Phil patted Harry on the back and said, 'That's more like it, old sport,' and then started talking about his latest clothes purchases.

Harry sat quietly, pretending to listen and nodding occasionally, while Phil talked on enthusiastically, flitting from one subject to another: men's clothes, rugby, wine, Christmas, Ginger. Harry just sat there, but all he could think about was one thing… one person.

Chapter 2
Three Weeks Earlier: Amy

Guy Boucher pulled into the car park at Newark station in his Ford Cortina, a twenty-first birthday present from his parents. He had come to meet Amy who was due to arrive by train at four that afternoon. She was coming home for the weekend, half way through her first term at college on the south coast. Guy had not seen her for six weeks and was looking forward to having her back: he disliked the fact that she was living so far away, and missed having the prettiest girl he knew on his arm when he was out and about, attracting admiring and envious glances from other men. They had exchanged letters once a week and spoken a couple of times on the telephone, but that was all – Amy only had access to one telephone at college, a pay-phone in the student common room for which there always seemed to be a queue. He parked the car and looked at his watch: three-forty – he was twenty minutes early. He decided to go and wait for Amy on the platform. He got out of the car, locked up and walked across the car park to the booking office. He checked the arrivals timetable on the notice board to find the right platform for Amy's train, bought a platform ticket from a nearby machine and walked out onto the platform. He found a vacant bench, sat down and lit a cigarette.

   Guy was twenty-two, nearly four years older than Amy. They had been going out together for six months. He was an incongruous looking young man: at a time when the swinging sixties were approaching full throttle, he presented himself to the world like a middle-aged man from the nineteen-fifties. He invariably wore either a tailored suit or grey flannel trousers together with a tweed jacket and club tie; his shoes, very often brogues, were always impeccably polished; and his almost black hair was cut in the classic 'Brylcreem Boy' style of the fifties: short back and sides, slicked back on top. And yet he was not at all bad looking: he was slim, above average height for a man and almost handsome in a baby-faced sort of way. In the estimation of those who knew him, he was a book that could very much be judged by its cover, for his old fashioned, staid appearance matched his personality and outlook on life almost to perfection – or so it seemed. This manifested itself in his physical relationship with Amy, which had never progressed beyond brief, and almost gratuitous, tight-lipped necking sessions, normally in his car. But he was committed to Amy, whom he regarded as a catch far beyond his imagining, and he was determined to keep her at all costs.

More or less on time, Amy's train approached the platform and slowly shuddered to a halt. Guy got to his feet and started to scan the crowd of emerging passengers for his girlfriend's face. Suddenly she was there, wearing a duffle coat and jeans, carrying a small suitcase and looking straight at Guy with a broad enchanting smile. He went towards her and took her suitcase. They embraced and kissed each other chastely on the lips. They chatted animatedly as he walked her to his car for the ten minute drive to Amy's home: a small semi on a suburban estate.

Amy's mother, Doris Anderton, was watching from the bay window in the living room at the front of the house when the Ford Cortina pulled up outside. She was a plump pretty woman in her late forties, with greying permed hair. Her husband, Amy's father, had died from lung cancer eight years earlier when Amy was ten, leaving Doris to bring up Amy and her fourteen year old brother on a small widow's pension and her modest earnings, working as a part-time assistant at the local library. Fortunately, there had been an endowment policy which had paid off the mortgage on the house, and so she had been able to keep the family home. It had been a difficult time for the middle-aged widow, who was fundamentally a kind hearted, gentle soul – and sometimes a little dizzy – but she had somehow managed to steel herself to the task of raising her children and maintaining her independence without having to call upon her wealthy older sister, Harriet, who had married a successful Wolverhampton solicitor. Aunt Harriet had, however, provided the two children with the occasional treat and the three seaside holidays they had enjoyed since the tragedy of their father's untimely demise.

Amy looked up at the house and waved when she saw her mother standing at the window. Doris waved back and then went straight to the front door to welcome her beloved daughter home after her long six week absence. She opened the door and Amy ran into her arms, while Guy kept a discreet distance behind her.

'Welcome home, my lovely little baby… welcome home!' exclaimed Doris, hugging her daughter tightly. 'How wonderful you're home. Let me look at you. Let me see. Oh you do look well, you do look well, my little sweetheart. They must be feeding you properly down at that college.' Amy loved her mother dearly, even though she often found her ways exasperating – she understood full well the sacrifices Doris had made to keep the family together and to nurture her. She melted happily into the soft embrace of her mother's ample bosom.

'Hello, Mum. It's lovely to be home. How are you?'

'All the better for seeing you, my darling… and look, Guy's here. Come along in, Guy, come in. Don't stand out there in the cold. There's a nice fire going in the front room… come in and get warm. It's so good of you to collect Amy from the station.'

'That's my pleasure, Mrs Anderton. We are courting after all and it wasn't too difficult to get out of the office for an hour this afternoon, although I shall have to get back before closing time at five-thirty. Dad's asked me to lock up for him.'

They all walked through the small reception hall into the front sitting room, where a fire was blazing in the hearth. Doris asked the young couple to sit down while she went into the kitchen to make a cup of tea and fetch the 'fat rascals' she had baked specially for Amy's homecoming. Amy and Guy sat down together on the sofa and held hands. Amy's home was spotlessly clean but it was plain to see that money was in very short supply: the furnishings and fabrics were old, faded and worn; the once white paintwork was yellowed and chipped; the few rugs and carpets that Doris possessed were threadbare; and the only sources of heat in the modest semi-detached property were the coal fire in the front sitting room and an anthracite boiler in the kitchen. After a while, Doris shouted from the kitchen, 'Amy, there's some post for you in the hall if you want to go and fetch it. There's an airmail letter from Australia too.' Amy got up and went to collect her mail. She rather wished her mother hadn't mentioned a letter from Australia – she knew who must have sent it. She returned with her mail, put it on the mantle piece and sat down again next to Guy.

'I'll open them when you're gone, Guy. I know you haven't got long,' Amy said.

'Yes, of course.' There was a pause. 'An airmail letter, your mum says... from Australia. That sounds exciting. Who's it from?'

'Well I won't know till I've opened it, will I?' Amy said with an icy edge to her voice, and then more softly, 'I expect it'll be from an old friend of mine. The whole family emigrated to Queensland last spring. She said she'd write when they got settled.' Guy seemed happy with this and changed the subject. Doris returned with her tray of refreshments, and the three of them sat round the fire and chatted while they consumed their afternoon tea. After a while Guy said that he'd better be getting back to the office to do a few jobs before the staff went home and he locked up for the night. He thanked Doris for the tea and took his leave of Amy who had walked him to the front door, but not before confirming the arrangements for the next day: a shopping expedition in the afternoon to buy Amy a new evening dress which she would wear to the Young Conservatives' formal dinner dance that evening.

Amy and Doris sat down together and talked for an hour or so, almost exclusively about life on the south coast at the College of the Immaculate Conception. Doris was a staunch Roman Catholic – although her husband had eschewed religion – and it had been her wish that Amy should go to a 'safe', single-sex, Catholic institution when it came to applying for college places. Amy had, of course, written home every week but Doris still wanted her to go over and elaborate upon all the happenings she had related in her letters. Then Amy helped her mother clear away the tea things before going upstairs to her old bedroom to unpack her suitcase and open her mail. Amy's bedroom was a tiny room at the front of the house – about seven feet square – just big enough to accommodate a single divan bed and bedside table, a small fitted wardrobe and some painted bookshelves. She put her case down in a corner, sat on the bed and looked at the letters: two bank statements, a card from her brother and an airmail envelope. She put the two letters from the bank and her brother's card to one side and studied the airmail envelope for a while before deciding to open it. This is what it said:

Dear Amy

I hope that you're keeping well. I'm sorry it has taken me so long to write, as I promised I would when we said goodbye, but life has been pretty hectic since we left England for Australia. First the long sea journey down here, then settling in at our new home, then making new friends and, of course, getting fixed up with a place at university here in Brisbane to study Economics. The academic year doesn't start here until January, so I'm working for Dad till then.

I expect you will now be well into your first term at college. I hope you're liking it, and doing well too. How did you get on in your 'A' levels? Anyway, life here in Queensland is pretty fantastic. The weather's great, the people are very friendly and there's lots going on. The beaches are fabulous and the swimming is great – you'd love it.

Enough of that, my main reason for writing is to tell you how much I enjoyed our week together last Easter, when you were staying with your aunt in Wightwick. I'll never forget the time we spent together and how lovely you were. I've had a lot to think about since we moved here, but you're always there in my thoughts. I don't think I've ever met a girl like you, in fact I know I haven't, and it's such a shame that we're now separated by thousands of miles of ocean. I hope one day I can make it back to England to see you again, or maybe you'll be able come out here to Queensland – you never know.

I hope you feel about me the same way I feel about you but, however you feel, please write back and let me know how you're getting on. I'll write again anyway.

All for now,

Lots of love

Danny
xxxxx

Amy read the letter several times before putting it down on the bedside table. Then she lay back on her bed, closed her eyes and allowed her mind to wander back to the previous Easter when she was spending the second week of her school holiday with Aunt Harriet at her big mock-Tudor house in the posh Wolverhampton suburb of Wightwick. Her Aunt, who had no children of her own, had invited Amy to stay so that she could have more peace, quiet and space in which to revise for her forthcoming 'A' level examinations. It was a week she would always remember:

Greengage Hill was a private suburban road of distinctly bucolic character. The substantial detached properties which ran along either side were set well back from the road behind high hedges in extensive grounds, all boasting manicured lawns and an abundance of mature trees and shrubbery. Aunt Harriet's house was a rambling, five-bedroom, mock-Tudor edifice, built in the nineteen-twenties. It had a long gravel drive leading up to the half-timbered façade and double garage. Next door there lived the Swift family in another mini-mansion, this one of neo-Georgian design. Mr Swift, originally from Australia but married to an Englishwoman, was a successful chartered accountant who had decided to sell up and move back to Queensland with his family, in order to take up a senior partnership with one of Brisbane's leading accountancy firms. His son, Danny Swift, had left boarding school at Christmas, having secured a place at Cambridge to study Economics. However, he had decided to forgo the privilege of a Cambridge education in order to go with his family to Australia. He was in residence at the Swift homestead when Amy Anderton arrived, just after Easter in the April of 1965, to spend the week with her indomitable aunt.

Harriet Ostime was an erect, handsome woman in her mid-fifties. Unlike her younger sister, Doris, she was a formidable personality whom few people, including her husband, Cyril, were prepared to gainsay. However, although she often came across as stern and uncompromising, she was a generous woman, capable of considerable charm and affection in the right circumstances. Having never had a family of her own, she was particularly fond of her sister's two children, and Amy was her favourite. She had decided that Amy's visit should not be exclusively limited to school work –

all work and no play etcetera – and thought it would be beneficial and a pleasant antidote to work for Amy to spend some time with her neighbour's son, who was only slightly older than Amy and was no longer away at boarding school. She was not concerned about any foolish romance developing between the pair, believing Danny to be a mature, charming and sensible young man who, in any event, was shortly to leave England for a new life in the antipodes. To this end she had invited Danny round for afternoon tea on the day of Amy's arrival so that the two could meet again – they had played together from time to time in the school holidays as small children, when Amy was in Wolverhampton staying with her aunt – and perhaps plan to see each other now and then: they might watch television together or play cards or maybe go for walks in the nearby coppice.

Amy and Danny saw a lot of each other that fine spring week. Amy would spend each morning at her school books and then in the afternoon Danny would call for her and they would go out somewhere, often for a walk in the coppice. Amy would return for high tea around half past five, after which she would spend another couple of hours revising. Danny would then come round at eight o'clock and spend the rest of the evening with Amy, returning to his parents' house at about half past ten. Most evenings they would watch television or play records on the radiogram under the watchful eye of Amy's aunt, but on two occasions Aunt Harriet and Uncle Cyril went out, leaving them alone together. Danny really fancied Amy, not just because she was very pretty but also because of her sweet, unsophisticated, girl-next-door ways. He made it his task to get as far as he could with her in the seduction stakes. The virginal Amy remained a maiden that week but she went further with Danny than she had ever done before with a boy – or would do again for some time to come.

Amy didn't love Danny – she wasn't even sure she really liked him. He was a handsome, athletic, blue-eyed, blond youth who gave the impression of being experienced and sophisticated beyond his years. He was a smooth talker who believed he could charm his way into any girl's underwear – or anywhere else: he firmly believed he had smooth talked his way into being offered a place at Cambridge when he went there for interview, because his 'A' level grades had been far from outstanding. Amy didn't care for glibness. She liked straightforward, plain speaking in boys – or anyone else, for that matter – neither was she particularly attracted to blond men, but she enjoyed her time with Danny and looked forward to seeing him: he was, for the most part, good company – interesting and entertaining; she liked the attention he always paid her; and he was different from the other boys she knew – more dashing, more sophisticated, more dangerous. Most importantly, there was something about him – and she couldn't explain exactly what it was – that aroused her animal instincts and stirred her dormant sexuality, and so when Danny began to make amorous advances towards her, she found it impossible to resist. He was the only boy ever to have touched her intimately – she liked it and wanted more – but she remained sufficiently in control of herself to prevent things from going all the way. In ensuing years, on the odd occasion when Amy felt the need to pleasure herself, it was often Danny Swift who was the subject of her fantasy.

The week at Aunt Harriet's house came to an end and it was time for Amy to return to Newark, something she would do with mixed emotions: on the one hand, she was resentful at having to give up her newly discovered delight in erotic pleasure; on the other, she was quite looking forward to being free of Danny who was just beginning to irritate her with his urbane, obsequious and sometimes overbearing presence. It had been arranged that Danny would drive Amy to Wolverhampton Station in his mother's car, which he duly did. When the couple parted company on the station platform – with a fairly passionate kiss and Danny promising to write as soon as he got to Australia – Amy boarded the train and settled in for her journey home, happy that she had experienced her unexpected and self-revelatory holiday fling, but also happy that it was now over and that Danny Swift would soon be far away, on the other side of the world. Three weeks later, she agreed to go out on a date with Guy Boucher, the persistent older brother of her school friend, Liz.

Amy was roused from her reverie by the sound of her mother calling up the stairs, 'Amy... Amy, my love, are you there? It's time to come down. Amy, sweetheart, are you there... I've cooked us some food. It's Friday fish.'

'All right, Mum, I'm coming. I'll just go to the bathroom and wash my hands and face.'

The two women dined together on home-cooked fish and chips with parsley sauce. Then they settled in for the rest of the evening by the fireside in the front room, watching television and chatting from time to time. Doris was filled with happiness at having her daughter's company for the evening once again. She had missed Amy greatly, having been on her own for the previous six weeks, with her son, Roger, permanently away in the Royal Navy and Amy away for the first time at college. She had found being on her own very hard indeed. Amy was also filled with a warm glow from being at home again with her lovely mum whom she loved so much. She had liked being away at college and the freedom and autonomy that gave her, but she had also experienced bouts of homesickness, living such a long way from home for the first time, and it was wonderful to be back. She wanted to go out into the world and experience things but, just at that moment, home was very much where her heart was.

The next day, Saturday, went very much according to plan – until later in the evening, that is. Amy spent the morning at home with her mother, helping with various chores, while Guy was busy working at the family business: Bulstrode and Boucher, the area's leading firm of auctioneers and estate agents. After lunch, Guy called for Amy in his car and took her into town to go shopping. They spent the afternoon looking round the best shops Newark had to offer. Amongst other things, Amy chose, and Guy paid for, a lovely evening dress for her to wear to the dance that evening. Although Guy was thrifty by nature, he enjoyed spending money on his girlfriend and seeing the delight on her face when he bought her something she really liked. He knew she had been brought up on very short commons, while he had always inhabited a world of plenty, and so buying Amy her first posh party frock gave him a tremendous kick. In fact, Amy was no longer quite as impoverished as she had been throughout her childhood and early teens. She had spent the summer before going to college working in the local department store, and had been able to save much of what she had earned; and now she was at college, she received a generous student maintenance grant which meant she never really went short of anything. She had also been given some money by her Aunt Harriet to help her through college. Nevertheless, Guy had plenty of money and Amy didn't – and, to some extent, this is what kept them together.

After the shopping spree, at about five o'clock, Guy drove Amy home so that she had plenty of time to get ready for the function later that evening. He dropped her off and then went back to his parents' house to make his own preparations, before returning a couple of hours later to collect Amy and drive her to the ball. It was being held at Loxley Hall Country Club, about a twenty minute drive from Amy's house. They chatted casually as they went, but Amy could feel the excitement and tension mounting inside her.

The ball lived up to all of Amy's expectations. She felt like a princess as she entered the glittering ballroom, bustling with immaculately dressed, well-heeled, young men and women from the area's wealthier families. She had taken great care in her preparations: bathing, shampooing, arranging her hair, meticulously applying her make-up, and then getting dressed in her beautiful new party frock and putting on her one pair of heels. She was wearing some earrings and a few items of jewellery she had borrowed from Aunt Harriet especially for the occasion, and was carrying a delicate little evening purse which her mother had been given as a twenty-first birthday present. She thought that Guy looked handsome in his dinner suit and cummerbund, and she liked very much his attentive demeanour during the course of the evening, and the thoughtful, yet unobtrusive, way in which he looked after her. She loved the attention and compliments she received from many of the other party-goers, both male and female, and felt a wonderful sense of elation at being present on such an occasion – wining, dining and dancing with Newark's young elite. There were one or two people she already knew, including her old school friend, Liz Boucher, who was there with her boyfriend, and so she never felt out of her depth, despite the newness and splendour of it all.

Amy was having the best time of her young life when, towards the end of the evening, Guy asked her to go with him to the Library, a quiet room at the other end of the building, because there was something he wanted to discuss with her in private. She was reluctant to go at first, aware that the party would be over at midnight and there wasn't long to go, but Guy looked so smart in his formal attire and had been so kind and caring towards her throughout the day and evening that she didn't take much persuading. They walked down a long corridor to the Library, which they found deserted, and sat down together on one of the sofas. Guy took Amy's hand. There was a prolonged pause while they sat looking at each other and Guy gathered his thoughts before speaking.

'Amy, there's something important I want to say to you… um, yes. Well the thing is, Amy…' He dried up. There was another long pause while Amy looked at him encouragingly, then he continued,

'You see I'm not quite used to this sort of thing and I don't know quite how to put it.'

'Don't worry, Guy,' Amy said kindly. 'Don't worry. You can say whatever you like. It's only me you're talking to.'

'Yes, I know, Amy, it's just that I'm finding this a bit more difficult than I thought it would be.'

'Come on, Guy,' Amy said, starting to get a little flustered. 'Spit it out. Say what you've got to say and let's get back to the dance. It'll be over soon and I don't want to miss it. I'm having such a lovely time, Guy, so please say what's on your mind and let's get back.'

'All right, Amy. It's like this… I've missed you very much while you've been away at college, and I'm just not seeing enough of you…'

'But you knew from the start that I was going away to college in September,' Amy interrupted. 'I told you on our very first date that I was going and we've talked about it lots of times since.'

'Yes, but that was before you went. It's different when you're away. I miss you. I need you and I want you here with me. I don't like you being all those miles away at college, not knowing what you're doing… what you're getting up to.'

Amy bridled. 'What do you mean, "getting up to"? I'm at an all girls' Catholic teacher-training college for God's sake – there are no boys there. We promised each other before I went away that we would stay girlfriend and boyfriend and that neither of us would go out with anybody else… and I've had no difficulty sticking to that. I hope you've been the same. And I'm very upset that you don't seem to trust me.'

'Well, there are all those men at the university; you've told me about them in your letters. Anyway, that's not the point… and I do trust you. The point is, I miss you and I want you here with me. I want you to leave college and come back home so we can be together. Amy… I want you to marry me.'

Amy was stunned. This was the last thing she expected Guy to say, and probably the last thing she wanted to hear. In fact, she didn't want this heavy conversation at all. She wanted some fun – she wanted to get back to the ballroom and dance. After a while she said very softly, 'Look, Guy, I'm only eighteen... yes, I know it's my birthday in a couple of weeks, but I'll still only be nineteen. I can't get married yet. I owe it to Mum, and to Aunt Harriet, to finish my course and get qualified. And anyway, I've promised myself I won't get married until I'm at least twenty-three and seen a bit of the world. I can't settle down until I've had some fun and achieved something in my own right.' By this time, Amy realised that all was lost as far as the party was concerned – the evening was ruined – and so she said, 'Tell me what you want, Guy. What exactly is it you have in mind? When were you thinking we would get married?'

'Next summer, after I've passed my final Chartered Surveyors' exams,' enthused Guy, encouraged by Amy's question. 'I'll be twenty-three by then and have a proper professional position in the firm, and a good salary. I'll be a partner before I'm thirty in one of the most profitable businesses in this part of Nottinghamshire, so you'll never want for anything: house, car, holidays, clothes... you name it. You can leave college now, come back to Newark and start making preparations for the wedding. You won't need a qualification because you'll never need to take a job. I'll look after you, you can have anything you want, but if you want to work while you're waiting to get married, Dad will find you a job in the business.'

'Oh yes... and what have your parents got to say about all of this?'

'They think it's a great idea. I've discussed it with them a number of times since you've been away. Of course, I want to speak to your mother as well and ask her permission to marry you, but Mum and Dad are all for it. They like you very much and they know you're a good Catholic girl. Just think, Amy, you'll be marrying into one of the leading Catholic families in the county. And my parents can't wait to be grandparents – Dad says he thinks you'll make the perfect mother for his grandchildren. Can't you see, Amy, it's absolutely perfect and it will make me so happy. Please, Amy, say you'll be my wife.

The idea of becoming a baby machine providing grandchildren for Mr and Mrs Boucher appalled Amy and, if a final straw were needed, that was it. Her immediate reaction to Guy's proposition was to finish with him there and then, but she managed to keep her emotions under control and take a few moments to collect her thoughts before responding. Amy had a dilemma: she didn't want to lose Guy as a boyfriend but she most certainly wasn't ready to get married and have children. Since the age of fourteen, she had been trying to devise a plan to escape the austerity she had grown up with and begin to enjoy some of the good things in life. She was not avaricious by nature – she had always been a happy-go-lucky, sweet-natured child – but over her teenage years she had developed a steely will to better herself. Going to college and qualifying as a teacher was part of the plan but she knew that working as a science teacher in a secondary modern school was not going to be enough to yield the sort of lifestyle she yearned for. She did not expect to be super rich but she did want to feel well off: to have the sort of life that her friend, and Guy's sister, Liz Boucher had – and Aunt Harriet too, for that matter. When Guy came along and she eventually gave in to his persistent requests for a date, she soon began to realise that he might well be the answer. She certainly didn't love Guy but she liked him well enough: he was always kind, thoughtful and attentive, and he was quite good looking in an old fashioned sort of way. For the most part she enjoyed his company and looked forward to seeing him, although she had had to admit to herself that she thought of him more as a brother than a lover. But, if she could hang onto him, she might grow to love him, and they might well be married one day.

'Look, Guy,' Amy said softly, after a long silence, 'I'm not going to promise to marry you. I'm nowhere near ready for it yet. I'm going to go back to college and I'm going to finish my course. I want us to stay girlfriend and boyfriend and be true to each other, and I hope you do too, and I'm sure there's a good chance we will get married one day, but I'm too young to make a commitment now. So let's try and get to see each other more often and make things work better for you... for both of us'

Guy looked crestfallen. After a few moments, he put his hand into his trouser pocket and produced a small jeweller's box, which he opened to reveal a sparkling diamond ring. He said, 'All right, Amy, I won't press you any further about getting married, but can we at least get engaged. Look, I've bought you this ring. Let's get engaged, then I'll know you're truly mine.'

Amy looked at the ring in amazement. Just for a moment she thought: yes, take the ring, it's gorgeous; get engaged and flaunt it in front of all your friends when you get back to college; get engaged and make the commitment. But she hesitated, and when, for no apparent reason, an image of Danny Swift flashed across her mind, reminding her there was another world out there, she knew for certain that it was impossible. She told Guy firmly that she couldn't accept the ring. But he persisted and, in the end, they reached a compromise. They agreed that Amy would take the ring but not wear it. They would remain a courting couple and, if they were still together in twenty months' time when Amy finished her second year at college, they would get engaged then – and she would wear his ring – with a view to marrying two years later when Amy would be twenty-two. In the meantime they would find ways of seeing each other more often when she was away during term time.

When they returned to the ballroom, everyone had gone, except for one or two members of staff who were busy tidying up and clearing things away. They collected their coats from the cloakroom and made their way to Guy's car for the journey home. The next morning, Guy called at the Anderton house to collect Amy and her mother so that they could all go to eleven o'clock mass together. After church he took them out for Sunday lunch at the King's Arms Hotel in Newark, and early in the afternoon he drove Amy to the station for her long train ride back to the south coast. She spent most of the journey reflecting on the events of the previous night – indeed, she had thought of little else since. Should she have followed her initial instinct to break free and finish with Guy? Should she have given in and agreed to leave college and get married, thereby securing her future beyond doubt? Should she, at least, have accepted the ring and got engaged? A torrent of conflicting thoughts went through her mind. In the end she satisfied herself that she had done the right thing or, at least, the best thing for herself. It seemed she had managed to secure the best of both worlds: she had kept her independence while still having Guy as her boyfriend and possible passport to a better future – any fleeting thoughts she may have had of Danny Swift had evaporated. The further away she got from Newark the more she started to relax and, by the time she was approaching her destination, she was feeling remarkably content. She would stick with Guy, get on with her academic studies and have some fun with her girl friends at college.

Later that evening, in her room at the student hostel, Amy had just finished relating the story of her weekend to a fascinated Ginger.

'So, you're engaged then?' was Ginger's assessment of events.

'No, Ginger, I told you: I haven't promised to marry him and I won't wear his ring.'

'I see… but you've got his ring – and a very nice one it is too – and you say you've decided to stick with Guy and that you may well get married to him in a few years' time… and in the meantime you're going to live like a nun while you're away at college, instead of having a bit of fun. That sounds like being engaged to me. And what's more, you say you don't even love him!'

'No, but I like him: he's kind and thoughtful and steady... and he's nice looking.'

'Well, I could never marry someone I didn't love. Anyone who gets wed for reasons other than love – or possibly lust – is destined for a lifetime of misery, mark my word.' Ginger was two years older than Amy and considered herself to be something of a woman of the world.

'You can talk, Ginger. What about you and Bobby? You only go out with him because he's got a car and a good job, not because you love him... not because you want to be Bobby's girl.' Amy said this with a sweet smile.

'That's different, Amy. "Going out with" is not the same as "getting engaged to". It's having a bit of fun with a lad who's got a few bob to spend and doesn't mind spending it on you. Anyway, I'm getting a bit fed up with Bobby... I think it'll soon be time to move on. And another thing: what's all this about being a "good Catholic girl"... and marrying into some bloody silly "leading Catholic family", for goodness sake?'

'Oh I know that's nonsense. I sometimes think I only go to church out of habit and don't really believe in all that Catholic mumbo jumbo... but that's not the point. What you don't seem to understand, Ginger, is what it was like for me and my brother growing up in Newark. We had nothing. You had two parents, both with decent jobs; you had holidays and clothes, pocket money and days-out, birthday parties and proper presents at Christmas. I want to have all these things and more... for myself and my children, if I ever have any. And if I stick with Guy, I might just get them.'

Ginger got up and walked over to Amy who was sitting on her bed. She sat down next to her, put her arm round her and said softly but earnestly, 'Listen to me, Amy: you're a very pretty girl – much prettier than me, damn it – and there are hundreds of men out there who would fancy you… and not just fancy you, they'd give their eyeteeth to have you as a girlfriend. I sometimes think I fancy you myself, only I'm not of the sapphic persuasion. So please don't waste it all. Make the most of it while you've got it, my sweet, because it won't last for ever.' She kissed Amy gently on the forehead.

The two girls talked for a while longer and then got ready for bed. After lights out, Amy lay on her back, reflecting once again on what had happened during her momentous weekend. She felt very fortunate to have found a friend like Ginger in her first term at college and glad to be back with her in their student room. She loved her mother and her home very much but, just then, she felt relieved and happy to be many, many miles from her hometown and Guy, and all that they entailed. She felt grown up and liberated – she was her own woman, in control of her own life. She turned onto her side, made herself comfortable and was soon fast asleep.

Chapter 3
November 1964: Harry

Steam rose from the communal trough, occupied by five naked young men luxuriating in the embrace of deep, hot, muddy water after their exertions on the rugby field during a cold, wet, November Saturday afternoon. There were three such troughs in the high-ceilinged, vapour-filled, Victorian changing room, all containing the bare bodies of members of the Regis College 1st XV who had just defeated their arch rivals, Barton School, in a hard fought close encounter on a pitch that was little more than a sea of mud. There was a tangible sense of exhilaration among the players at having come out on top in their annual grudge match. Henry Irving rose to his feet, climbed from the trough and walked naked and dripping to a row of showers, located along a tiled wall on one side of the room, in order to rinse himself off. He dried himself, got dressed in his prefect's uniform, stored in a locker on the far side of the room, and went to one of the heavily misted mirrors where he cleared a patch of glass with his hand before combing his still wet hair. He exited through a side door and emerged from the humid warmth of the changing room into the teeming rain and ice-cold wind of a late autumn Gloucestershire evening, and then ran across a long grassy terrace towards the east wing of the old main-school buildings which accommodated Beauchamp House, Harry's term-time home for over four years. He entered the building through an arched basement doorway and climbed a stone staircase to the main floor. He strode to the end of a long corridor where the prefects' common room was located and there he found Jon Geary, his good friend and fellow member of Harry and the Hawks, in the process of brewing tea and making toast, in anticipation of Harry's arrival.

'Here he is then, the Cliff Morgan of Regis College 1st XV... bang on time. I hear we won. How did you enjoy rolling around in freezing mud all afternoon? I understand it's very good for the brain.' Jon despised rugby union, a sport he regarded as fit only for thugs and perverts.

'Very funny! I can see you managed to keep warm and dry... and if you want to know, it was actually a very exciting and hard fought victory. I feel quite elated.'

It was a longstanding convention at Regis College that boys not engaged in Saturday afternoon sport should turn out to watch the 1st XV play, if there was a home match, whatever the weather. In order to avoid this, Jon had managed to secrete himself away in one of the college music rooms for the duration of the afternoon before going to the common room at about five o'clock to prepare their teatime snack. Jon was a powerfully built youth with rugged facial features who had once been the school's under-fifteen boxing champion. However, on entering the sixth form he had decided to eschew sport in favour of more aesthetic pursuits, in particular music, at which he excelled – his ability to play a number of instruments to a high standard, coupled with a rich baritone singing voice, had earned him a choral scholarship to Oxford, which he would be taking up the following academic year. However, despite his undoubted musical gifts, he still very much enjoyed thrashing the drums in Harry's fairly basic pop group.

'I've made us some tea, and there's some toast on the go,' Jon said, passing Harry a mug of tea and taking one for himself. They went and sat down on a couple of the leather armchairs that were scattered haphazardly about the room

'I'm sorry to hear about your letter from Cambridge,' Jon went on, changing the subject from rugby. 'It's a bit of a bugger, I'm sure.'

Harry had received a rejection letter from Emmanuel College in the post that morning.

'Oh well, I'm not really surprised. I don't think the classics prof was particularly impressed with my enthusiasm for modern pop music, which I suppose I went on about a bit too much at the interview. He seemed much more interested in knowing what I thought about Caesar's *Gallic Wars* and Ovid's poetry, and as I didn't have any sort of opinion on either, and wasn't able to make one up – well, not a plausible one anyway – I guess I was pretty much doomed to failure. Now, if he'd wanted to ask me about The Beach Boys or Johnny Kidd and The Pirates or even Billy Fury, things might have been different.'

'So, what do you think you'll do?'

'I'll take up the place I've been offered at Wessex... which is fine, but I'm really pissed off about that bastard, Swift, managing to con his way into Trinity. His exam grades were no better than mine, pretty much the same in fact, but he still managed to pull the wool over their eyes with his smarmy smooth-talking bullshit, and get offered a place. As far as I can work out, adults – and girls too, for that matter – don't seem to be able to see through the poncy bastard. That's how he became house captain, I suppose. But I know all about Danny Swift: he's nothing but a sadistic bully... a complete shit.'

Because Harry had come to Regis College as a scholarship boy, having won one of two annual awards reserved for the sons of Church of England clergymen, he had been put into a higher year group so that the level of teaching would match his perceived academic ability. He had found himself in a class of older boys who had already established themselves at the school and forged friendships. He was a small, physically immature thirteen-year-old, whereas most of his peers were fourteen or fifteen, many of whom had developed men's voices, started to shave and generally grown bigger and stronger. One of these was Danny Swift, who had taken it into his head to bully Harry. He had persistently picked on the younger, much weaker new boy, taunting him with names such as 'piss-poor pauper' and 'little orphan bastard' – he had discovered that Harry was the adopted son of the Reverend and Mrs Irving – and he would regularly and gratuitously punch him, often in the solar plexus, causing severe winding. Danny Swift's bullying of Harry during his first term at Regis had become almost unbearable, but when Jon Geary befriended Harry shortly before Christmas, the tide had very quickly turned. It soon became apparent that having Jon as a friend was the ultimate protection for a small boy in the lower-fifth form at Regis College: nobody messed with Geary, the school boxing champ. By the time Harry reached the sixth-form, he had undergone his adolescent growing spurt and had outgrown Danny by three inches.

'No doubt about that,' agreed Jon, 'Swift's a complete and utter shit. Anyway, I expect this means you'll be leaving school at Christmas?'

'Too right, I will – along with you and Swift. I only came back into the third year sixth because Dad wanted me to try for Cambridge – he wanted me to go to his old college, you know. Now that's over with, I'm getting out of this prison as soon as I can. I'm not staying on for another two terms of celibacy just to take my 'A' levels again and have another crack at Cambridge. I'll go to Wessex next academic year and that'll be fine. The worst thing about it is I could have gone there this year... I could be there now, getting laid. Coming back here has been a real bugger in terms of trying to get laid.'

'I thought getting laid was the purpose of tonight's little escapade.'

'It is... it is! But I'm not sure Rosie will succumb to my charms. This is only our first proper date, you know, and I'll only have a couple of hours to work on her. Then again, it was her idea to invite me round to her house this evening while her folks are out, so she might just be up for it.'

Harry planned to slip out of school that evening while the rest of the senior school were watching a film show in the Great Hall. He had arranged to meet Rosemary Hunt, the daughter of Major Hunt, a staff officer at Black Down Army Camp, located just beyond the school playing fields. He was to walk to her house on the army base, arriving at about seven-thirty, and spend the evening with her. Harry had met Rosie at the annual Regis College school dance, earlier in the term – she had been one of a group of sixth-formers from Gloucester Girls' High School who had been invited to the event. Harry and the Hawks had been playing throughout the refreshment interval and he had managed to 'get off' with her during the second half of the evening. Jon was to cover for Harry in the unlikely event that he was missed during his absence.

'Well, I wish you well in your endeavour, Harry. And I shall expect a full report on how you've fared when you get back.' Jon was always very keen to hear about the rare romantic exploits of his friends, even though he never seemed to take any interest in girls himself.

Jon and Harry continued to talk for another half hour or so, drinking tea and eating buttered toast, and then they strolled over to the school dining hall for the evening meal. When that was done, Harry climbed the stairs to the Beauchamp House senior dormitory where he shared a cubicle with Jon Geary. He washed his face, brushed his teeth, buffed his shoes and put on the trousers from his Sunday suit. The only mufti he had with him at school was his favourite black polo neck sweater, which he also put on. He combed his hair in the mirror, trying to shape his locks into something that looked passably fashionable, before descending the stairs to the house cloakroom in the basement of the building to collect his mackintosh and wellington boots. By this stage in the evening, the rest of the senior boys were assembling in the Hall in readiness for the film show: some cartoons followed by a screening of *I'm All Right Jack*. Harry put on his raincoat and boots and, carrying his shoes to keep them clean, slipped quietly out into the cold November evening.

It had stopped raining by then, but it was dark and overcast which enabled Harry to make his way unnoticed across the terrace and down onto the extensive school playing fields. He crept discretely round the perimeter of the grounds until he came to a gate which led onto Chaplaincy Lane, where the school chaplain's cottage was located. On the other side of the lane lay Black Down Camp. He crossed the lane onto the sprawling army base, where he changed into his shoes and hid his wellingtons behind a hedge. He knew where the officers' houses were sited and set off in that direction, along thoroughfares lined with nissen huts and wooden barracks. When he got to the officers' quarters, a cluster of detached houses arranged round a grassy square, he saw Rosie standing in a wide, brightly lit, picture window at the front of her house, waiting for him. She was a slim ponytailed girl, dressed in slacks and a loose fitting sweater. She waved when she saw Harry approaching and went to the front door to let him in.

Rosie led Harry through to the living room and asked him to take a seat on the sofa. Set before him on a coffee table were two small tumblers and a bottle of elderflower wine which Rosie had purloined from her father's abundant supply of homemade wines, stored in his garage. She drew the curtains, put on an LP to play softly, sat down beside Harry on the sofa and poured them each a glass of wine. Harry thought things looked very promising. It was gone seven-thirty by this time and Harry knew he needed to be back in school by ten at the latest if he was not to be missed; this meant he had around two hours to spend with Rosie before he would have to set off back to Regis. They chatted happily enough for quite some time, taking occasional swigs of Major Hunt's wine, but then things seemed to take a turn for the worse. The wine was beginning to make Rosie rather garrulous and she suddenly started talking with great enthusiasm, and for no apparent reason, about Danny Swift: how dishy he was; how all her friends at school fancied him; how charming he was and nice to talk to; and how many of her friends had wanted to dance with him at the Regis school dance. Things hit rock bottom when she asked Harry if he might be able to fix up a meeting with Danny for her and some of her friends. Harry blustered and prevaricated but, in the end, had to come clean and admit that he wasn't at all friendly with Danny Swift and therefore would not be in a position to act as a go-between for her and her friends. They sat next to each other in silence for some time, Harry having concluded that all was lost in the 'getting laid' department, when all of a sudden Rosie, who by this stage in the evening had consumed three full glasses of wine, looked up at the mantelpiece clock and, realising that time was pressing, suddenly turned to face Harry and kissed him firmly on the lips. After the initial shock, he started to respond and, as their kissing became more passionate, so Rosie's responses became increasingly abandoned. Harry thought, it's now or never, and started to manoeuvre her into a prone position on the sofa. He met no resistance. He was just getting to grips with her when the sound of a motor car pulling up on the gravel drive outside could clearly be heard.

Rosie sat up abruptly, pushing Harry onto the floor in the process.

'Bugger! That's my parents... home early. You'll have to go.' She went to the window and peered out from behind the curtain. 'Yes, it's them. Quick... the French window!' She pulled Harry to his feet and ushered him to the French doors on the other side of the room. She pulled back the curtain, unlocked one of the doors and pushed him unceremoniously out into the cold night air of Major Hunt's back garden, throwing his coat out after him. Then, without uttering another word, she slammed the door shut and drew the curtain. That was the last he ever saw of Rosemary Hunt.

It didn't take long for Harry to collect his thoughts. He gathered up his mackintosh and crept quietly round the side of the house to the front garden. He checked to make sure the coast was clear and, seeing that it was, crossed the road and proceeded to make haste across the army camp towards Chaplaincy Lane. Once there, he retrieved his boots from their hiding place, crossed the lane and entered the familiar, but darkened, territory of the Regis College playing fields. He made his way quietly and discreetly back to Beauchamp House the same way he had come earlier in the evening, entering the building by the basement back door.

The Saturday evening film show came to an end, and the two hundred or so boys of the senior school began to file out of the Great Hall under the supervision of two prefects, one of whom was Jon Geary, standing in for Harry. After the last of the boys had passed through the double doorway at the rear of the hall, Danny Swift appeared and approached Jon.

'Where's your friend, Irving?' he demanded. 'He's supposed to be on duty tonight. I didn't see him in the film.'

'I've swapped duties with him,' Jon replied curtly, not bothering to turn to look at Danny.

'Okay, but where is he? He wasn't in the film. He better not have broken bounds and sloped off somewhere, because if he has, he'll be in big trouble.' Danny sounded more like a headmaster than a school prefect.

Jon turned towards Danny and looked him straight in the eye. 'He went up to the dorm to lie down. He's a bit knackered after the rugby match this afternoon.'

'Well he better be there, because if he isn't I'll have to report him to the master-on-duty, and he'll be for it.'

Jon walked slowly up to Danny and, with his rugged face only inches from Danny's, said, 'Are you calling me a liar, Swift? Because if you are, you'll live to regret it. Now sod off!' With that, he turned and marched out of the hall to finish off his duty stint, ushering stragglers up to their dormitories.

When Danny arrived a few minutes later in the entrance to Harry's cubicle in the senior dormitory, he was disappointed to find Harry, lying on his back on the bed with his hands behind his head.

'What the hell are you doing here, Irving? You were supposed to be on duty tonight.'

'I swapped with Jon.'

'Why weren't you in the film, though?'

'I hurt my leg, playing rugby.'

'I see. Did you get a chit from Matron?'

'Nope.'

'You know the rules, Irving. Everyone needs a chit if they're to be excused from Saturday evening activities... including prefects. I'm going to have to report you for this.'

Harry was not generally given to aggressive behaviour, even with those he disliked, but he was still smarting from his time with Rosie: he was frustrated and annoyed at having fallen at the final fence in the 'getting laid' stakes; and irritated beyond measure by the revelation that Danny seemed to have achieved almost pop idol status among the sixth-form girls of Gloucester High School. He sat up on his bed and glared at Danny. 'Do what the hell you like, Swift, I don't give a toss. I'm leaving this prison at the end of term, and it makes no difference to me whether I go now or in four weeks' time. Now piss off and leave me alone.' Danny turned and left the room, and that was the last Harry heard on the matter.

The following Friday, Harry was on morning prefect duty, which involved going round the house dormitories during break time to inspect the beds and make sure the boys had made them properly. He was checking the beds in one of the junior dormitories – a long bare cavernous room containing thirty hospital beds – when he heard a loud thwack, followed by a high pitched squeal coming from the washroom at the far end of the dorm. He went to investigate and when he opened the door to the communal bathroom and looked in, he saw a junior boy called Clode, bent over one of the bathtubs with his blazer pulled up at the back. A few paces behind him was Danny Swift, wielding a leather slipper in his right hand. Harry watched as Danny took a run-up and delivered a second resounding blow to Clode's trouser-clad buttocks. Clode yelped, stood up, clutching his backside, and then, at Danny's command, bent over again.

'What on earth do you think you're doing, Swift?' demanded Harry.

Danny turned and glared angrily at him. 'What does it look like I'm doing, Irving? I'm beating Clode. What business is it of yours? The little toe rag is a complete disgrace: dirty shoes, hands in his pockets, torn blazer, bed not properly made. He needs knocking into shape.'

'Not by you,' Harry said as he walked over to Danny's victim. 'Come on, Clode, up you get'. He straightened the young boy up, adjusted his blazer for him and told him to clear off.

'Who the fuck do you think you are, Irving, interfering with the perfectly proper punishment of a junior boy by his house captain? You'll pay for this.'

'Will I? We'll see. I know what you are, Swift. You're a pervert... a nasty, sadistic pervert. God knows what you'll do to satisfy your sordid little perversions when you've left school. There'll be no small boys' arses to beat.'

'Listen, Irving, if I want to thrash Clode, or any other little faggot for that matter, I will, and you're not going to stop me. You're just a wimp, Irving, a great big wimp. You may have grown a bit, but you're nothing but a big long streak of piss. You were a little softy when you came here and you're a big softy now – little orphan 'Arry, the piss-poor pauper.'

Harry was not just bigger than Danny, his body had become hard and his muscles toned from nearly three months of fairly brutal rugby training for the 1st XV. He strode towards Danny who was standing, slipper still in hand, by the bathtub used for Clode's punishment, and for the first and last time in his life, unleashed a vicious right hook, aimed at Danny's head. The blow connected perfectly and Danny slumped to the floor. Harry turned round, leaving his victim where he lay, and walked out of the room, rubbing his sore fist as he went.

Three weeks later Regis College broke up for the Christmas holiday, when Harry, Jon and Danny left school for good. Nothing more had been said about the incident in the washroom, either by Danny or Harry – Danny explained the swelling and subsequent bruising to the left side of his face by saying he had taken a tumble in one of the washrooms and hit his head against the side of a basin. Harry returned home to his adoptive parents' rectory near Swindon, where he found a temporary job working as a packer in a food processing factory. He continued to pursue his ambition to 'get laid' but, even though he was now liberated from the highly restrictive regime of an early nineteen-sixties boys' boarding school, he fared no better in his quest than he had done while at Regis. He enjoyed a number of liaisons with local girls, including another close run thing with a pretty girl chorister in his father's church choir, but never managed to break his duck. He was still a virgin when he arrived at Wessex University at the beginning of October 1965.

Chapter 4
May 1966

Harry was sitting up in bed watching Flic get dressed. He had spent the night with her in her room at the student house she shared with three other women undergraduates from the university. She was a jolly girl – a fleshy, pug-faced bleach-blonde from Liverpool, in the final year of a degree in Spanish. Harry had been seeing her, off and on, since the end of the Michaelmas term, shortly after his abortive encounter with Amy Anderton, but she made no secret of the fact that she also saw one or two other lads, as well as having a 'proper boyfriend' back home in Knotty Ash. However, she had a particularly soft spot for Harry, who was quite a bit younger than she was, and had taken great delight in inducting him into the joys and mysteries of coital relations – he had finally broken his duck in the 'getting laid' department on their first night out together. She had then gone on to tutor him in some of the sexual techniques she had acquired since losing her virginity at the age of fifteen: most importantly, when and how to apply a condom to the male organ without spoiling the erotic excitement of the build-up to coupling, and without the risk of the thing coming adrift during the act itself. Harry had been particularly naïve, if not downright negligent, about the need for contraception in his earlier abortive attempts at 'getting laid', and had probably been very fortunate in his failure.

Harry liked watching Flic get dressed almost as much as he liked watching her get undressed. He particularly liked watching her put on her stockings. He sat there, naked except for a sheet covering his legs and nether regions, and enjoyed the show.

'Come on, lazy bones, shift yer bum!' Flic said when she had finished dressing. 'There's a lecture I want to go to at eleven and I'm not leaving you here on your own. The other girls won't want some stray male roaming about the place.'

'Okay, Flic, if you say so. There's a class I could go to at eleven as well, and I'm due to meet Phil at twelve, so I suppose I may as well get moving.'

'I'll make us a cuppa while you're getting dressed, then we can walk up to college together.'

It was a short distance from Flic's house to the university campus, a leisurely stroll for the two students. They walked along tree-lined University Road until they reached the Languages Faculty where they parted company. Flic went in for her lecture and Harry continued on towards his own department further along the road. When he reached the Students' Union building, he decided to pop in and see what was going on. It was the Monday of the second week of the summer term. There would be two more weeks of formal classes, followed by a short break for revision, and then exams at the beginning of June. After that there was another lull in proceedings for a couple of weeks, before the publication of exam results at the end of the first week in July, marking the end of the academic year. Most lectures and seminars at this time of year took the form of revision classes, which Harry regarded as a bit of a waste of time, and so he wasn't particularly bothered if he missed his eleven o'clock session.

Harry entered the Union building and decided to go and check the pigeonholes in the Junior Common Room to see if he had any letters or messages – not that he was particularly expecting anything. The pigeonholes stretched along a section of one wall in the JCR and Harry went to the box marked 'I'. He sifted through the mass of paper in the box until he came across an unstamped envelope with his name handwritten in blue ink on the front. He looked at the envelope, turned it over in his hands a few times, puzzled about what it might contain, and then went over to a row of easy chairs where he took a seat and opened it. Inside was a letter from Jerry Somers, a brash would-be entrepreneur in his mid-twenties, who had taken over the management of The Saxons, the university's student pop group, shortly after the Christmas break. Harry had played three gigs with the band during the previous term, standing in for Rod Burt, the guitarist and lead singer, who had decided that his studies were more important than playing in a pop group – Rod was a final year student who was apparently 'on for a first', a very rare achievement in those days. He had cried off for three of the band's last five engagements and, as a result, Harry's persistent badgering to join the group had finally paid off when he was asked to step into Rod's shoes and cover for his absences.

The letter, written in formal style, advised Harry that Jerry Somers had managed to arrange a recording session for The Saxons at Joe Meek's London studio – apparently Joe Meek was a friend of a friend of Jerry's. The recording session would take place in three weeks' time, exactly a week before Harry's first exam. Rod Burt had announced that he would be neither willing nor able to make himself available to go to London for the day, so close to his final examinations, in consequence of which the rest of the band and Jerry had unanimously agreed that Rod should be asked to stand down from the group and Harry invited to take his place and play at the recording session. The letter went on formally to invite Harry to join The Saxons as its permanent guitarist and vocalist, with immediate effect, and to communicate his acceptance of the offer by telephoning Jerry on the number provided within five working days.

Harry didn't need to think about it, and he certainly didn't need to take 'five working days' to make his decision. As far as he was concerned, it was a no brainer: a recording session with Joe Meek, England's most renowned independent record producer, meant hitting the big time in his books. Although Meek was past his heyday, he was still famous for his hits with the likes of John Leyton, The Tornados and The Honeycombs. His recording of *Telstar* by the Tornados had been the first British pop tune to reach number one in the USA charts, where it had stayed for several weeks. Harry went straightaway to one of the payphones in the Union lobby and made the call, accepting Jerry Somers' offer. By then it was too late for him to consider going to his eleven o'clock class, even if he had wanted to, and so he went instead to the refectory and bought himself a cup of coffee. He sat down at one of the many tables in the big bright dining room and passed the time before his planned midday meeting, sipping his drink, musing on his unexpected good fortune and fantasising about fame and fortune to come. Shortly before noon, he set off for the Bassett Arms to meet his friend, Phil.

The two friends had seen relatively little of each other during the Lent term. Phil had moved out of the digs he shared with Harry and Hedley Stevens, following a blazing row he'd had with their obtrusive landlady, Mrs Scrutton, just before the Christmas vacation. He had managed to find himself a very pleasant little bedsitting room on the ground floor of a Victorian villa not far from the university. He had also become increasingly preoccupied with his relationship with Ginger, spending most of his free time in the evenings and at weekends seeing her, rather than drinking beer in pubs with Harry. At weekends, Ginger would often stay overnight with Phil in his bedsit, which had gradually become something of a love nest. Harry was very much looking forward to seeing Phil whom he hadn't seen since before the Easter break, although it was Phil who had contacted Harry to arrange the meeting.

Harry arrived in the lounge bar of the Bassett Arms bang on twelve to find Phil standing at the bar, dressed in a fashionable, dark blue, Italian suit, ordering pints of beer and pork pies, their customary public house lunchtime sustenance. After the usual greetings, they took their pies and pints over to one of the tables and sat down. Harry was so bursting with the news of his nascent career as a pop star that, without even asking Phil how he was, he launched into a detailed account of what had transpired that morning. After he had been talking virtually non-stop for twenty minutes or so, enthusing about the various opportunities that recording with Joe Meek were about to open up for him, Phil decided it was time to interrupt.

'Well, old sport, that is excellent news. Very good indeed... and I'm absolutely delighted for you. But I wanted to see you because I have some rather important news of my own I want to discuss with you.'

'Christ, Phil, I'm sorry... I've been prattling on for ages like a complete pillock. I'm ever so sorry Phil... yes, of course, tell me your news.'

'Okay, Harry, here goes: Ginger and I are going to get married next month.'

Harry, who was in the process of taking a swig from his pint glass, choked and spluttered on his beer. 'What?' was all he could think of to say when he eventually regained his breath.

'We're getting married in June, down in Kent – a big reception at my parents' place.'

'But why are you getting married... and why so soon?'

'Well I should have thought that was obvious, old sport: Ginger's pregnant.'

'Pregnant! Pregnant! I don't believe it. Didn't you use anything? Didn't you take any precautions?'

'At first I refrained from using French letters in deference to Ginger's Roman Catholicism. We relied on the so-called safe period, instead. By the time I realised that Ginger didn't give a toss about papal edicts and was more than happy for me to use johnnies, it was too late... she was up the spout.'

'I see. Yes, I see. But do you want to marry Ginger... and, well I mean, what will you do?'

'Well I'm twenty-one now; I could wait another ten years and I don't think I'd find anyone who suits me as well as Ginger does. She's great company and she's always willing when it comes to the old hanky-panky. I think the answer to your question is: yes, I do want to marry her. And as to what we'll do... well, I'll leave university and Ginger will give up her teaching course. I'll go back into the family business and we'll settle in Kent. It was my idea to come here and do a degree after I'd done a couple of years in the wine trade and, I have to say, I've found the whole experience a bit of a disappointment, apart from meeting Ginger, of course... and you too, old friend.'

'And what do your folks have to say about all this? Are they happy about it... well, I suppose they must be, if you're going to have a big bash in their back garden to celebrate?'

'If the truth be told, old son, they're as pleased as Punch. They're amazingly liberal and open minded about this sort of thing, for a couple of old birds. Dad never wanted me to go off to university in the first place, so he's delighted that I'll be back in the family business. He's knocking on a bit and he'll be wanting me to take over from him fairly soon. And I have to say, they both seem thrilled at the idea of becoming grandparents. They've both turned sixty and I'm an only child, so I think they had come to the conclusion that grandchildren might never happen – it seems the "safe period" worked out pretty well as far as they're concerned. Mum's a bit fed up that there won't be a big church wedding – just a few folk at the local registry office – but there'll be a big party afterwards at home... you know, a big marquee in the garden and a couple of hundred guests. They've got over five acres of grounds.'

'Well, I suppose I ought to congratulate you... Hell, what am I saying!' Harry jumped to his feet. 'Congratulations, Phil!

Congratulations, my very good friend.' He shook hands heartily with Phil. 'Of course, I shall miss having you here at university... not that I've seen that much of you of late.'

'You'll be busy enough with The Saxons, I should think, and, if that takes off, you'll be out of here pretty sharpish yourself. Anyway, there's something else I want to ask you about. I'd like you to be my best man. You're not the first choice, mind: my best friend from school is a lieutenant in the Royal Tank Regiment, and he'll be away on NATO manoeuvres in West Germany on the day, so he can't do it. But you're the next on the list... and I'd really like you to do it. And so would Ginger, you being there when we first met and all that.'

'Er, well... when exactly is the wedding? I've got exams coming up, remember.'

'I've checked all that and it's on 17th June, two days after your last exam.'

'You know, Phil, I'm very grateful... and honoured to be asked. But I've never done anything like this before... you know, making speeches and all that sort of thing. There'll be lots to do, I expect, and it's so soon after my exams, and well... I won't have time to get everything ready.'

'Nonsense! All you've got to do is turn up at the registry office with the ring, listen to a short, boring ceremony and sign the register as a witness; then make a bit of a speech at the reception, responding to my toast to the bridesmaids; and then have a quick dance with bridesmaids – a piece of cake. You'll be perfect... and you've got to say yes.'

'Oh, I don't know, Phil, I...'

'... and there are going to be two bridesmaids: one is Ginger's sister, Blanche, who's thirty, married and a bit of a bruiser by all accounts... and the other is a certain Amy Anderton.'

* * * *

When Amy returned to college towards the end of April for the start of the summer term, Ginger wasn't there. At first, Amy thought she must be staying the night at Phil's bedsit, but when she hadn't shown up by Wednesday of the first week of classes, Amy decided to make some inquiries: first with the college registrar and then with members of the teaching staff, including some of the nuns. Nobody seemed able or willing to tell her what had happened to her friend. Of course, there were rumours among the students who knew Ginger, but nothing concrete. Two days later, one of the nuns, Sister Christina, a spiteful Irish woman who worked in the Principal's Office, approached Amy as she was leaving a morning lecture, took her to one side and furtively related her version of the mystery of Ginger's disappearance. She told Amy that Ginger had been, in secret, to see the Mother Superior and Principal of the college on the first day of term, and told her that she was pregnant. The Reverend Mother, who was apparently outraged at the revelation, had first admonished Ginger in the most severe terms for her sinful behaviour and then expelled her from the college in disgrace, with immediate effect. She was to come back to college to collect her belongings at a time to be agreed with her personal tutor when most of the students would be busy with classes or exams and there would therefore be little risk of Ginger contaminating them with her profane presence. Sister Christina then proceeded to warn Amy about the dangers of becoming too friendly with the likes of Ginger – a sluttish ungodly young woman – and suggested that Amy might like to go to the college chapel to give thanks to the Almighty for being delivered from such an abhorrent impure influence on her young life.

Amy was stunned. There must have been an element of truth in what Sister Christina had just told her, even though the nun was well known among the student body as a rumour monger and troublemaker, but she found it hard to believe that Ginger was pregnant or that she had been expelled. She had to talk to Ginger and find out what had happened. The only contact number she had for her friend was her home telephone number in Coventry – there was no telephone at Phil's bedsit – and so she decided she would try and reach her there by phone that evening, when trunk call charges would be much cheaper than peak daytime rates. However, before that, she would skip her afternoon classes and catch a bus to Phil's place, on the off chance Ginger might be there and she would then be able to talk to her in person. She made her way to the hostel room she shared with Ginger in order to deposit her books and collect her purse and coat before walking to the bus stop outside the college gates. When she opened the door to her room, she found Ginger calmly sitting on her bed putting things into a suitcase. Amy's amazement and delight at finding her friend sitting there was almost matched by her surprise at Ginger's appearance. Amy had always thought of Ginger as being slightly bohemian in the way she presented herself to the world – flat shoes, sloppy sweaters, longish skirts and little in the way of cosmetics – and so to find her looking rather like something from Vogue magazine, dressed in heels, a fashionably tailored skirt and jacket, and wearing make-up and lipstick, was strange, to say the least.

'Ginger, you're here… thank goodness. I was so worried about you,' Amy said after her initial shock. Ginger rose from the bed, walked across the room to the doorway where Amy was standing and gave her a big hug.

'I'm sorry, Amy,' Ginger said. 'I tried to contact you to tell you what was happening, in fact I rang your home in Newark the Saturday before term started and spoke to your mum, but you had already left for college. I've been at home in Coventry trying to sort things out with my parents.'

'But what is happening, Ginger?' Amy said as they went to sit down. 'Sister Christina said you'd got yourself pregnant and been expelled from college in disgrace.'

'Did she now? She would say that, wouldn't she, the spiteful old bag. Well, she's right about one thing... I am pregnant. But I haven't been sacked... I've resigned. I went to see the Mother Superior last Friday to tell her I was leaving college, but I didn't tell her why – that I was pregnant and getting married – until she continued to press me on the matter. She looked a bit disapproving at first, but she was really quite sweet about it in the end. She wanted to be reassured that I was marrying a good Catholic man and that the baby would be brought up in the faith... and so I lied and said that Phil was from one of the "leading Catholic families" in Kent – I thought I'd borrow your Guy's famous expression – and that the baby would indeed be a new recruit to the one true church. I didn't mention that I was getting married in a registry office to an absolute pagan.' Ginger chuckled.

'Wow, Ginger! This is a lot to take in. I can hardly believe what I'm hearing: married, pregnant... and leaving college.'

'Not quite in that order, Sweetie.'

'No... no, I guess not. So what happened? Tell me how it all happened.'

Ginger went on to relate the whole story: how she had started having sex with Phil shortly after the Christmas break; how they hadn't bothered to use any form of contraception for the first few weeks because she had, at first, encouraged Phil in his mistaken belief that she might object to the use of condoms on religious grounds; how she hadn't been unduly worried about getting pregnant because she'd already more or less decided she wanted to 'bag' wealthy Phil for a husband; how they'd found out she was pregnant in April during the Easter vacation, and Phil had immediately proposed; and how they had both decided to give up their courses, get married and set up home in Kent, where Phil would return to working in the family business. Next Ginger enthused about the plans for the wedding: a small ceremony before the registrar followed by a lavish reception in a marquee in the grounds of the Semarks' country house, with around two hundred guests. Amy listened intently to the story and, when it was finished, sat for a moment in silence. It had suddenly struck her that Ginger would soon be gone and that the friendship she treasured so much might then be as good as over. A tear ran down her cheek.

'I'm very happy for you, Ginger,' Amy said with a slight sob, 'but is it really what you want? You've always told me you'd only ever get married for love... or lust. Do you love Phil?'

'No, not really, but we get on pretty well and he's absolutely loaded. The family are so rich they'd probably make Guy's lot look like a bunch of mendicants. And I don't mind having sex with him – which he likes to do quite a lot – although I wouldn't call it lust on my part. I don't enjoy it particularly, but he's very sensitive and gentle about it, and doesn't ever ask me to do anything kinky or unpleasant... well not yet, anyway.' Ginger paused when she became aware that Amy was a little tearful, and then said, 'Oh, sweet Amy, what's the matter, you're crying?'

'I'm sorry, Ginger. I know I should be so happy for you, if this is what you want. It's just that I'm sad you're going – you know, leaving college – and I'm going to lose you as a friend,'

'Don't cry, sweetie. And don't be silly, we'll always be friends. I think of you as my very best friend... so much so that I want you to be one of my bridesmaids at the wedding. There'll only be two: my big sister, Blanche, and my best friend, Amy. You've got to say yes. Promise me you'll do it.'

* * * *

The transit van, hired by Jerry Somers to transport The Saxons and all their gear to the metropolis, pulled up outside 304 Holloway Road in Islington, North London – home to Meeksville Sound Ltd, Joe Meek's recording company – just before 10.00 am on the last Monday in May. The group – Spud Chrisp, drums; Dave Cant, bass; Ken Walker, organ and guitar; plus Harry – had loaded up and set off from the Wessex University Students' Union early that morning, allowing plenty of time to get to London, negotiate the rush-hour traffic and find their way to the recording studio in time for their ten o'clock appointment. Jerry, a dapper little fellow dressed in a dark suit and tie, parked the van in the street and led the way to the front door of the premises, which turned out to be the entrance to a leather goods shop. They entered the shop where they were instructed by an assistant to go through to the back and climb the stairs to the flat on the first floor. Joe Meek's studios came as a complete surprise to all of them, Jerry Somers included: here was a renowned record producer, who had topped the charts throughout the world, including the USA, operating from a shabby rented flat above a high street retail outlet. The accommodation was quite large, covering three floors, but most of the rooms seemed to be crammed with weird-looking items of recording equipment, together with amplifiers, drum kits and various other musical instruments. One room was given over for use as an office by Major Banks, Meek's business partner and financial backer. The most eccentric aspect of the place was the flat's bathroom – and home to its only water closet – which doubled as the studio's echo chamber, used to produce the distinctive Joe Meek sound which featured on records such as *Johnny Remember Me* and *Telstar*. The whole place had a dusty, musty, run-down, Heath Robinson feel to it.

Meek himself was a stout man in his late thirties, with an abundance of almost-black, slicked-back hair. He was a moody taciturn man who hardly spoke a word to the members of the band until after the recording session was over. There was no need to unload the minivan, except for the two guitars and bass, since all the amplification, keyboards and drums they might need were available in the studio. The session lasted about four hours, during which time the band stood on the landing outside the bathroom playing their instruments and singing, while Meek sat in his control room twiddling knobs and adjusting the controls of various pieces of electronic equipment. Jerry sat in an adjacent room quietly observing proceedings. Six tracks were put down during the session, each one requiring several takes: three were covers of American rock and roll numbers, and three were songs that Meek had on his books. Harry disliked the Meek numbers, which he thought were lightweight and banal, more like novelty pop songs than rock and roll. When the session was over, Jerry and the group were told to take a walk along Holloway Road to a nearby café, where they could get a cup of tea and a sandwich, while Meek played around with the tracks for an hour or so to achieve the sounds he wanted.

They returned an hour later to find Meek waiting for them with the news that he thought two of the tracks they had recorded would do very well for release as a single: one for the A side one for the B side. Harry hoped he had selected a cover of *Rocky Road Blues*, an old Gene Vincent song they had recorded – although it was just a very basic twelve bar blues, Harry felt the band had put in a pretty impressive, gutsy performance. However, Meek had chosen a couple of the numbers he had provided, and announced that he was going to submit a song called *Everyone But Me* to one of the major record distributing companies for release as the A side. Nobody said anything, but you could tell all the members of the group were disappointed with the choice, despite the group's communal elation at the prospect of getting a record released. Harry was particularly disappointed, even though he had been given the lead vocal on the proposed track. Of course, nobody, especially Jerry Somers, was going to turn down the chance of a recording contract and so they all kept mum. So far, Meek had addressed all his remarks to Jerry, but now he turned to the group as a whole and said, 'You're gonna have to change your name, boys – Saxons is no damn use, and anyway, there's already a professional jazz band called The Saxons, so the record companies won't wear it.'

This came as a blow to the band, and there was a prolonged silence while Meek just stood there, staring at them. Eventually, Spud Chrisp, the band's thickset curly-haired drummer, chirped up with: 'What about The Angles, then? You know…Angles and Saxons?'

'No… that's too like The Angels. There's already The Band of Angels,' was Meek's response to this suggestion.

There was another long silence until Harry eventually put up his hand. Meek nodded at him.

'Um… I had a group at school,' Harry said tentatively. 'We were called Harry and The Hawks.'

Meek thought for a moment. 'Harry and The Hawks, eh? *Everyone But Me* by Harry and The Hawks. Sounds great. Yep… that'll do great. Harry and The Hawks it shall be.'

Jerry Somers signalled his agreement on behalf of the band.

The look of outrage on the faces of the three original Saxons was something to behold – although Joe Meek didn't seem to notice. They knew Meek had made up his mind and there was no point in protesting. It was a fait accompli. They were just rookies in the pop world, completely in awe of the 'legendary', and probably unhinged, Joe Meek. All they could do was look daggers at Harry.

Chapter 5
The Wedding: June 1966

Castle Court, home to the Semark family, was a rambling, ten-bedroom, Arts and Crafts mansion, set in several acres of grounds in rolling Kent countryside. The building had a multi-gabled exterior with half-timbering, intricately carved woodwork, leaded windows – many with stained glass detailing – and fine decorative brickwork. At one end, a battlemented tower served as the main entrance to the house, as well as being its tallest feature. Amy arrived there, together with Ginger, her sister and parents, on a fine English summer's afternoon, the eve of Ginger's wedding. She was due to spend the next two nights with the Semarks – Ginger would be there on the first night, and her parents and sister for both nights. Phil had moved out before their arrival into a local country hotel where he was to spend the night with Harry. Mrs Semark had decreed that, despite the countless nights Phil and Ginger had already spent together, it would simply not do for her son to sleep under the same roof as his bride-to-be the night before his nuptials. Ginger's father, who had driven down from Coventry that morning with his wife and two daughters, had picked Amy up from the nearest railway station before driving on to Castle Court. On locating the property, he turned in through a pillared gateway, next to a porter's lodge, and proceeded up a long woodland drive to the mansion where they found Jim and Sylvia Semark, standing outside the heavy oak front door at the base of the tower, awaiting their arrival.

The Semarks were a genial pair, dressed in tweeds and brogues, both with snowy white hair. They were small of stature, but slender, and erect. Jim Semark was the ageing image of his son, Phil. They greeted their guests cordially, inviting them in and ushering them through an oak panelled hallway into the main family drawing room, beautifully lit by two enormous leaded bay windows, one with French doors leading onto a sandstone terrace. The room contained an eclectic array of solid wooden furniture and soft furnishings; the walls were papered with William Morris prints. Jim Semark asked everyone to sit down while he went to find the housekeeper to organise some afternoon tea. While they were waiting, Sylvia offered her guests a cigarette from a silver cigarette box kept on the ornate mantelpiece. Everyone accepted and so Sylvia passed the box round and then went to each of her guests in turn to light his or her cigarette with an elaborately shaped silver table lighter.

The atmosphere during this time, and throughout afternoon tea, was pleasant enough on the surface, but there was an unmistakeable, underlying tension. Amy was aware of this, and noted that it was Ginger who was taking the lead in keeping the conversation flowing. Amy did her best to help her friend out in this regard, and the Semarks seemed to warm to her accordingly – it was already apparent that they were very fond of Ginger. However, Ginger's parents, particularly her father, appeared reserved and somewhat distant. Ginger's sister, Blanche, a broad, stocky, square-faced woman, very like her father in appearance and unlike Ginger, scarcely uttered a word. Amy put the family's conduct down to the difficult time Ginger had had with her parents since announcing to them that she was pregnant and intending to get married. They were devout Roman Catholics and were shocked to discover that one of their daughters had fallen from grace. They had always imagined that she would get married, virgo intacta, to a Catholic man in the family Catholic church in Coventry, with a full nuptial mass, just like her sister had done. The fact that she was to have a shotgun marriage to a non-believer in a registry office in Kent was something they found hard to come to terms with. Also, it had come as a great blow to them that Ginger was to give up her course at college. They were both practising physiotherapists and put great store by studying, getting professionally qualified and working for a living, consequently they were not at all happy at the idea of their younger daughter marrying into money rather than making her own way in the world. And, to cap it all, they were staunch, old fashioned, Labour Party supporters who felt ill at ease in the company of well-to-do, upper middle class, Kentish gentry, such as the Semarks.

When tea was over, Ginger's mother, a small, shrewish, wiry woman, whom Ginger resembled, asked Sylvia if she and her husband might be shown to their rooms so that they could unpack and freshen up. Amy took the opportunity to do likewise. She was shown to a pleasant room in the east wing of the property, overlooking an extensive area of lawn, in the centre of which was pitched the wedding day marquee. Beyond the lawn was a large orchard, and, beyond that, views over open countryside. She took her shoes off and sat down in an easy chair by the window so that she could collect her thoughts. She was glad Guy had not come with her and that she was by herself. She and Guy had fallen out briefly when she had announced that she was going to be Ginger's bridesmaid in Kent on 17th June. It was the weekend of The Holy Trinity Church summer fete, which would take place on Saturday the 18th. Guy was a member of the organising committee, consequently it was an event he could not miss. To make matters worse, on the evening of the 17th, Guy's grandparents were having a small party to celebrate their golden wedding anniversary, which Guy had assumed he would be attending with Amy as his escort, even though his grandparents lived in Nottingham and Amy had never met them. Amy had determined that being her best friend's bridesmaid was much more important to her than going all the way to Nottinghamshire to attend Guy's parish church fete or the golden wedding of a couple she had not met and did not know. After a considerable amount of wrangling and recrimination, she had put her foot down, Guy had reluctantly given in, and the couple had agreed to 'do their own thing' that particular weekend. It was the nearest Amy and Guy had come to having a blazing row in over a year of courtship – so bland had their relationship become that a row was no more likely to occur than an eruption of romantic passion.

Amy's thoughts turned to Harry – he was seldom far from them. She knew, of course, that he was to be Phil's best man and that the following day she would be seeing him again for the first time since their meeting back in November – she would probably have to dance with him again. She knew that, if there was such a thing as love at first sight, this was what had happened to her the night they met, but she also knew that since then she had strived with singular determination to put the incident and her feelings for Harry behind her, and focused determinedly on her relationship with Guy; and so part of her was reasonably confident that seeing Harry again would not throw her emotions back into turmoil. But there were still things that troubled her about tomorrow's encounter. What would Harry's feelings be for her? She knew, via Phil and Ginger, that he had really liked her when they first met and had wanted to see her again, but that was more than six months ago, and she also knew, from the same source, that he had been out with other girls in the meantime, including an older, Liverpudlian girl with whom he had formed some sort of relationship. And would he prove to be a disappointment when she saw him again? Would he be the same tall, handsome, straightforward, self-deprecating, boyish and funny young man who had swept her off her feet six months ago, or had she managed to create an idealised mental image of Harry which he could not live up to?

However, what troubled Amy most of all was her growing frustration with her relationship with Guy. They had kept their agreement of making a special effort to see more of each other during college terms: Amy had returned home for three weekends between Christmas and Easter, and Guy had travelled to Wessex twice during the same period to see Amy, staying at a bed and breakfast near the college. She still liked him and found him nice looking and pleasant company: he was considerate, generous and always solicitous of her well-being. And there was that ever-present, underlying determination to escape her childhood penury, and the belief that she could grow to love Guy who would one day marry her and provide the good things in life she coveted so much. The trouble was she couldn't fathom Guy's feelings for her. She knew, or thought she knew, that he loved her in his own fashion, and was desperate to keep her as his girlfriend and future wife, but he didn't seem to desire her physically in any way. He told her she was the most beautiful girl in the world, but never showed the slightest sign of passion or lust. He had never tried to touch her chest or put his hand under her skirt or pat her bottom; they had never seen each other in the slightest state of undress; and their tight-lipped necking sessions had, if anything, become shorter and less frequent, rather than developing into something more intimate. Despite Guy's frequent assertions that he one day wanted to have children, particularly a 'son and heir', they had never once discussed any aspect of their physical relationship. Amy had experienced, albeit briefly, erotic pleasure in her short dalliance with Danny Swift, and she knew without question that she needed some passion in her life. Although she was not particularly sexually attracted to Guy, she felt that, if he were to show some physical interest in her and if, as a consequence, she were to feel that she was the object of his desire in some way, this might spark an element of reciprocal desire on her part, which, in turn might sow the seeds of love. But nothing ever happened and Guy continued to show complete indifference to the pleasures of the flesh. Amy sometimes felt that she was nothing more than a trophy girlfriend, destined to become a trophy wife and vessel for Guy's children – if he could ever get round to doing the necessary deed.

And so, although a part of Amy was quietly confident that her self-discipline and determined focus on a future with Guy would see her safely through her imminent reunion with Harry, there was another side to her which harboured a sense of mounting excitement at the prospect of seeing her supposed true love again. If Harry did indeed turn out to be the boy she had fallen in love with, the deep sense of dissatisfaction she had developed with the lack of passion in her love life might well prove to be her Achilles heel when it came to warding off the onslaught of her natural instincts and emotions.

* * * *

Dinner was over at the George Hotel where Harry and Phil were each enjoying a post-prandial double Scotch, seated at a table in the quiet cocktail bar. The George was an old country hotel in Cranbrook, the nearest town of any size to Castle Court, where the two friends were staying on the eve of the wedding. Harry would also be staying there for the night after the wedding, because all the bedrooms at Castle Court would be occupied by various members of Phil's extended family, as well as Amy, Ginger and her family. The pair had only seen each other once since early May, when Harry had agreed to be Phil's best man, because Phil had that same day formally resigned his university place and returned to Kent. As a reward for agreeing to officiate at the wedding, Phil had told Harry he could move into his bedsit – the rent for which was fully paid up until the end of July – an offer which Harry had jumped at. He had moved out of Mrs Scrutton's digs the very next day and had been resident in the bedsitting room ever since, a state of affairs which had proved most conducive for the purposes of entertaining Flic – when she was available.

The conversation over dinner had been mostly focused on the wedding arrangements, in particular Harry's duties as best man, which appeared to be rather more extensive and demanding than Harry had anticipated, given Phil's description of the role when he had agreed to take it on. It seemed that he was to be a general master of ceremonies during the course of the reception and that there were various protocols and rules of etiquette which needed to be complied with, and with which Harry was not at all familiar. The dinner had turned out to be rather more of a seminar than a social occasion, with Phil as the tutor and Harry his student. However, things had lightened up somewhat once the meal was over, and the conversation had moved on from the wedding to Harry's progress at becoming a pop star.

'So, old sport, what's the latest on the record deal?' Phil asked. 'Have you heard anything more from your Mr Meek?'

'No, not yet. He said he'd get in touch with Jerry Somers, just as soon as he's finalised a deal with one of the big record distributors, but I haven't heard anything from Jerry. Anyway, I only finished my exams a couple of days ago and I've been pretty much preoccupied with those for the last few weeks.'

'Yes, I expect you have. Thank God I'm free of all that malarkey, that's all I can say. But you know, Harry, I've been thinking. You need to get the money side of things sorted out with that brash little bugger, Somers, before he starts ripping you off. I bet you still haven't signed any sort of contract, eh?'

'Well no – none of us has, as far as I know. But he's always paid me fair and square when we've had a booking, and he paid all the expenses for going to London for the recording session.'

'That's as may be, old son, but it'll be a very different matter if and when the big money starts coming in from record sales. Remember, that fellow Meek has got your recordings nicely locked away in that tinpot studio of his. He can do anything he likes with them and you've got nothing to prove what, if anything, you might be entitled to, once he's got a deal with Decca or Parlophone or whoever it might be, and the cash starts rolling in.'

'Well, I suppose you're right, but there's nothing I can do about it at the moment. I've just got to put my faith in Jerry and hope he'll play fair with us. After all, if the record's successful, he'll want more from us, and then we'll have something to bargain with, particularly as we haven't signed anything yet saying he's going to be our manager for ever. It cuts both ways, you know. Anyway, it all might come to nothing, in which case it doesn't really matter... and I've had other things on my mind recently.'

'Like, for instance, Amy?'

'Exams, actually, Phil. I've invested quite a bit of effort in my university work the last few weeks, and I hope I've done okay. I don't want to disappoint my old dad. Academic success means a lot to him, and I want to please him if I can.'

'Yes, I'm sure, and that's all very laudable, but what about pretty little Amy Anderton. You'll be seeing her again tomorrow, and I think I'm right in saying you were more than a little taken with her when you met her last November. I have it on the highest authority that she will be unaccompanied when she performs her duties as a bridesmaid tomorrow, because her boring estate agent boyfriend is otherwise engaged in the wilds of the East Midlands. Could be your big chance for a bit of hanky-panky with one of the prettiest girls around.'

'I don't think so, Phil. I'm not in the business of breaking up people's relationships. And anyway, if I'm as busy at being best man as you seem to think I'll be, there won't be any time for chatting up Amy, or anyone else for that matter... Mind you, that's not to say I'm not looking forward to seeing her. She's certainly the nicest girl

I've ever met. I really did like her, there's no doubt about that.' Harry sat pensively staring at his glass of scotch.

'Look, old son, you're not going to be that busy, particularly after the meal's over, and all the speechifying is finished. And don't fret yourself over Amy's bloke. According to Ginger, he's a boring bugger who doesn't like sex. I haven't told you this before, Harry, but Ginger seems to think that you're the fellow Amy's really got the hots for, so this could be your big chance to get in there.' Phil finished his whisky and signalled the barman to pour two more.

'Well, we'll see… and anyway, as I've told you before, I'm not looking to get snarled up in some sort of serious relationship with a girl, particularly if things are about to take off with the pop group, and particularly now I'm quite experienced in the shagging department. The sort of understanding I've got with Flic suits me quite well at the moment, even if she is probably screwing every other bloke in Wessex… and Liverpool for that matter.'

'Yes, I'm sure Felicity Tustin is most accommodating, judging by her reputation in the University, but I still think you might be about to miss a golden opportunity with the lovely Amy. Still, there you are… it's up to you.' Phil said this as he got up and walked to the bar to collect the two whiskies he had ordered. He returned to their table and sat down. 'Now, I think a reasonably early night is called for, old sport, seeing as tomorrow is my wedding day. We both need to be prepared for the rigours of the day, so let's enjoy our drinks and then turn in. And who knows what tomorrow may bring.'

* * * *

As soon as he saw her he knew. She looked quite lovely in her bridesmaid's outfit: a perfectly tailored, pale blue, sleeveless dress cut three inches above the knee, as fashion dictated. Her hair had been beautifully styled, elegantly arranged on top of her head, and she moved gracefully in her shoes with little heels in a colour to match her dress. Harry knew he had to find an opportunity to be with her and make her his, at least for the day, but he realised he would need to be patient and choose his moment carefully. He had much to do during the course of the day, and he wanted to make sure he discharged his duties well. He would just have to bide his time. Although there were only nine people at the registry office – Phil and his parents, Ginger and her family, Amy and Harry – everything seemed to happen at such a pace that Harry never once found an opportunity to address a remark directly to Amy. The marriage was booked for twelve-thirty, and Ginger and her bridesmaids were the last to arrive along with Ginger's father who had acted as chauffeur. Harry and Amy acknowledged each other by exchanging nervous smiles as Amy entered the Registrar's marriage room. The short ceremony was followed by the signing of the register, with Blanche and Harry acting as witnesses. Then the small party were hurried to their cars by Jim Semark for the return journey to Castle Court: the newly weds went with Jim and Sylvia in Jim's Bentley, which had been decked out with ribbons for the occasion; the rest went with Ginger's father in his Austin Cambridge. Harry hoped he might sit on the back seat with Amy and Blanche, preferably nestling against Amy, but Ginger's father insisted that he sit in the front, because of his long legs, and that the three women occupy the back seat. Throughout the twenty minute drive, Ginger's father kept Harry engaged in conversation, mainly about life at Wessex University, in which he seemed to be inordinately interested, thereby depriving Harry of any opportunity to turn round and say something to Amy sitting behind him.

 As soon as the cars arrived at Castle Court, Jim Semark whisked the bride, bridesmaids and Ginger's parents off to the entrance hall so that they could prepare a line-up to greet their guests who would start arriving within ten to fifteen minutes. Harry was packed off to the marquee to make sure that the catering and waiting staff had everything ready for the wedding feast, including checking that the seating plan and place names were in order. He then returned to the main house to satisfy himself that the champagne reception, which was to take place in the grand dining hall, was properly organised. He was still busily engaged in his administrative duties when the first guests started to arrive.

Castle Court on a sunny, slightly breezy June day was an almost perfect setting for a wedding reception. The Arts and Crafts mansion set in immaculately manicured grounds against the backdrop of the rolling hills of the Weald of Kent and a blue and white sky, was about as close as you could get to many people's idea of an English idyll. The wedding guests filed past the welcoming party in the entrance hall and were then ushered into the dining hall where champagne and canapés awaited them. Many of the guests spilled out through open French doors onto the sandstone terraces which ran along one side of the house and from there onto the lawns surrounding the pristinely white marquee. Most of the guests were friends, relatives and business associates of the Semarks, but there was a significant contingent of younger people in attendance: college friends of Ginger, and some of Phil's school and university pals, including Hedley Stevens, the rude young man who had broken up Harry's tete-a-tete with Amy the previous November.

The bride and groom were at the end of the welcoming line. Ginger was wearing a dress similar to Amy's only in pale ivory, rather than Amy's and Blanche's pale blue. Phil wore a light grey, three-piece suit – he and Harry had been to a tailor in Wessex to have identical suits made for them, all at Phil's expense. It took some time for all the guests to arrive and be formally received, and so by the time the welcoming party felt able to break up in order to go and mingle with their guests, it was almost time for Harry to bang the gong and summon everyone to the feast.

As the afternoon wore on, Amy became increasingly frustrated by the lack of opportunity to get together with Harry. She had been taken completely by surprise by the surge of emotion she experienced on seeing him – tall, slim, boyish and handsome – standing next to Phil, as she entered the marriage room. She simply couldn't believe how much she fancied and desired him. The fear of disappointment she had harboured evaporated at once, and instead a passion she had never known before overwhelmed her – her defences were well and truly down. When she was sitting behind Harry in the car, on the journey back to Castle Court after the ceremony, all she had wanted to do was put her hand out and run her fingers through his thick, mid-brown hair – now significantly longer than it had been when they first met. Yet there she was, about to enter the marquee and sit down for the wedding breakfast, and still she hadn't exchanged a single word with him.

The interior of the marquee was furnished with a score of round tables, each providing places for ten guests, and a long top table facing the assembled diners. The bridesmaids were placed at the opposite end of the top table from the best man, separated by the bride and groom and their respective parents, and so, throughout the meal and the ensuing speeches and formalities, there was no opportunity for contact or conversation between Amy and Harry. The banquet and subsequent formalities went off without incident. Harry's best man speech, about which he had been extremely nervous, seemed to be well received: the audience laughed at his jokes and applauded warmly at the end. And when it was all over, Harry made an announcement inviting guests to adjourn to the bar, which had been set up in a room in the main house, so that furniture in the marquee could be reconfigured for dancing. After everyone had gone, Harry's final duty was to liaise with the dance band as they set up their gear on a small platform at one end of the tent, then he would be free to seek an opportunity to speak to Amy. Nearly five hours had elapsed since the start of the day's proceedings, and at last he might be able to make a move.

The guests returned to the marquee to watch Ginger and Phil take to the floor to kick off the dancing. Harry was aware that protocol required him to have a dance with each of the bridesmaids, and so he decided to ask Blanche first and get it over with quickly before turning his full attention to Amy. Blanche was sitting with some of Ginger's college friends, talking loudly and rather too much, when he approached her and asked her to dance. She appeared remarkably excited by his invitation, in fact her demeanour had changed dramatically since Harry had last observed her at the registry office, when she had looked taciturn and unsmiling. She had become giggly and garrulous. It was not long before Harry realised she was very drunk.

'I'm so glad you asked me first, Harry,' Blanche slurred, in a drink-fuelled attempt at coquettishness, clinging firmly to him in a sort of shuffling waltz. 'You're such a pretty boy and I felt sure you'd ask Amy. But you chose me, you naughty boy, you. I expect you like older women don't you? That's it, isn't it, Harry? You like someone with a bit of experience. Ooh... you're so naughty. Of course, everyone keeps saying how lovely Amy looks, and I was sure you'd ask her first. But I think I look just as nice and that's why you chose me. You do think I look nice, don't you, Harry?'

'You look very nice, Blanche – very nice indeed.' Of course, Harry didn't think Blanche looked nice at all. At her best, she could hardly be described as attractive, and any bloom of youth she might once have had was well and truly in the past, but in her bridesmaid's outfit, the same one that looked so elegant on Amy's slender figure, Blanche looked rather bizarre. It was quite out of place on her stocky frame and thickset, muscular legs – a bulldog dressed up as a gazelle. And to compound matters, she had become increasingly dishevelled as the alcohol had taken its toll: her intricate hairdo had come slightly adrift, her lipstick was smudged, and the bodice of her frock was dotted with drink stains. But none of this stopped her coming on strong with Harry, and, if he had supposed that his dance with Blanche would be over quickly, he very soon had to think again. She simply wouldn't let go of him. Even when he tried to excuse himself each time the dance band finished a number, she held on to him with a ferocious, almost animal-like tenacity and demanded 'just one more little trip round the dance floor with your little Blanchie'. And all the while she was making suggestive remarks, repeatedly saying how good she felt, being away from the children and her 'dull, moronic husband' for the weekend, and how nice it would be if she and Harry were to get together later in the evening and spend some time together, although she never specifically invited him to go to her bedroom. She would look up at him while they were dancing with her version of doe eyes, fluttering her eyelashes and telling him what a pretty boy he was and how much she would like to 'mother' him.

After four dances Harry, who was by now getting desperate, made up his mind that, the next time the band stopped playing, he would break free from Blanche, however rude and physically forceful he had to be, and make his escape, but half way through the number she suddenly started to loosen her grip. Harry let go of her and stood back. Blanche just stood in front of him, swaying slightly, with a glazed look in her eyes.

'I need the toilet!' she suddenly announced, her drunken words barely comprehensible. 'Take me to the ladies.'

'I can't do that, Blanche,' replied a startled Harry, suddenly feeling completely out of his depth. 'Look, I'll go and find your mother. She'll know what to do.'

'No, I don't want her... I want you. Take me to my room then. I need to lie down.'

However much Harry wanted to escape from Blanche, he was not one to shirk his responsibilities to others – he was, after all, a child of the rectory. The least he could do was assist Blanche away from the dance floor and find her somewhere to sit down. He put his arm around her waist and guided her carefully and slowly out of the marquee and into the open, where she could get some fresh air. There were some wooden benches by the edge of the lawn just below the terrace, near steps that led up to the doors of the dining hall, and so he led her towards these. Just as they reached one of the benches, Blanche announced that she was going to be sick. Harry quickly diverted her towards an adjacent rose bed, where she leant forward and proceeded to evacuate the contents of her stomach over one of Jim Semark's prize floribunda rose bushes in full bloom. Harry gently sat her down on the bench, instructing her to stay where she was, and went off to find her mother.

To say that Amy was disappointed when, from the other side of the dance floor, she saw Harry go and ask Blanche for the first dance would be an understatement of some magnitude – she was gutted. But she managed to persuade herself that Harry was probably just fulfilling an obligation to dance with both bridesmaids and that it would soon be her turn. So she had a dance with Phil's father and one with one of his uncles, and then a couple of jigs with his thirteen year old cousin, Simon, all the time affecting an air of jolly conviviality. But inside, all she wanted was Harry to come and sweep her off her feet. Then she watched Harry put his arm round Blanche and leave the marquee with her. She couldn't understand what was going on. How could he be interested in Blanche, of all people? After all, there were quite a few attractive young women at the reception, even if he didn't want Amy herself. She was not a judgemental sort of girl but she had found Blanche extremely difficult to get on with during the course of the day, and considered both her demeanour and her appearance to be quite off-putting. Perhaps Harry had developed a penchant for older women, as a result of his relationship with the Liverpudlian student she had heard about from Ginger. She went and joined a group of college friends who were standing by the bar, set up on a long trestle table on one side of the marquee, where she asked for a glass of wine before endeavouring to join in the conversation. But she was feeling sad and upset, and needed to collect her thoughts. After ten minutes or so, she decided to find somewhere she could sit by herself for a while and think things through. She made her way to one of the exits from the marquee and was just about to leave when somebody approached her from behind and grasped her firmly by the arm. She turned round and found herself confronted by Hedley Stevens.

'Where are you off to?' demanded Hedley, with a leering smile on his face. 'I've been waiting to have a dance with you. Don't I know you from somewhere?'

Amy recognised him instantly as the obnoxious young man who had taken Harry from her, the night they had met. 'Yes, I've seen you once before. You were rather rude to me then. What do you want?'

'I want you dance with me. I'm sorry if you thought I was rude. I remember now. It was back in the autumn when I collected Irving from the university coffee bar. He had behaved like a bit of a prat that evening, you know, not turning up for his lift to London. Anyway, come and have a dance with me, it's far too early for you to be sloping off.'

She could have excused herself by saying she was going to the ladies' cloakroom, because she certainly didn't find the prospect of dancing with Hedley particularly appealing, but she was still in a confused state and feeling weary from all that had happened, so she reluctantly acquiesced and took to the dance floor with him.

Meanwhile, Harry had found Blanche's mother sitting quietly with her husband on a sofa in the sparsely populated dining hall – they were obviously not enjoying socialising with the Kentish gentry in the marquee. He explained the situation to them and they both agreed to go with him to look after their daughter. They found her slumped on the bench, fast asleep and snoring gently. Harry excused himself, saying that there were one or two things he needed to take care of, and then hotfooted it back to the marquee. Once inside he scoured the throng for Amy, and very soon spotted her unmistakeable figure on the dance floor – dancing with Hedley Stevens, of all people. Hedley and Amy were on the far side of the floor from Harry, Amy with her back to him. They were on their second dance and it was already quite apparent to Amy that Hedley wasn't simply being sociable but was making a play for her, in his rather crude, naïve way. She was determined to get away from him as quickly as possible, without being unduly discourteous, but she was finding him very persistent. From his position, Harry couldn't tell whether or not Amy was happy dancing with Hedley – although what any girl could possibly see in him was beyond Harry's comprehension – and he was nervous of dashing his chances with her by rudely interrupting a liaison she was enjoying. However, by the time the band had finished their current number, frustrated by the way events had unfolded during the course of the day, he threw caution to the wind and strode determinedly across the floor to where the couple were standing.

   Amy was just beginning to make her excuses to Hedley, who appeared not to be taking the slightest notice of what she was saying, when Harry arrived on the scene. He took Amy's hand in his and said very firmly, 'Excuse me, Stevens, but I'm afraid you'll have to give way. The next dance with Amy is mine. I've been in serious dereliction of my duty as best man in taking so long to ask her to dance, and I'm afraid you'll just have to stand aside.' The band struck up again, with a slower number this time, and Harry whisked Amy away from Hedley and into the crowd of dancing couples, leaving Hedley nonplussed and angry. He held her gently but closely, and she melted into his embrace, putting her head against his chest, free at last from the anguish that had built up inside her, and overwhelmed with happiness. They swayed softly together throughout the number without uttering a word. It was only when the band stopped playing that they looked smilingly into each other's eyes and started to speak.

'Hello, Amy.'
'Hello, Harry.'
'I'm sorry it took so long.'
'Thank heaven you're here now.'
'Thank heaven you're here with me.'

They danced some more and then decided to leave the party for a while to take a stroll through the gardens. It was early evening at the end of a bright, warm, June day. They held hands as they walked across lawns and through woodland pathways until they were sure they were out of sight of the revellers at the reception, and then they turned to face each other. They embraced and kissed for the first time. For Harry it was a magical moment, finally to have Amy in his arms, kissing her sweet, full, warm lips, after all that had happened during the course of the day. For Amy it was also a moment of perfect bliss, and when their mouths opened slightly and their tongues touched, her whole body reacted, almost violently, with a sensation of pure pleasure. It was as if an electric shock had shot through her. She gasped out loud and literally went weak at the knees. She clung to Harry as they continued to kiss, locked together in mutual passion. They stayed close to each other for the rest of the evening, firmly resolved that nothing would separate them.

Chapter 6
After the Wedding: June/July 1966

They slept together that night in Amy's room at Castle Court. They did not make love in the fullest sense – Harry had learned from his teacher, Flic, never to 'proceed to penetration' unless fully prepared in the condom department – but they were intimate in many ways, spending the night blissfully wrapped in each other's arms.

The wedding party had wound down after the bride and groom had departed for their honeymoon in Phil's new Jaguar, a wedding present from Jim and Sylvia. By nine o'clock, all of the guests who were not staying the night had left, and those who were staying had assembled in the drawing room for a light buffet supper, which had been laid on by the Semarks' domestic staff. Harry had been offered a room at Castle Court for the night by Sylvia when they were at the registry office, just before the marriage ceremony, because one of her relatives had phoned earlier in the day to say that she and her husband were not going to be able to make it to the reception, thereby leaving their allocated room vacant. This meant that there was no need for him to return that evening to the George Hotel in Cranbrook. Amy had excused herself from the supper party shortly after ten-thirty, saying that she was tired out and needed to turn in after the excitement of the day. About fifteen minutes later, Harry announced that he too was going to retire. He said goodnight to those of the party who were still up, and then proceeded to find his way to Amy's room where she was in bed waiting for him, still wearing her slip.

The next day, after breakfast, Amy and Harry set off for Wessex. Harry had acquired Phil's old Morris Minor as a best man present. Phil had offered him a choice of valuable gifts in consideration of his services, including a new gold watch, but Harry, knowing that Phil was soon to be the recipient of a brand new Jaguar, had tentatively suggested that he would like Phil's old car. At first Phil had resisted, saying that the Morris was worth virtually nothing on the second hand car market, even though it had been carefully maintained, was in good condition and ran well, and that he wanted Harry to have something of value. In the end they agreed that Harry should have the Morris together with a year's insurance and road tax, paid for by Phil. Thus, the young lovers took their leave of the Semarks and Ginger's family – except for Blanche, who had not yet dared to show her face that morning – by driving away together down the long Castle Court drive. Jim and Sylvia stood on the front doorstep waving them off. When the Morris was out of sight, they turned and smiled at each other with a knowing look in their eyes, then turned and went back into the house, holding hands.

After calling at The George so that Harry could collect his things and check out, the pair took a leisurely drive along the south coast to Wessex. There were three more weeks of the official summer term remaining, which they planned to spend together in Harry's bedsit. Neither of them was willing to contemplate life beyond that: Amy had scarcely given a thought to the small matter of what she was going to do about her relationship with Guy, and Harry had almost blanked out all thoughts of pop stardom. They were totally immersed in their passion for each other. They went first to Amy's college so that she could check her mail and messages and collect some things. Then they went to the Students' Union at the university so that Harry could also check his pigeonhole. Neither of them had communications of any significance and so they drove to Harry's place where they parked the car in the street, right outside the front of the house, and went inside. They scarcely emerged during their first week together, other than to buy provisions and make a couple of sallies to The Bassett Arms.

Harry's – formerly Phil's – bedsit was the downstairs front room of a Victorian semi-detached house in a tree-lined road of similar properties. It was a large, high-ceilinged room with a bay window facing the street, an old granite fireplace and ornate plaster mouldings round the ceiling. Although quite grand, it was run-down and sparsely furnished. It contained an old, creaky, three-quarter bed which sagged in the middle, a couple of old leather armchairs, a table and upright chair, and a fitted wardrobe. Other amenities included a washbasin, a Baby Belling electric cooker and a Gas Miser fire. One corner of the room was taken up with Harry's guitars, amplifiers and p.a. equipment. However, there were posters on the walls, which Phil had left, a number of cushions scattered about the room, and lots of books, all of which made the place feel more habitable. And on their first excursion to buy provisions, Amy bought two boxes of candles, which, when lit, gave the room a cosy, more intimate ambience.

Amy lost her virginity on their second night together in the bedsit. Harry had been patient and gentle in his lovemaking and, tutored by Flic, sensitive to Amy's needs and pleasure as well as his own. Their first full sex had been good for both of them, and it just got better as the days went by. When not making love, they talked – about virtually everything: their homes, families, friends, schools and courses; religion, politics, music, books and films; food, drink, holidays, fashion and hairstyles; television and radio programmes; and so on and so on. But one subject they did not broach in any detail, until several days had elapsed, was the troublesome question of other boyfriends and girlfriends. They had both mentioned in passing various dates they had each had in the past, before going to college and university, but not the more serious matter of current liaisons. It was Amy who raised the matter. It was Friday morning, a week after the wedding, and they were lying in bed together under the sheets smoking cigarettes, having just made love.

'Harry, are you going to tell me about the older girl from Liverpool you've been seeing? Ginger told me about her... she knew about her from Phil.' She put her cigarette out and rolled over towards Harry, putting her head on his chest. 'Tell me about her, Harry, and I'll tell you about Guy. I know Phil will have told you I've got a boyfriend back home.'

'You mean Flic... Felicity Tustin. Yes, I should have said something about her before, I know, but she's not a proper girlfriend, Amy, she's just a friend really. Anyway, she's just taken her finals and she'll be leaving Wessex soon. She may have already gone if she isn't staying around for graduation – she's just finished a four year languages degree. There's not much to say really, Amy. I started seeing her shortly after our meeting last November... she used to flirt with me in the student common room. But she's not my girlfriend – she says she's got a regular boyfriend in Liverpool – and I know for sure that she's been seeing a couple of other blokes at Wessex. As I say, she's just a friend really... well, a sort of friend I have sex with now and then.'

Amy fell silent for a moment, and then said quietly, 'I see. So you're having sex with her. Where does that leave me?'

'Amy, there's no comparison. She's not in the same league as you,' asserted Harry, sitting up in bed. 'I don't love her, I don't think of her as my girlfriend and I don't know if I'll ever see her again. She may have gone home to Knotty Ash, for all I know. But you're special, Amy. There's no other girl like you. You're quite wonderful. I haven't said this before, Amy, but I think I'm in love with you...in fact I know I am. I love you, Amy.'

'And, I love you, Harry. I love you so very much.' She snuggled up to him, and then they kissed. They lay back down on the bed and held onto each other tightly, almost as if they were both afraid the other one might somehow disappear.

'So… what about Guy?' Harry asked after a while.

'Oh, Guy… it's quite a long story really,' Amy said, releasing Harry from her arms and sitting up. 'He's my boyfriend in Newark. I've been going out with him for over a year now.' She then went on to tell Harry the whole story, emphasising the fact that she didn't love Guy, and never had done, and also that there was virtually no physical aspect to their relationship, other than a little kissing now and then. She told Harry that she thought Guy would be devastated if she finished with him and that he was banking on their getting married, even if he had to wait another four years. The telling of the story made both Amy and Harry focus for the first time on what might happen when their three weeks together came to an end, which it surely would. They would both have to go their separate ways, at least for a while, at the end of term when they returned to their respective family homes for the long summer vacation. There were some big decisions to be made. In the end they decided to procrastinate. They had two more weeks together which they didn't want to spoil. They would make a decision on their future at the end of that time and, in the meantime, just enjoy each moment they had together. However, despite their candour in talking about their respective relationships with Flic and Guy, neither of them had come completely clean: for some reason, which she couldn't quite fathom, Amy had not wanted to reveal her short, intimate fling with Danny Swift; and Harry hadn't told Amy that it was Flic who had taught him all he knew about making love, something that was now proving to be very much to their mutual benefit.

The other matter that Harry had said nothing to Amy about was the possibility, however slight, that he might imminently be going to leave university to become a full time pop musician. Overcome by his passion for Amy, he had pushed this to the back of his mind. He had told her about playing a few gigs with The Saxons and that he was now a permanent member of the group, and mentioned that they had been up to London for a recording session, but he hadn't told her who the session was with and what the outcome had been. It was just something he had said in passing and which neither he nor Amy had pursued. All he really wanted to think about was Amy – and he certainly didn't want her to be put off by thinking he might soon be going away on tour and leaving her behind at college, particularly when the likelihood of any sort of record deal seemed, with the passing of time, to be increasingly unlikely. So Amy was completely in the dark about Harry's possible pop career.

The following week the young lovers decided to take a trip along the coast to Bournemouth for a few days, funded by the money Harry had earned – and saved – playing with The Saxons. Harry had been to the resort on a number of family holidays with his parents, staying at a private hotel near Boscombe Pier, and seemed to know it well. He was sure there would be a great many guest houses and small private hotels with inexpensive rooms vacant in late June, before the school holidays began. So they visited Woolworths in town to buy a cheap, imitation wedding ring for Amy to wear, costing half a crown, packed a small suitcase and drove down to Bournemouth, where they checked into a small B&B near Fisherman's Walk in Southbourne for three nights – as Mr and Mrs Irving. The plump, taciturn landlady who ran the place seemed unconvinced by their claim to marital status, but took their money anyway, got them to sign the visitors' book and showed them to a double room. She didn't say much but, when she did speak, she finished virtually every sentence with a loud ironic 'Mr and Mrs Irving'. But Harry and Amy didn't mind – they enjoyed their little summer vacation by the sea: sitting on the beach, taking long walks along the promenade and swimming in the still cold English Channel. They walked along the cliff top, holding hands and looking out across Poole Bay – the Isle of Wight with The

Needles, overlooked by the 'polar bear', to the east; and the Isle of Purbeck and Old Harry Rocks to the west. They went on the pier, played pitch and put and crazy golf, ate ice cream cones and dined on fish and chips in the evenings. At the end of their short, sunny, seaside break, they drove back through The New Forest, stopping to examine the Rufus Stone en route, and resumed their reclusive life together in their little love nest.

On the Thursday morning of their last week together in the bedsit, Amy and Harry went to get their exam results from lists which had been posted on notice boards in their respective academies. They had both passed comfortably, and so to celebrate, they decided to push the boat out and go for a meal at the Berni steakhouse in town. The restaurant was relatively peaceful at lunchtime, when they arrived, and they were shown to a quiet table in an alcove at the back of the room. They ordered steaks and a bottle of red wine, and proceeded to tuck in to their celebratory feast. During the course of the meal, Amy asked Harry to tell her more about his time at Regis College. She was quite fascinated by some of Harry's stories about the eccentricities of life in an independent boys' boarding school – quite different from her experience at a state-run girls' day school. Harry was telling her about some of the characters he had known at school when he happened to mention in passing the name, Danny Swift.

'Did you say Danny Swift?' Amy interrupted.

'Yes... why?'

'Well, I knew a boy called Danny Swift too. His parents lived next door to my Aunt Harriet in Wolverhampton. And he used to go to a boarding school, although I don't remember which one. I don't think he ever actually told me.'

Harry was somewhat taken aback by this revelation and cautiously asked, 'What was he like then, this Danny Swift of yours?'

'Quite tall – not as tall as you, though – slim, athletic and very blond... and he liked the sound of his own voice. He was going to go to Cambridge but his family were moving to Australia, so he decided to give up his place and go with them.'

'That sounds remarkably like the Swift I knew,' Harry said, already feeling ill at ease with the idea of Amy being friendly with the only person he had ever really detested. 'Was his full name Daniel Willoughby Swift, by any chance?'

'Yes, yes it was... it still is I suppose. He must be the same boy as your school friend. Well fancy that – what a coincidence!' Amy enthused, quite oblivious to Harry's growing state of discomfiture.

'How well did you know Danny Swift then?'

Amy had consumed nearly a third of the bottle of wine they were sharing – quite a lot for her. She was feeling mellow: happy, relaxed... and off-guard. It seemed to her the right moment to tell Harry about the week she had spent with Danny at Aunt Harriet's house, the Easter before going to college.

'Well, I haven't told you this before, Harry, but I had a bit of a fling with Danny in my last year at school. It didn't amount to much in the end, it was more like a holiday romance really... it only lasted a week. I was staying with my aunt, revising for 'A' levels.' Amy went on to tell Harry the whole story. She made it clear that she had never fallen in love with Danny, and, in many ways, hadn't really liked him, particularly his glibness. But, without going into details, she let it be known that he had excited her sexually and that he had been the only boy other than Harry with whom she had ever had any serious carnal contact. Of course, she made it clear that she had not allowed Guy to go all the way with her, and that she had remained a virgin.

A dark cloud descended over Harry as the story unfolded. He looked at Amy as she spoke, and saw the girl he loved: the loveliest, funniest, sweetest, sexiest girl he had ever known, or could ever imagine knowing. Yet the idea that she had allowed Danny Swift, the most loathsome of individuals, to touch her intimately and to arouse her sensually, appalled him. His idea of Amy had suddenly become tainted, as had his love for her. If Amy had been telling him about anyone else, anyone at all – someone she had done the deed with even – it would not have mattered. It would have just been something that had happened before he knew her, with someone he didn't know – but Danny Swift! Harry hadn't necessarily expected Amy to be a virgin, although he was pleased when she said she was. After all, he had been having sex with Flic two or three times a month, sometimes more frequently, since the end of November, and before that there had been one or two others with whom he had done some fairly heavy petting during his quest to get laid, and so he had never expected any girl he went out with to come to him untouched by human hand. But this was something different: this was Danny Swift.

When Amy finished her tale, Harry hardly seemed to react at all. He did his best to conceal his feelings. He didn't want to appear jealous or vindictive, and, in any case, Amy could not be blamed for something that had happened long before they had met, and without her having the slightest knowledge of what had transpired between Danny and himself during their schooldays. He asked Amy, as nonchalantly as he could, what had become of Danny, and found some comfort in learning that he was now living on the other side of the world in Queensland, even though she admitted to having exchanged letters with him. Amy was surprised when Harry then changed the subject and started talking about their trip to Bournemouth. It seemed strange to her that he wasn't more intrigued by the small-world coincidence of her having had a brief relationship with one of his 'school friends' and didn't appear to be interested in finding out more about it. But she didn't pursue the matter and allowed their conversation to move on to other things. They finished their meal, left the restaurant and drove back to Harry's bedsitting room.

As the afternoon wore on, Harry became increasingly morose and withdrawn. The more he thought about Amy being with Danny Swift, the more it rankled with him. Doubts filled his mind: how could Amy have allowed herself to be sexually aroused by the likes of Danny Swift; why hadn't she told him about her fling with Danny before, when she talked about other boys she had been out with in the past; was it true that she hadn't loved or particularly liked Danny, or was it more likely that she had actually fallen for him, and that the liaison had only ended because he had emigrated to Australia; and was she telling the truth when she insisted that she hadn't let Danny go all the way with her, or had she, in fact, lost her virginity to him and not Harry? He was plagued with uncertainties. Amy couldn't help but notice his change of mood and, after a while, she came over to where he was sitting, sat on his knee and put her arms round his neck.

'What's the matter, sweetheart? Why do you look so sad?' she asked, softly and sweetly.

'Oh, I don't know, Amy. I suppose it's because we've only got one more day together, and then, the day after tomorrow, you'll be going home to Newark and I'll be off home to St Bart's Rectory. We still haven't made any plans for the future or decided what we're going to do about each other... you know, you and Guy and all that.'

'I know, Harry, I know... I feel the same. But please don't let's spoil our last day together by discussing it now. Tell you what: I'll make us both a special meal tomorrow evening; we'll light some candles, have a bottle of wine and talk the whole thing over then. I'm sure I know what I really want but I haven't really given myself time to think things through properly. Let's give ourselves another day together and then have the conversation tomorrow evening – our last evening together for the time being – over a nice, cosy dinner.'

Harry mulled Amy's proposal over for a moment and then agreed; he too needed time to think. Later on they decided to go out to the pictures to see *The Good, The Bad And The Ugly* which was showing at The Tivoli cinema in town, before returning to the bedsit for a relatively early night. They didn't make love that night – the first night since they had begun having sex together. Amy had started her period, and this was the reason for their abstention, although Harry was relieved for other reasons: he felt emotionally drained from anguishing over Amy's revelation about Danny Swift, and was in no mood for sex, even if Amy had been available.

The next morning, the couple went to a local grocery store to buy supplies for their evening feast, and then to The Bassett Arms for a ceremonial final glass of beer there. In the afternoon, Harry decided to make one last trip to the university in order to check his mail in the Students' Union, and sort one or two things out in his academic department. He wondered if there might just be an outside chance of some sort of message in his pigeonhole from Jerry Somers. If not, he would assume that the game was up as far a record deal with Joe Meek was concerned. Amy decided to stay in the bedsit and do some preparation for dinner.

Shortly after Harry had left for the university, there came a loud knocking at the front door of the house. Amy ignored it, assuming that one of the other tenants in the house would go and answer it but nobody went and, after a while, there was further knocking, followed by somebody outside tapping on the bay window of the bedsit. Amy decided that she had better find out what was up. The blinds were down at the window and so she exited the bedsit and went to the front door to see who was there. She opened the door and was confronted by a tarty-looking young woman with bleached hair, dressed in a skimpy top and a skirt which Amy thought was far too short for her rather plump thighs. She knew immediately who it was.

'Oh hello! I don't know you, do I?' Flic said in her Liverpool brogue, striding through the open door, past Amy, and into the hall.

'You must be a new tenant. I've come to see Harry in the downstairs front room. Do you know if he's in?'

'No... he's out actually,' Amy replied, following Flic into the hall. 'He's gone up to the university to check his mail.'

'Hold on a mo,' said Flic suspiciously, noticing that the door to Harry's bedsit had been left ajar. 'His door's open.' She paused for a moment and then turned to face Amy, looking her up and down. 'Don't tell me,' she continued, 'you've been staying here with him, haven't you? Are you some sort of girlfriend... is that it?'

Before Amy could answer, Flic pushed open the door to Harry's room and marched in. Amy followed on behind her.

'Look, I don't know who you are,' Amy said, trying to exert some sort of control over proceedings, and knowing perfectly well who Flic was, 'but, as I've already told you, Harry's gone up to the university. Do you want to leave a message or something for me to pass on to him... before you go.'

Flic scrutinised the room with a proprietorial air, noticing the little female touches that Amy had introduced: an immaculately made bed, plumped up cushions on the chairs, cleaned basin and cooker, crockery and cutlery washed up and put away, candles in saucers dotted around the room, and clothes folded and tidied away. 'Well this looks like a proper little love nest, doesn't it? I'm Flic, by the way. I expect Harry's told you about me. Anyway, who are you?'

'I'm Amy, Harrry's girlfriend... and yes, Harry has told me about you.'

'Harry's girlfriend, eh! Well Harry hasn't told me about you. You're quite a pretty little thing aren't you? Have you been having it away with my favourite little posh boy, then?'

'I don't think that's any business of yours.' Amy said, blushing.

'Well I don't know about that, seeing as I thought I was Harry's girlfriend, and I've just come round for a bit of end-of-term hanky-panky with him.' Flic sat down on one of the old leather chairs, staring at Amy. Amy just stood there, looking totally forlorn and not knowing what to say.

'Look, chuck, I don't want to seem horrid,' Flic continued, 'but what has Harry said about me?'

'He said you weren't his girlfriend,' Amy replied. 'He said you were just a friend who he had been to bed with now and then, and that you had a regular boyfriend in Liverpool. And he said you saw other boys as well. I've been here with Harry for three weeks now, all day and all night, and, if you must know, I'm in love with him.' She walked over to the bed and sat down, tears in her eyes.

'I see. Okay then, I suppose that's not too far from the truth: I have got a feller back home... and I do like boys – that's well known, I think. But I've become rather fond of Harry, even if he is a bit too young for me. He's sort of become my favourite. He's so sweet... and handsome. I'd give up Stan, my boyfriend in Liverpool, for Harry any day if I thought he was available, but he'll be off on tour soon, I expect, so this might be the last time I see him for some time.'

'What do you mean, off on tour?' Amy said, sitting up straight with surprise.

'Hasn't he told you... you know, about the record deal and all that?'

'No. I don't know what you mean.'

Flic told Amy the whole story about the band's trip to London, the recording session at Joe Meek's, the promise of a record deal and the name of the song, the change of name for the group, and the fact that Harry was the lead singer on the chosen track. She told her how excited and full of it Harry had been when he got back from London, and how he expected there would be a national, or possible even a European, tour to coincide with the release of the record. This would mean Harry giving up his course and leaving Wessex. Amy sat listening in disbelief.

'I can't believe he hasn't told you any of this, pet,' Flic said.
'Well, he did tell me about going to London with the group for a recording session, but nothing much more – nothing about a record deal with Joe Meek or a tour or leaving university. I don't understand it. We're supposed to love each other.'

Flic suddenly felt full of compassion for Amy. She could see how confused and distressed she was – and how young and beautiful she was too. She went over to the bed, sat down next to her and took her hand.

'I can see how upset you are, chuck, so I'm not going to stay around and upset you any more. I was looking forward to seeing Harry today and spending the night with him, but that's too bad. I'll just have to go and see one of my other fellers instead – they're nothing like as nice as pretty boy Harry, of course, but one of them'll just have to do. You got here first, so I'll let you have him. I can tell you really love him, and I can understand why – and I can see why Harry might be nuts about you – so I'll give in this time. I'm not usually one for letting someone get one over on me, but I'll make an exception in your case.'

'Thank you, Flic,' was all Amy could think of to say.

'Let me give you some advice, Amy, before I push off. I'm sure you love Harry all right, but be very careful before you give your all to him. He could break your little heart, he could, if this pop group thing takes off. So you just be careful… sometimes there's more to life than fellers and love and sex. You be very careful, my sweet.'

Flic stood up and walked to the bedsit door. She turned to Amy and said, 'I probably won't see Harry again, so say goodbye to him for me, will you? I've enjoyed seeing him, and teaching him all about sex – he was a good pupil… quick and eager to learn. I'll miss him. And you take care now, my pretty one, and remember what I've said. Right, I'll be off. I need to make sure I've got a date for tonight, so I'd better get a move on. Bye then, chuck.' And with that she left the room, closing the door behind her. Amy heard her shut the front door of the house and walk off down the street, her heels clicking on the paving stones.

When Harry checked the undergraduate pigeonholes in the Students' Union, he found, to his surprise, an envelope addressed to him in familiar blue ink. It was a message from Jerry Somers. He held the envelope in his hand, staring at it for some time. He felt just as he had done when he received his 'A' level results in the post, two years earlier. He decided to bite the bullet and open it, which he did slowly and nervously. His hand was shaking as he read the contents. Jerry wrote that *Everyone But Me* by Harry and The Hawks was to be released on the Pye record label on or about 4th August, to be followed shortly thereafter by a six month tour of Europe and the UK, supporting The Tornados, another band from the Joe Meek stable. There was to be a week of rehearsals, immediately prior to the start of the tour, at a venue to be confirmed; living accommodation would be provided. The letter clearly stated what the weekly rate of pay for members of the band would be during the course of the tour – a handsome amount, on top of living expenses which would be handled by Jerry – but nothing was said about the band's entitlement to payments in respect of record sales.

Harry could hardly believe his luck. He really was about to embark on a career as a pop singer. He put the letter away in his pocket and hurried back to his car, which was parked in the student car park adjacent to the Union building, before driving back to his pad. His excitement at potentially realising the second of his great ambitions – getting laid having been the first – and the prospect of fame and fortune to come completely dominated his thoughts. He was aware, of course, that explaining the situation to Amy was not going to be easy, and that she might well cut up rough at the idea of his being on the verge of giving up university and leaving her behind in Wessex for the next two years of her course. But as far as Harry was concerned, if he was forced to choose between pop stardom and Amy, there was only one winner. He might well have thought differently if the Danny Swift revelation had not been at the forefront of his mind but, much as he wanted to keep Amy as his girlfriend, he was not going to give up the opportunity of a lifetime for a girl who could be seduced by the likes of Danny Swift. Hopefully he would be able to have his cake and eat it but, if not, it was Harry and The Hawks for him.

Amy was sitting in one of the armchairs, listening to the radio, when Harry arrived back at the bedsit. They greeted each other in the usual way, as if nothing had happened during the couple of hours they had been apart. They chatted for thirty minutes or so about nothing in particular, each one anxiously trying to pluck up courage and seeking the most judicious moment to say what needed to be said. It was Amy who struck first.

'I met your friend, Flic, this afternoon, Harry! She came here looking for you.'

'What, Flic... here? But, I thought she must be back in Liverpool by now. I haven't heard anything from her since exams finished.'

'Well, she's still here in town. She said she had come round for some end-of-term hanky-panky with you.' Amy went on to relate the story of Flic's visit, much to Harry's embarrassment, and then she said, 'So, Harry, what's all this about a record deal with Joe Meek... and leaving university to go on tour?'

'Oh, that... she told you about that, did she? Well, I did tell you we'd been up to London for a recording session.'

'Yes, you did. But not who with, and not that you'd been offered a record deal, and not that you were seriously planning to leave university and go off on tour. Where do I fit in to all of this?'

'Well, we hadn't actually been offered a record deal or a tour. Joe Meek said he was going to try and get one of the big record labels to take us on, and our agent, Jerry Somers, said a record deal would lead to a tour and other commitments, so we'd need to make ourselves available. But I hadn't heard anything about it from Jerry for over five weeks, so I thought the whole thing was probably off. That's why I didn't tell you about it.'

'So, there's no deal then, and no tour, is that it? And you'll still be here at university next term so that we can go on seeing each other?'

There was a painful pause while Harry fumbled in his pocket for Jerry Somers' letter. He looked at Amy, sitting opposite him, looking as lovely as ever, and felt her slipping away from him. He handed her the letter. 'You'd better read this. I got it today.'

Amy and Harry spent the rest of the evening in difficult and often emotional discussion about their future. They ate their special meal and drank their bottle of wine – Amy even lit the candles – but it was far from the romantic evening it might have been. There were recriminations and expressions of disappointment, but no real anger. The atmosphere was more one of despair at the prospect of their magical love affair slipping through their fingers. They each expressed their love for the other and their desire to continue their relationship, but Harry was gently insistent that he was not willing to give up his 'chance of a lifetime' to make it in the world of pop music. Amy understood how important this was to Harry but, by the same token, was not willing to commit herself to finishing with Guy and giving up her future financial prospects for the sake of someone who was going to be away on the road most of the time in the ensuing months, and who was prepared to gamble his future on the vagaries of the pop music industry. Their anguished dialogue had no conclusive outcome: neither of them was prepared categorically to finish their affair, yet neither was willing to give ground on his or her entrenched position. In essence they did little more than agree to let things drift. They would be parting company the next day. They had each other's home address and telephone number, and so they would leave things open and let destiny take its course.

The next morning they packed their belongings ready for their separate journeys home in the afternoon. Harry crammed all of his things, except for his musical equipment, into two suitcases, then drove to the university to store away his guitars and amplifiers in one of the Students' Union music rooms. Amy returned to her college hostel to collect her things. She had been allocated the same room for the following academic year – although she hadn't been told who her new room mate would be. This meant that she was not required to clear the room, and so she too could manage with just a couple of suitcases. Harry drove her to the station in time to catch her train, before setting off on the two hour drive to St Bartholomew's Rectory near Swindon. Their parting had been far from easy – it had been awkward and upsetting. Amy could scarcely contain her distress during the long train journey north to Newark: several times she felt tears starting to roll down her cheeks. But she was able to compose herself and remain firm in her resolve not to yield to an almost overwhelming desire to throw caution to the wind and give everything up for the sake of Harry. She was sustained in this by the advice her Aunt Harriet had given her the previous September, shortly before she left home to start college, and her aunt's revelations about her beloved and sorely missed father.

Chapter 7
September 1965: The Tale of Amy's Father

Aunt Harriet climbed the stairs of her sister's semi-detached house in Newark, and knocked on Amy's door. She had been staying with Doris for the weekend in order to see her niece before she left home for college the following Saturday. She knew Amy was in her little bedroom, going through some things and trying to decide what to take with her for her first time living away from home. Amy said 'come in' and Aunt Harriet entered to find her niece sitting on the bed, looking at some photographs. The one she was holding was of her father, taken just over a year before he had died.

'Can I have a little word, dear?' Aunt Harriet said gently, sitting down on the bed next to Amy with an envelope in her hand. 'I've got something here for you, but I wanted to have a little private chat with you as well, before you go away to college.' She handed Amy the envelope.

'Thank you, Auntie,' Amy said, looking surprised.

'I don't want you to open it now, Amy. Open it later, after I've set off for home.' Amy put the envelope down on her bedside table, along with the photograph of her father. 'Your mother tells me you're going steady with a nice young estate agent in town. That's the young man you went out with last night, I suppose?' Aunt Harriet had not yet met Guy.

'Yes, Auntie, his name's Guy. I've been going out with him since May.'

'Well that's good. Mum says he's a good steady young man from a well-to-do family, and that he's got very good prospects.'

'Yes, that's right. When he passes his final exams next May, he'll be a qualified chartered surveyor. He reckons he'll be a partner in the family firm before he's thirty.'

'Excellent. And do you like him?'

'Yes, of course, Auntie. I wouldn't go out with him if I didn't.'

'No, of course not... but do you think you love him?'

Amy thought for a moment before responding. 'I'm not really sure what it feels like to be in love with a boy, Auntie, but I think the answer is: no, I don't love him. I suppose I would know if I did.'

'I see. Well I'd like to give you just a little bit of advice about young men and love and marriage, before you go off on your own, all the way down south. You'll meet a lot of boys down there, I'm sure, from all sorts of backgrounds. I know you're going to an all female college, but there will be hundreds of young men at the nearby university, and you're bound to meet and mix with some of them. The thing is, Amy my love, you're such a pretty little thing and there are bound to be boys who will want to take you out, and I don't want you to come across some handsome heartthrob type who might turn your head. You mustn't get swept off your feet by some clever young fellow who turns out to be feckless and unreliable. My advice to you, my dear, is to hang on to your steady, solid, young estate agent who can provide you with a decent future, just like Uncle Cyril has done for me. I didn't fall in love with Uncle Cyril at first, you know, not even when we got married. But he was good and steady and hard working, and I grew to love him. He's always been good to me, and he has been a wonderful provider. As you know, Amy, my only regret is that we didn't have children. But that's why you're so important to me.'

Amy hadn't given much thought to the prospect of meeting boys when she got to college, and so her aunt's counsel did not seem particularly important or relevant to her at the time. As far as she was concerned, Guy was her boyfriend and that was that – she wasn't looking for anyone new. So she simply said, 'Yes, Auntie, I'll stick with Guy, as you say.'

'That was a photograph of your father you were looking at when I came in, wasn't it?'

Amy nodded and sighed slightly.

'You were ten when he died, weren't you, Amy? What do you remember about him?'

'I loved him lots. I think about him often. He was always gentle and kind and loving. He played with me whenever I asked him to and he was always lots of fun. I know he was a bit soft with Roger, and Roger used to take advantage of him and misbehave – until Mum sorted things out – but, as far as I was concerned, he was perfect.'

'Does your mother ever talk about him?'

'Not very much, I think it makes her sad. But when she does, she just says what a good, kind man he was, and how handsome he was, and how much she loved him.'

'Well, you're daddy was handsome, my dear, and he was kind, but there are things about him you probably don't know.' Aunt Harriet sat and thought for a moment, and then went on, 'Look, I'm going to tell you some things about your father that your mum will probably never have mentioned to you, not because I want to spoil your memory of him – it's quite right that you should have loved your father and have fond memories of him – but because I think you ought to know the whole story before you go off to college on your own. They're not particularly bad things, just things that might put a different complexion on how you look at life, particularly when it comes to boyfriends and getting married and that sort of thing. You see, the trouble with your father was that he didn't live in the real world. He was a dreamer.' Aunt Harriet then went on to tell the tale of Amy's father – as she saw it:

Arthur Anderton was born in 1914, the son of a wealthy Bradford industrialist who owned a successful dye works in the city. It was just before the outbreak of the Great War. His mother had died in childbirth, something for which his father never quite forgave him, and so for the first seven years of his life he was raised by a nanny, known as Fletcher, whom he grew to love. She was in late middle-age when she came to the Anderton household to look after baby Arthur, and she would remain there until she died fifteen years later, by which time she had become Mr Anderton's housekeeper. His father was a remote figure who, when not away on business, spent his time in his large private library where he also took his meals, removed from the goings-on in the rest of the household. At the age of seven, Arthur was sent away to a boarding preparatory school near Huddersfield and then at thirteen to Repton School in Derbyshire. When he was sixteen, his father married again, this time to a much younger woman, and a year later a baby girl was born – Arthur's half-sister, Eliza.

Despite being a dreamer, Arthur was a bright boy who did well at school, well enough to earn a place at Oxford University to read English Literature, a place he took up in the Michaelmas term of 1933. By this time he had grown into a handsome, if somewhat gaunt, young man, although he was by now deaf in one ear as a result of a vicious kick to the head, received while playing rugby at school. He had also developed a passion for poetry and had spent much of his spare time at school and in the school holidays penning different types of verse – he had even attempted to write a play in blank verse, in what he perceived to be the style of Shakespeare. By the time he arrived at university, he had become obsessed with his poetry writing, convinced that his destiny was to become a man who would make his living by the pen. He soon discovered that there was little at Oxford University that pleased or suited him. He found his studies dull, his tutors overbearing and pretentious, and his fellow students immature and irritating. Shortly after the start of his second year, he decided to cut his losses and go to London to try his luck as a professional poet, and so he left university and headed for the capital. He had an allowance from his father – intended to support him through college – and so he could just about afford to sustain himself in a rented room in Highgate while he established himself in the world of literature. He hawked his writings round the London publishing houses and sent samples of his work to various magazines which published poetry; he spent a great deal of time in various inns and coffee houses where he supposed the literati hung out, hoping to make contact with kindred spirits and those with influence in the publishing world; and in the evenings, he beavered away at new pieces of poetry in his cold, bleak rented room, on an ancient typewriter he had acquired – but all to no avail.

It was not until he was at home for Christmas in December, 1934, that he told his father what he had done. His father, who had long been exasperated by his son's lack of conventional drive and ambition, and who regarded his achievement of gaining a place at Oxford University as his one saving grace, was outraged at the news. He declared that he would disown Arthur unless he agreed to return to university – if the university would allow it – and resume his studies, at the earliest opportunity. Arthur refused to do so. That would have been that, and he would have been cut off without a penny if his young stepmother had not intervened on his behalf. Instead, he was cut off with a once-and-for-all gift of £500, a not insignificant sum at the time. Otherwise, he was no longer welcome in the family home, and he was told by his father to regard himself as disinherited. Arthur never saw his father again and never returned to his Bradford home.

For the next few years Arthur lived in London, continuing, with diminishing enthusiasm, the hopeless pursuit of his dream of becoming a professional poet, while frittering away his modest fortune. Eventually the money ran out and he started to take low-paid, unskilled jobs in order to keep a roof over his head and food in his belly. By the time war broke out in 1939, he had abandoned the capital and found himself working as a shop assistant in a bookshop in Nottingham, a city to which he had moved in pursuit of a young woman he had fallen in love with – and by whom he had soon been discarded. A few months later, he received his call-up papers for military service, but failed the medical on account of his one deaf ear and a heart murmur which his medical examination had revealed. He returned to his job in the bookshop and joined the local Home Guard. He met Doris, Amy's mother, in late 1940. She was working as a secretary in Nottingham, her home town, and was a frequent browser and occasional buyer in Arthur's bookshop, which was near the office where she worked. She had just had her twenty-third birthday.

Doris was a pretty, slender young woman to whom Arthur took an immediate fancy. He would endeavour to engage her in conversation whenever she visited the bookshop. Doris found Arthur extremely attractive – handsome, charming, gentle and funny – and very soon fell for him. However, she was already engaged to Walter Hanson, a young solicitor who was a friend of Cyril Ostime, Aunt Harriet's husband. At the time, Walter was serving as a lieutenant in the infantry, having volunteered for military service at the outbreak of war, and had recently been posted to the Middle East along with his regiment. Arthur and Doris started to meet each other during their lunch breaks at one of the local pubs, and were soon deeply in love. Doris decided to break off her engagement with Walter, and did so by sending him a 'Dear John' letter, which he received just a few months before being killed in action in an Allied operation against the Vichy French in Lebanon. The couple got engaged and were married in October, 1941, at Doris's local Catholic church, just in time for Doris to avoid being called up, as a single woman, to join one of the women's auxiliary services. Their first child, Roger, was born in September of the following year.

At the end of the war, Arthur managed to secure the post of assistant manager of a bookshop in Newark. The job was not very well paid but it provided a steady income, and there was enough to keep the little family housed and fed. With the help of Cyril Ostime, who had influence with the Tipton Building Society, Doris and Arthur were able to obtain a mortgage on a small semi-detached house in Newark – the house in which Amy would grow up and which would remain the family home. Amy, the couple's second child, was born at the beginning of November, 1946. It was a constant struggle, bringing up two small children on Arthur's modest income, plus the family allowance, but things improved slightly when Amy was six and Roger ten, and Doris was able to take a part-time job at the local library, working hours that fitted in reasonably well with the children's school times – although there was still some juggling that needed to be done, arranging childcare cover with various friends and neighbours on those occasions when school was out and Doris had to be at work.

Arthur, who had become a heavy smoker, was diagnosed with lung cancer early in 1956, and died a year later, throwing the family back into near penury.

When Aunt Harriet finished telling the story, Amy fell silent. There was so much of her family history about which she knew nothing. Her mother seldom talked about the past and Amy had never been sufficiently interested to want to ask questions and find out. She had been told that her father's parents had both died before her own parents had met, and that there were no aunts, uncles or cousins on his side of the family. She was completely unaware of her father's youthful obsession with poetry and his futile endeavour to fulfil the ambition of becoming a poet; neither was she aware that he had come from a wealthy family and gone to Oxford University, and that he had given everything up, including the prospects of a handsome inheritance and a lucrative career, in pursuit of this forlorn ambition. Amy had also once been told by her mother that, before she had met Amy's father, she had been engaged to a soldier who was killed in the war; but Amy had never been told that her mother had, in fact, broken off the engagement in order to be with Arthur Anderton, nor that her fiancé had been a solicitor who might well have been able to provide her with the sort of lifestyle that Aunt Harriet had enjoyed.

It was Aunt Harriet who broke the silence. 'I'm sorry, my dear, have I upset you? Perhaps I shouldn't have told you all of this. Perhaps I should have kept it to myself. Doris has never asked me to keep these things a secret from you and Roger, but I know she has never told you much about your father's past or his family history, and I just thought it was time you knew. Perhaps I should have kept quiet.'

'No, Auntie, I'm glad you've told me. I needed to know these things. And it doesn't make me love Daddy any less. I love him more, if anything. It's such a sad story... and a happy one too: sort of bitter sweet.'

They talked for a while longer and then Aunt Harriet said she had better go and pack her suitcase, ready for her journey back to Wolverhampton later that afternoon. Amy stayed in her room, reflecting on her aunt's revelations. There was much to take in and come to terms with, but most of all, the story of her father bolstered her in her resolve never to allow herself to fall into the poverty trap that had ensnared her mother... and her childhood self. She would follow her aunt's advice and stick with her steady estate-agent boyfriend.

That evening, after Aunt Harriet had left, Amy went to her room and opened the envelope she had been given. Inside was a floral notelet on which her aunt had written a most affectionate good luck message. And attached was a cheque in the princely sum of £150, 'for my dear Amy to help you through your first year at college.'

THE SUN, THE MOON AND HARRY

Chapter 8
July 1972: Amy

'Good morning, Mrs Boucher. Lovely morning,' declared Bob Allen, the baker, as Amy entered his shop on a bright, late July, Saturday morning. 'Turned out nice again, as George Formby used to say. What can I do you for this morning, m' duck – the usual?' Bob said virtually the same thing every Saturday – except when it was raining.

'Yes please, Mr Allen. A large split-tin loaf and six teacakes... and may I have a fresh cream Victoria sponge as well, this week. It's for Mum. I'm going round to hers for a cup of tea later, and she can't resist one of your cream sponges.'

'Right you are, duck.'

It was six years almost to the day since Amy and Harry had parted company, and she hadn't seen him or had any contact with him since, other than seeing him on television in late August, 1966, when Harry and The Hawks made their one and only television appearance – on *Ready Steady Go* in the twilight time of that once iconic show's dwindling popularity – but she still thought about him every day. She looked very much the same as she had as a nineteen year old: her hair was slightly different – she had grown it longer, over her shoulders, and abandoned her rather severe, mid-sixties fringe in favour of the softer look of a side parting, with her hair swept across her forehead – and her figure had filled out ever so slightly, but otherwise she had hardly changed. She was wearing flared jeans and a floral blouse, in autumnal colours, and looked very much a seventies girl as she went about her Saturday morning shopping.

Amy left the baker's shop with her purchases and returned to her car, parked just outside in the street, for the short drive back to her house in Balderton, a village on the outskirts of Newark. It was just gone noon when she arrived home and pulled up on the tarmac forecourt where she saw Guy's BMW parked in front of the double garage. Guy always went to work at the main branch of Bulstrode and Boucher, Auctioneers and Estate Agents, on Saturday mornings, and so she was surprised to see him home before one-fifteen: Guy was now a partner in the family firm and took his stewardship of the business very seriously. Amy's heart sank slightly to see her husband back so early. Her home was a large, two-storey, detached house, built in 1968, with plain brickwork and extensive areas of glass, enabling visitors to see straight into the main reception rooms when approaching the front door – the bedrooms on the first floor were protected from prying eyes by what seemed like acres of net curtains. The featureless façades of the property formed an almost perfect square, topped with an ill-advised flat roof. It had been designed by an architect friend of Guy's parents as an ultra-modern residence, Amy having had very little say in its appearance or layout. Nevertheless, she had taken enormous pride and satisfaction in her new home when the newly-wed couple moved in, on their return from honeymoon.

Guy was sitting at the table in the large, stark, open-plan kitchen area, looking at the morning paper, when Amy came in through the front door. Since their marriage, he had grown a moustache and put on weight, giving him the sort of austere appearance and gravitas which he imagined suited his professional and social status. He was wearing a white shirt and tie but had removed his suit jacket, which was hanging on the back of his chair – a rare concession to the warm July weather. He looked up as Amy entered the room carrying her shopping bags, but made no offer to help. The couple greeted each other without any physical contact or endearments.

'Hello, Guy. You're home early. Is anything wrong?'

'Hello, Amy... no, nothing's wrong. I told you at breakfast that I had to be at the tennis club at one-thirty. I'm umpiring a junior tournament this afternoon... as I informed you earlier. Is there going to be any lunch before I go out?'

'Oh yes, the tennis club, I forgot. I'm sorry. Um, yes, I'll get us some salad when I've put the shopping away. It'll be ready in about twenty minutes.'

'Is that all – salad? Isn't there anything hot? You know I like a hot lunch.'

'No, Guy. It's summer and we're having salad.'

'Oh, I see.'

'Okay, Guy. If you must have something hot, I'll do you some scrambled eggs on toast.'

Guy thought for a moment. 'All right, scrambled eggs will have to do.'

Amy busied herself with the shopping, putting things away in various cupboards. After a while Guy said, 'I do wish you'd listen to what I'm saying when I'm telling you things, Amy. You always seem to be in a world of your own. You must pay proper attention when I'm talking to you. If the members of staff at work ignored what I'm saying the way you do, they'd be sacked. I hope you've remembered what's happening this evening.'

Amy thought: well sack me then... getting sacked sounds pretty good to me. And then she said, 'Yes, Guy, I have. There's a do on at the tennis club connected with the tournament and it probably won't finish until about eleven.'

'Yes... at least you haven't forgotten that. And don't forget we're going round to my parents tomorrow for Sunday dinner, after mass.'

'I haven't forgotten, Guy. I'm hardly likely to, am I, seeing as we go there every other Sunday. But I shan't be going with you to mass. I've arranged to go round to Esme's for coffee tomorrow morning.'

Esme Poppleton was one of Amy's colleagues from the primary school they both taught at; Amy and Esme had become good friends.

'What... missing mass again! That's the second time this month, you know. Really, Amy, this won't do. It doesn't do my standing in the church community any good at all when I have to turn up to mass unaccompanied by my wife – no good at all. And my parents will be very concerned about your moral wellbeing. I really don't think that going round for coffee at that Protestant woman's flat on a Sunday morning is any excuse for missing mass.'

'I'm a grown woman, Guy, and I shall do as I please, as long as it doesn't inconvenience anybody else.' Amy had become irritated by her pompous, overbearing husband, as she often was lately. 'And Esme isn't a Protestant... she isn't anything. Just because we teach in a C of E school doesn't make either of us Protestants. We'd be Anglicans, if anything, anyway.'

'Well, it inconveniences me, if you must know – your not going to mass. It inconveniences me a great deal.' There was a long pause while Guy waited for a response. Amy remained silent and got on with starting to prepare the lunch. 'You should never have taken that job at a Church of England school,' Guy went on, starting up on one of his favourite hobbyhorses. 'You should have found work in a good Catholic school, like I told you to at the time. It'll be your downfall, that infernal school will. It's already led to a fall from grace in the eyes of the church, and if it goes on like this much longer, without your going to confession, you'll be denied communion... and then where will you be? And look what it's done to our marriage. It's the reason we haven't got children: God's judgment on you for your sinful ways.'

Amy had heard all of this before, and she could barely stand to listen to it again. But she kept her calm, despite the profound frustration and unhappiness his words caused her. She said nothing and silence prevailed.

The couple lunched together in silence, but when Amy started to clear the plates away, Guy said, 'I want to remind you, Amy, about what you must do tomorrow, if my parents start going on about our starting a family and having children. They haven't done it for a while, I know, but I could tell from talking to Mum on the phone yesterday that the wretched business is playing on her mind again. You're to change the subject, okay? Steer the conversation onto something else. Just say that we're not quite ready yet and move on. I don't want there to be the slightest suggestion that we don't want or can't have children, or any talk about our need to get started with a family, just like my sister has done with her two little brats, or any of that sort of talk. Do you understand, Amy? They're my parents and I expect you to respect my wishes.'

'Yes, Guy, I think I can manage that. I always do.'

'Right... well I'm going now. I expect you'll be asleep when I get home. I do hope the double bed in the guest room is made up for me so I can go to bed in there. Goodbye, then.'

'Goodbye.'

Guy got up, put on his jacket and left the table, without making the slightest contribution to clearing up or washing the dishes. Amy breathed a sigh of relief when she heard him exit the house through the front door. She went into the living room, where she poured herself a glass of Scotch, sat down on the sofa and lit a cigarette. She sat there, sipping whisky and smoking, and pondered her fate. She realised how unhappy she was and knew she had to do something about it, but she couldn't work out exactly what. She didn't, as yet, feel trapped or completely miserable: she had her teaching job which she loved, and her friends from the school staff, whom she liked very much and who were, unwittingly, a significant source of solace and support to her; she had all the material possessions and comforts she could ever have wished for; she had the house to herself most of the time, with Guy being busy at work during the week, and involved with the church and the tennis club most weekends and often in the evenings; and anyway, she knew Guy's religious principles meant he would never agree to a divorce. She had come to the conclusion that she had lost the great love and passion of her life when she had lost Harry, and that she was unlikely ever again to find someone she could love the same way. But she didn't yet feel ready or able to leave Guy and everything she had strived for, by striking out on her own, as her friend, Esme, had done. So, instead, she sipped her whisky and, not for the first time, started to reflect on how life had brought her to this not very pretty pass.

When Amy returned to Newark in the summer of 1966, she waited anxiously, hoping and praying that Harry would contact her, either by phone or by writing her a letter, but he did neither. She knew he would almost certainly be on the road somewhere, touring – either in Britain or Europe – and the chances of her making direct contact with him were extremely remote. She regularly toyed with the idea of telephoning the rectory and leaving a message for him with his parents, or writing to him there, but something inside her always stopped her at the last moment – she had actually composed a letter to him and placed it in a stamped addressed envelope, but on three separate occasions she had drawn back from posting it, on the brink of dropping it into the post box. Deep down she felt it was up to Harry to make contact: it was he who had decided to give up university and go off on tour, risking everything on the throw of the pop stardom dice, and leaving her behind at college for the next two years with little hope of seeing very much of him. It had been his decision, not hers, and it was for him to regenerate their romance, if indeed he truly loved her.

After five weeks of tearful waiting, her despair turned to anger, not only with Harry for failing to get in touch with her but also with herself for not casting aside her pride and trying to contact Harry. It was then that she made a firm, if profoundly painful, resolution to put Harry and her brief affair with him behind her and get on with her life in the way she had always planned. She telephoned Guy, whom she had continued to go out with fairly regularly, and from whom she had managed to conceal the extremes of emotion that she had been experiencing since her separation from Harry, and arranged to meet him for lunch the following day. At the meeting, she told Guy, who knew nothing of her affair with Harry, that she wanted to confirm their engagement and start wearing his ring. She went on to say that she was prepared to get married after she finished college in the summer of 1968, providing he would agree to her working as a teacher for at least a year after they were married, with no immediate plans to start a family. Guy was delighted at Amy's change of heart and agreed immediately with her terms, becoming highly animated in his enthusiasm about the engagement and all the subsequent plans and announcements that needed to be put in place. He was particularly keen to emphasise how thrilled his parents would be when they received the news.

During the ensuing weeks, Amy managed, with some difficulty and after contending with considerable bureaucracy, to transfer her teaching course from The College of the Immaculate Conception to a teacher-training college near Southwell in Nottinghamshire, with full credit for having completed her first year of the course. This would enable her to live at home in Newark and travel to classes by bus. Her best friend, Ginger, had abandoned her course in Wessex; her lover, Harry, had left the nearby university; and she had no desire to return to the south coast with all the painful, heart-rending associations the place now held for her. Her new college was both secular and co-educational which pleased her greatly, freeing her from the stifling constraints of a Catholic, women's institution, run by nuns. Living at home in Newark would also enable her to concentrate on her relationship with Guy and her plans for the future, thereby helping to dull the sense of longing she felt for her lost love.

Things went well enough for Amy, and very much according to plan, during the following three years: her engagement to Guy continued in an amicable, if passionless and chaste, manner; she successfully completed her training and qualified as a schoolteacher in the summer of 1968; the following September she and Guy were married at the Holy Trinity Catholic Church in Newark, followed by a lavish Reception at the Loxley Hall Country Club; and that same September she was appointed to her first teaching post at a Church of England junior school in nearby Farndon. Her love for Harry never died but the pain and the pining slowly faded as she came to terms with the future she had chosen for herself. And, thankfully, many of her material ambitions were realised: on their return from honeymoon, the couple moved into a brand new, five-bedroom, detached house in one of the most desirable areas in the environs of Newark; Amy had her own car, a brand new Mini; there were foreign holidays and regular trips to the theatres and smart restaurants in Nottingham; the couple developed a busy social life, centred very much on couples connected with Guy's tennis club, the church and his professional life; and Amy never wanted for money, receiving an allowance from Guy, as well as keeping all of her earnings from teaching. She was leading the sort of life she had always envisioned – the sort of life Aunt Harriet had enjoyed and had wanted for her.

Amy's private life was a different matter, however. Although Guy continued to be a generous and amiable consort during the early days of marriage, he remained apparently uninterested in the sexual side of their life together. The marriage had been consummated during their honeymoon, but the coupling had been a perfunctory affair with Guy apparently wanting nothing more from Amy than her willingness to act as a vessel for his seed. Thereafter, during their first year of cohabitation, the sex act was performed on very few occasions – always at Amy's instigation and only during 'safe periods'. To make matters worse, there was very little romance in their lives. Guy would buy her expensive presents for birthdays and Christmas, and be demonstratively affectionate in public, holding hands and touching her tenderly, but in private there were no demonstrations of romantic affection, tactile or otherwise, making her feel increasingly that she was turning into the trophy wife she had often feared she might become. And so she was not growing to love Guy, as she had hoped she might do, rather she was beginning to like him significantly less than she had once done.

Matters deteriorated further when the couple agreed, at Guy's insistence, to start trying for a baby. After they had been married a year, Guy reminded Amy, fairly bluntly, that he had agreed to her working for just one year after she had qualified, and now that the year was up, it was time to start a family – he insisted that he had only consented to abandoning 'immediate plans' for a family, which had always been his particular wish, for the one year in which it had been agreed that Amy might work as a schoolteacher. A major row ensued. Amy asserted that she was not ready to become a mother, and that she enjoyed her teaching and was not willing to give it up. She insisted that the 'one year' of post-qualification work that they had agreed on was a minimum, not a maximum, and that there was never any agreement, express or implied, that they would start a family after just a year of marriage. Guy remained intransigent, however, reminding Amy that she had always known how paramount the birth of a son and heir was in his hopes for the future, and in his idea of marriage – and how important this was to his parents – and that she, as a good Catholic wife, should understand this and succumb to his wishes, reminding her that she had sworn before God in her marriage vows to 'honour' him, which included honouring his legitimate wishes to become a father. The dispute continued for over a month, the arguments on both sides being revisited regularly. In the end, Amy gave way on the issue of trying to start a family, on condition that she was not required to relinquish her teaching job until after she became pregnant, and then not until her condition warranted her giving up work. She agreed to this, not because she had been persuaded by Guy's arguments, nor because she believed there was any sort of marital, moral or religious obligation on her to concede, but because she felt sure that he was so utterly uninterested in sex that the likelihood of her becoming pregnant was the remotest of contingencies.

To her considerable consternation and distress, Guy suddenly became not just keen but insistent on exercising his conjugal rights, beginning almost as soon as their accommodation on starting a family had been settled. They would have sex, after a fashion, usually twice a week, sometimes more often, except when she was menstruating, but the act never amounted to anything more than Amy lying on her back with Guy humping on top of her until he could deposit his semen. There were no endearments, there was no foreplay or eroticism of any kind and, although Guy was never rough with her, no tenderness. She disliked it from the start and looked forward to the arrival of her period, when she could get some relief from having to yield to her husband. But the coupling was always over very quickly and so she was able to bear the unpleasantness without too much difficulty. It was a constant source of wonder to Amy, that Guy, who apparently had no interest in sex, was perfectly potent when motivated by the prospect of procreation.

This routine continued for about a year without Amy becoming pregnant, and then for a further year with coitus taking place less frequently, again without any positive results. It was at this stage that Guy's coldness to Amy – at least, in private – began to gain momentum, spurred on by his belief that it was Amy who was responsible for their inability to procreate, and that divine intervention was the cause of her infertility: a judgment upon her for straying so often from the tenets of the one true church. Amy suspected that she was capable of conceiving and that, if anyone was infertile, it was Guy. But, although the matter of testing for fertility had been discussed, he steadfastly refused to be tested. As far as he was concerned it was Amy's sinfulness that was the cause of their problems, and there were no circumstances under which he was going to submit himself to the humiliation of a fertility test. As a result, neither of them was tested. Sexual relations ceased and, although in public Guy continued to put on a show of affection towards her and be tactile with her, in private there was no physical contact between husband and wife of any sort. And that was how it had been for almost a year on the day that Amy sat with her glass of whisky, contemplating her predicament.

When she had finished her whisky, she spent the next couple of hours doing some household chores before setting off in her car to see her mother for afternoon tea, taking with her Bob Allen's Victoria sponge. As she pulled up outside the little semi-detached house, she was surprised not to see her mother watching out for her in the front room bay window, as was her custom. Amy had a key to the house and so she let herself in through the front door. The old family home had been spruced up in recent years, thanks to Amy's generosity and marital prosperity: the whole interior had been redecorated; there were fitted carpets throughout; and a new three piece suite in the living room. Best of all, as far as Doris Anderton was concerned, was the arrival of a brand new colour television which Amy had recently bought for her to replace the black and white rental set she had used for many years. Amy called out for her mother and, when there was no reply, walked through the hall and into the kitchen to find her sitting at the table, her eyes bloodshot from crying, a forlorn expression on her round, gentle face.

'Mum! What on earth's the matter? You've been crying.' Amy went up to Doris and put an arm round her shoulder.

'Oh, I'm sorry, sweetie,' sobbed Doris. 'Come and sit down at the table. I've had some rather sad news.' Amy joined her mother at the kitchen table.

'What is it, Mum? What can have happened to upset you like this?'

'I'm afraid it's Uncle Cyril, Amy. I've only just heard myself from your Aunt Harriet.' Doris paused for a moment, trying to collect herself, and then went on, 'It's Uncle Cyril, sweetheart. I'm afraid he's passed away. He had a very bad heart attack last night, and was rushed to hospital. The doctors thought they had stabilised him overnight, but he had another attack early this morning and died. It's a complete shock, you know, Amy. Cyril was never ill – I can't remember him ever missing a day's work through illness. Harriet must be in a state of shock, though she seems to be bearing up at the moment. They were very close, you know, even if Harriet was always rather bossy with him.'

Amy was genuinely shocked at the news, and also sad, although she was more upset for Aunt Harriet than for herself. She had experienced real grief from bereavement when she had lost her father as a ten year old child, and would not claim to be grief-stricken at the passing of her uncle Cyril, however unexpected his death was. She liked her uncle very much, and knew him to be a kind generous man, and a loving husband, but there had been relatively little contact with him over the years, while she was growing up, because it was always Aunt Harriet who took her and her brother on excursions, holidays and other treats, Uncle Cyril rarely being in attendance. Similarly, when Aunt Harriet came to stay with the family in Newark, she always came alone. But Amy knew very well how devoted Aunt Harriet was to her husband – even if she didn't always show it – and so Amy was truly saddened to contemplate how bereft her aunt must feel.

'Oh, I'm so sorry, Mum. Poor Aunt Harriet... it must be dreadful for her.'

'Yes, it must, darling. But you know, pet, I'm really very sad too. I've known Uncle Cyril for such a long time. I knew him before I knew your father, and even before Harriet married him. Your father was probably still at Oxford when I first knew Cyril. He was the best friend of my first fiancé – you know, the soldier who was killed in the war. They were articled clerks together in Nottingham, in the same firm of solicitors. I was only sixteen or seventeen when I first met Cyril and I always liked him. And he helped Arthur and me such a lot when we were newly weds, and particularly when we moved to Newark with you two tiny tots. We'd never have been able to buy this house without Cyril's help. And it was Cyril who organised the endowment policy which meant I could keep the house when your poor dear daddy died. Oh... he was such a good man, and so kind to me. I shall miss him such a lot, even though I haven't seen much of him in recent years – poor Cyril; poor Harriet.' Doris started to sob again, and Amy comforted her. It seemed to Amy that, in those few moments, her mother had revealed more about her past than she had ever done before.

Later that afternoon, when they had finished their tea and slices of sponge cake, it was agreed that Amy would drive over to Wolverhampton during the ensuing week to comfort her aunt and help her with any tidying up of Uncle Cyril's things that needed to be done; she would also help her aunt deal with the various formalities and arrangements that had to be seen to, in the wake of Uncle Cyril's death. It was the school holidays and so Amy was free to go, whereas Doris was still working at the local library. Amy stayed with her mother for most of the evening in order to keep her company: she cooked some macaroni cheese for their evening meal after which they sat and watched the colour television together. At around nine-thirty, Amy decided that Doris had calmed down sufficiently for her to take her leave and return home.

Half an hour later, Amy was sitting in her own living room, watching a news bulletin on television, when she heard Guy's key in the front door. She was surprised and irked to find him coming home at least an hour early – she had hoped to be in bed and asleep by the time he returned to the house. Guy came into the living room looking flustered, his face drained of colour, and sat down in his customary armchair. Nothing was said for several minutes, until Amy got up and switched off the television.

'What's the matter, Guy? Why are you home so early?' Amy asked, breaking the silence between them. 'You look a little upset. Has something happened?'

'Yes it has, as a matter of fact,' Guy responded, in an unusually subdued tone of voice. 'I've been verbally abused by the parents of one of the junior members at the club.'

Amy looked at Guy quizzically for a moment and then said, 'What do you mean "verbally abused", Guy? What are you talking about… what on earth happened?'

'Well, I was talking to a couple of the committee members – Tom Harvey and his wife, Lillian – shortly after the buffet supper was over, when, all of a sudden and apparently out of nowhere, this couple I didn't know from Adam came up to me, looking red faced and furious, and started yelling abuse at me. They used the most offensive language, calling me all sorts of names, and in the end they had to be restrained by two of the stewards and some of the other club members, who escorted them from the premises. It was over pretty quickly, but it was absolutely dreadful while it lasted.'

Amy was quite taken aback. She had never seen Guy so upset and flustered. For a moment, her mood softened towards him.

'Dear me, Guy… how awful. I'm so sorry. What exactly did they say? You must have been terrified.'

'I can't remember exactly – just lots of vile, offensive names... and lots of effing and blinding. They must both have been very drunk – drunk out of their minds. And yes, it was very intimidating. But worst of all it was so embarrassing... in front of all those club members. I'll never live it down... never.'

'But why, Guy? What was it all about? Who were these people?'

'I had no idea at the time, but somebody told me afterwards that the couple were Jimmy Hartley's parents. Jimmy's a difficult little beggar who got knocked out of the semi-finals of the under-sixteen singles tournament this afternoon, when I was umpiring. I know he didn't like some of the decisions I made that went against him, and he certainly didn't like it when I had to caution him for improper conduct and abuse of the racket. And then, at the end, when he'd lost the match, he definitely appeared to react very badly. I can only assume his parents blamed me for him losing, got drunk and wanted to take it out on me. You see, Amy, some of the parents take these tournaments far too seriously, and they're ridiculously protective of their spoilt little sprogs. But I've never known anything like this before. This really was way over the top.'

Amy continued to sympathise with her deflated and subdued husband, until all that could be said about the incident had been said. Then she decided it was time to tell Guy the news about her uncle.

'Guy, there's something I need to tell you, as well. As you know, I went round to Mum's this afternoon for tea, and she had some rather bad news: it's my Uncle Cyril... he died this morning from a heart attack. He was in hospital at the time, being treated for another attack he'd had the night before. He'd been rushed to hospital by ambulance after the first attack. Mum's very upset...she'd known Uncle Cyril nearly thirty-five years.'

Guy, who had been sitting quietly, staring at his feet, looked up at Amy and said, 'Oh dear, Amy, I'm sorry to hear that... very sorry indeed.'

'Thank you, Guy. The thing is, Aunt Harriet will be quite bereft and probably in a state of shock at the moment. The neighbours are with her right now, but she's basically on her own now Uncle Cyril's gone, and Mum and I are the only family she's got – and Roger too, of course, but he's away at sea at the moment. So, it's been agreed that I'll go over to Wolverhampton next week for several days and look after her. I expect I shall have to deal with most, if not all, of the formalities, if Aunt Harriet's in a bad way. And I shall probably have to make the funeral arrangements as well. Now, I know you don't like, or approve, of my being away from home without you, but I'm sure you'll make an exception in this case.'

'Oh... yes, of course, Amy, you'll have to go. Mr Ostime was, by all accounts, a very fine man – and a very successful solicitor. I know from business contacts that he was highly regarded by members of the Wolverhampton Law Society, and in the profession generally. Yes you must go. Um, you will, of course, let me know when the funeral is. We must be there together.'

'Yes, of course, Guy. I shall come home, anyway, a few days before the funeral, and then we can go back to Wolverhampton together for the ceremony.'

'Good – I don't suppose there'll be a requiem mass?'

'No... Uncle Cyril wasn't a Catholic, and Aunt Harriet is lapsed. I don't really know what sort of ceremony it will be. I shall have to discuss it with Auntie.'

'Yes, I remember now. Your mother told me: she married a Protestant and then lost her own faith – a terrible thing really.' There was a pause and then he added, 'That's probably why they never had children – God's will.'

Amy stiffened, and the sympathy she had felt for her husband after the unpleasant incident at the tennis club immediately evaporated. How could Guy make such a vile and uncalled-for observation about her beloved Aunt, particularly in the prevailing circumstances? It was, of course, really intended as a sideways swipe at Amy herself – it was as if he couldn't help it. She immediately stood up and announced that she was going to bed, telling Guy that the spare bed had been made up for him and he should sleep there; and with that she left the room and retired for the night.

The next day Amy excused herself from Sunday roast with her parents-in-law, and headed off to the West Midlands after morning coffee with her friend, Esme. For the rest of that week, she busied herself sorting out matters at Aunt Harriet's house in Wightwick. Harriet Ostime was a robust woman and, although shocked and grief-stricken by her husband's unexpected and untimely death, she was strong enough to assist her niece in the many tasks that needed seeing to. Amy took on the harrowing job of telephoning the innumerable friends, business associates and distant relatives who Harriet felt should be notified of her husband's sudden demise. Amy and her aunt went through Uncle Cyril's papers, wardrobe and personal effects together – a difficult and time-consuming endeavour, precipitating many a tearful outpouring of grief on Harriet's part. She had decided that she wanted a complete clearout of her husband's clothing and personal possessions, because, much as she had loved Cyril, she couldn't bear the thought of having all these things around her in the house as a constant reminder that he was gone for ever. Fortunately, Cyril had kept meticulous records and made detailed arrangements in respect of his financial affairs, much of which was in the hands of one of the partners at his law firm, who was also the executor of his will and in charge of probate arrangements, and so Amy was saved a considerable amount of work in that regard, other than liaising with the executor. The registering of the death, the placing of press notices and the making of funeral arrangements were left entirely to Amy. Cyril's will provided that he wished to be buried in the graveyard at the local parish church in Wightwick, and so she set about the task of arranging the ceremony, interment and post-funeral gathering – to take place on the Friday of the following week. Harriet decided that the wake should be held at her substantial house on Greengage Hill, with external caterers being called in to provide the food and drinks.

By Saturday, Amy had done as much as she could to help her Aunt, for the time being at any rate. Amy's mother, who had arranged to take the following week off work, was coming over to Wolverhampton to spend the days leading up to the funeral with her bereaved sister. So Amy felt it was a good opportunity for her to return home to Newark for a few days, leaving her aunt in the safe and loving hands of her younger sister. Amy collected Doris from Wolverhampton station on Saturday morning to take her to Greengage Hill and, after lunch, set off by herself on the drive back to Nottinghamshire.

She returned with Guy on the eve of the funeral. The next morning at eleven o'clock, Aunt Harriet supported by Amy, Guy and Doris processed behind the casket, borne by six pallbearers, into the fourteenth-century parish church for the funeral service. The church was packed to overflowing. After the ceremony, when everyone had gathered around the freshly dug grave in the churchyard for the burial, Amy noticed among the throng of mourners a tallish young man, with a blond moustache, dressed in the blue-grey uniform of an RAF officer – he was standing alone some distance away, at the back of a large group of people on the opposite side of the grave from Amy and her close relatives. She glanced across at him once or twice and became aware that he was trying to catch her eye. She tried to avoid his gaze but was unable to curb her curiosity, and every so often she would look across to where he was standing. Each time she did this, she found him staring directly at her. After a while, it occurred to her that she recognised him from somewhere, but couldn't think where. And then it suddenly dawned on her who the young man was – he was Danny Swift.

Chapter 9
August 1972: Amy

What was Danny Swift doing in Wolverhampton? He was supposed to be on the other side of the world in Queensland. And what was he doing at her Uncle's funeral? She had done all the ringing round of friends and relatives, notifying them of Uncle Cyril's death and the date of the funeral, none of which, as far as she knew, had involved her contacting anyone remotely connected with the Swift family. And why was he dressed in the uniform of an RAF officer? For a start, Danny was an Australian and, in any case, he had set his sights on going to university to read economics before joining his father's accountancy firm with a view to qualifying as a chartered accountant. Amy couldn't understand it, but there was no doubting who the dashing young officer was – he was Daniel Willoughby Swift.

Amy acknowledged Danny by looking at him with her head tilted ever so slightly to one side, raising her eyebrows and letting the faintest hint of a smile flicker across her lips. Danny responded by raising his right hand and flashing one of his well-honed, charming-young-man smiles: a slightly crooked, one-sided grin, coupled with a twinkling of the eyes – his practised take on Clark Gable's legendary come-to-bed look. Amy experienced a ripple of excitement at this simple, subtle exchange of greetings, and then quickly regained her composure to concentrate on the serious matters in hand. After that, she avoided looking in Danny's direction again while the mourners remained gathered at the graveside. There was no opportunity for the pair to speak to one another until later on at the Ostimes' residence on Greengage Hill, when Danny approached Amy shortly after everyone had repaired there for the post-funeral reception. She was in the grand conservatory, talking to one of Aunt Harriet's neighbours, Mrs Jenkins, a stout grey-haired woman in her late fifties, whom she had known since she was a girl.

'Hello, Mrs Jenkins, do you remember me?' Danny declared, as he walked up to the two women, taking Mrs Jenkins' hand and shaking it gently. 'Daniel Swift, I used to live next door to the Ostimes... on the other side of their house from you.' Danny had not acquired even the slightest trace of an antipodean accent, and spoke with the public school English of his youth.

'Yes, of course, Danny. How could I forget such a handsome young man? And my, don't you look wonderful in that uniform? All the girls love a man in uniform... wouldn't you agree, Amy?'

'Yes, you look very dashing, Danny.'

'Yes, you do indeed, Danny,' Mrs Jenkins agreed. 'And what are you doing here in England? We all thought you had moved permanently to Australia.'

'I'll tell you in a minute, Mrs Jenkins, but first, I must just say hello to my favourite girl of all time,' Danny turned his attention to Amy. 'Amy Anderton, just look at you, the prettiest girl I ever knew, and now... the most beautiful woman – even in your mourning clothes. It's wonderful to see you, Amy, even on a sad occasion like this,' he leant forward, placing his hands on Amy's shoulders, and kissed her on both cheeks. 'You know, Mrs Jenkins, Amy and I were really quite close before I went off to Queensland. We'd known each other since we were both knee high to grasshoppers.'

'Hello, Danny... it's lovely to see you too.' Amy smiled demurely at Danny and meant what she said. 'Actually, it's Amy Boucher now. I've been married for four years.'

'Yes, so I've heard. Well, it obviously suits you. You look wonderful on it, that's all I can say; any little ones?'

'Not yet, Danny. I'm not quite ready for that yet.'

'Quite right,' interposed Mrs Jenkins. 'You have some fun while you're still young, Amy... plenty of time for children and all that malarkey when you're a bit older. I think women start their families far too early these days. You know – married at twenty, pregnant within months, motherhood at twenty-one; and some even younger.'

'Quite so, Mrs Jenkins. Anyway, Danny, tell us what you're doing here in Wolverhampton and how you came to know about Uncle Cyril's funeral... and why you're wearing that RAF uniform, for goodness sake. You're supposed to be a chartered accountant in Brisbane. We can't wait to hear, can we, Mrs Jenkins?'

'No, Amy, we can't. Come on, Danny, explain yourself.'

'Oh well, it's all quite simple really. When I left university in Brisbane – with a good degree in economics, by the way – I couldn't face the prospect of shutting myself away in an office for the foreseeable future, doing accounting. I was in the university's air force squadron while I was an undergraduate – something I'd very much enjoyed – and so I applied to join the Royal Australian Air Force as an officer cadet. They had a special entry scheme for university graduates. Anyway, I was accepted, and six months later I was commissioned as a pilot officer. I'm a flight lieutenant now. Then, back in January, the opportunity arose for young officers to do a six-month secondment with the RAF in England, and I couldn't resist the chance of coming back home for a while, so I put my name down and, hey presto, here I am. I arrived in Blighty back in March. I'm stationed at RAF Cosford, just a few miles from here. I suppose having dual nationality helped... you know, having an English mum and all that.'

'Wow... I'm amazed, Danny,' enthused Amy. 'I never thought to see you again... and living so near Greengage Hill. But how come you're at Uncle Cyril's funeral? I did most of the phoning round, telling people he'd passed away, and you certainly didn't hear about it from me.'

'Well, I got to know through the grapevine, actually. That's how I heard about Mr Ostime's death, anyway. And then I read the notices in the *Express and Star* and so I knew when and where the funeral was going to be held. My parents used to be very friendly with the Ostimes, as you know, and so I thought I really must come and pay my respects.' Danny then turned to Mrs Jenkins and, affecting a conspiratorial air, lowered his tone and said, 'Actually, Mrs Jenkins, I really came in the hope that the lovely Amy Anderton might be here, so I could get to see her again and, you know, maybe ask her out for dinner or something... and here she is.' Amy blushed.

'Oh, Daniel, you really are wicked,' Mrs Jenkins said, giggling girlishly, 'but quite charming. It's just as well Amy's married, otherwise she wouldn't stand a chance – she'd be bowled over,' and turning to Amy, 'wouldn't you, dear?'

'Probably, Mrs Jenkins, but then Danny always was full of flannel, weren't you Danny?'

Before Danny could answer, Mrs Jenkins glanced at her watch and said, 'Look, I'd better go and find my husband. He'll be wondering where I am. I can see you two young ones are anxious to do some reminiscing with each other, so I'll leave you to it. I'll talk to you both later on. Bye.' Mrs Jenkins took her leave of Amy and Danny, and disappeared into the crowd in search of Mr Jenkins. Amy and Danny faced each other and smiled, Danny with his Clark Gable grin.

'Can you still wiggle your nose, like Samantha from *Bewitched*, Amy?' Danny asked. 'Now that really did beguile me – never failed. It's one of THE biggest turn-ons ever. Go on Amy, nobody's looking, do it for me now.'

'I expect I can, Danny, although I haven't done it for years... and I don't propose to do it now, delighted though I am to see you. And you really must stop flirting with me. As I've told you, I'm a married woman – married for four years – and my husband's here, somewhere.'

'Yes, I saw him with you at the funeral service. He looks a bit of a dull fish to me. Four years is a long time, Amy, do you still get on with him?'

Amy was lost for words at such a direct observation and question. She stood silently for a moment, while Danny looked into her eyes, a quizzically mischievous smile on his face. After a few seconds she spoke. 'That's actually none of your business, Danny, and not really an appropriate question, particularly on an occasion like this. It is very nice to see you, Danny, but please don't spoil everything with your foolishness.'

Danny knew what the answer to his question was from Amy's response – it was 'no' – and he was satisfied. He put both hands in the air, in a gesture of surrender, and said, 'Okay, Amy: pax – no more flirting! But we really must get together and talk over old times. I'm here at Cosford until early September, before I fly back to Oz, so we must fix a time to meet – something innocuous like going out for lunch together: no strings attached, no hidden agenda, just two old friends who haven't seen one another for seven years, meeting to reminisce. My duties at the airbase are quite flexible; I have a lot of autonomy, so I'm sure we'll be able to fix something up. What do you say?'

Amy thought for a moment and said, 'All right, Danny... yes, that would be really nice. I'm on my school holidays until the first week in September, and I shall be coming over from Newark, probably every week, to stay with Aunt Harriet for a few days to make sure she's all right. So yes, we must make contact and fix something up when I'm in Wolverhampton. I'll be back here next Wednesday, probably.'

'Excellent. Look, Amy, I haven't got your Aunt's telephone number.' Danny felt inside his breast pocket and took out a ball-point pen and a scrap of paper. 'Tell me what it is and I'll write it down.' Amy told him the number and he wrote it down. Just as Danny was pocketing the pen and paper, Guy appeared in the conservatory and approached them.

'Amy, there you are... I was wondering where you'd got to, where have you been?' Guy said in a slightly agitated and demanding tone of voice.

'Guy... um yes, well, I've been here pretty much the whole time, talking to Mrs Jenkins actually, and now to my old friend, Danny.'

Guy looked at Danny, unable to conceal his hostility, and said, 'I'm Guy Boucher, Amy's husband. I don't believe we've met.'

'This is Danny Swift, Guy.' Amy jumped in quickly, before Danny could say anything. 'He's a very old friend of mine. I've known him since I was five or six. He used to live next door to Aunt Harriet and Uncle Cyril, and now he lives in Australia. Don't you Danny?'

'Flight Lieutenant Daniel Swift of The Royal Australian Air Force, at your service, Mr Boucher,' Danny said in a clearly ironic tone of voice, accompanied by an exaggerated air force salute. The pointedly mocking tone of Danny's greeting was not lost on Amy, but went apparently unnoticed by Guy who seemed to relax somewhat, softening the unpleasant glare he had been giving Danny. He offered Danny his hand.

'Pleased to meet you, Daniel,' Guy said, shaking hands with him.

'Likewise,' replied Danny.

'You're an old friend of Amy's then? I must say, she's never spoken about you to me, as far as I can remember, have you Amy?'

'Probably not,' Amy replied. 'Guy's been in Australia for over seven years and I'd completely lost touch with him. We were playmates as children. It's a complete surprise to see him here at Uncle Cyril's funeral.'

'Yes,' said Danny. 'It just so happens that I'm over here on secondment with the RAF at Cosford, and so I've been able to come to the funeral. I'm flying back to Queensland next month. My family were neighbours of Mr and Mrs Ostime for fifteen years, you see. Anyway, I must go and circulate. It's been lovely seeing you again, Amy, and having a bit of a chat about the old days. Do try to keep in touch. Goodbye,' Danny gave Amy a formal handshake, and then turned to Guy. 'Nice meeting you, Guy. Take good care of Amy now, there's a good fellow!' Danny shook Guy's hand and left the room – and then, having achieved his objective, left the gathering on Greengage Hill more or less immediately and returned to Cosford.

'He seems rather a smooth customer,' was Guy's judgment, after Danny had left. 'And rather rude, I thought. Who does he think he is, telling me to take care of you?'

'I don't know... it's just his way, I expect,' Amy said, dismissively.

'By the way, Amy, what was he writing down when I came into the conservatory? You were saying something to him and he was writing it down on a piece of paper, which he put in his trouser pocket. What was that all about?'

'Oh, he came out with the usual nonsense about wanting to keep in touch after he gets back to Australia. He asked me for our address so that he could send us a Christmas card, so I told him what it was and he wrote it down. I couldn't see any harm in it. I remember he said the same sort of thing just before the family left England for Queensland seven or eight years ago, but I never heard from him again... and it'll be the same this time. It's all talk with Danny.' Guy seemed quite happy with Amy's explanation, and the conversation moved on to other things. Soon the couple drifted back into the spacious, oak-beamed drawing room, where most of the mourners were gathered, and mingled with the crowd.

When the reception was over and everyone had gone, Doris and Amy did some tidying, while the caterers were busy clearing away the buffet. Aunt Harriet sat quietly in the small morning room, weary from the harrowing events of the day, while Guy watched television by himself in the drawing room. They all ate a light supper together, prepared by Doris, and then retired relatively early for the night. Amy had made sure that she was sleeping in the small, single bedroom she always used when staying with her Aunt – the same room she had invariably slept in as a child – thereby avoiding the unpleasantness of sleeping with Guy. The previous weekend, she had made up one of the main guest rooms for her husband to sleep in when he came for the funeral, and he had made no objection when, on their arrival at Aunt Harriet's house, Amy had shown him to his very comfortable, but separate, quarters.

As Amy lay in her bed reflecting on the day's events, her thoughts were dominated, not surprisingly, by the encounter with Danny Swift. She couldn't work out exactly how she felt about him – her feelings were ambivalent, as they always had been. He was still the same, garrulously glib young man he had been as a youth, but his urbane manner and supreme self-confidence were more convincing, more natural – and yes, more charming – than the rather artificial, affected sophistication of the teenage Danny. After a while she concluded that she had rather liked him and, if the truth be told, been more than a little thrilled by the encounter. She enjoyed being flirted with by the handsome dashing Danny, and it was this that had made it so easy for her to slip naturally into the deviousness she adopted with Guy about her conversation with Danny and the prospect of a further encounter with him. Yet she couldn't quite understand her motivation in seeking to cover up and lie about her arrangement with Danny – other than a desire to put one over on Guy – because she had no conscious intention of embarking on some sort of illicit liaison. But the subterfuge of the proposed encounter seemed to make it all the more thrilling – a shiver of excitement ran through her at the prospect. After lying in bed for some time without being able to drop off, Amy resurrected the old fantasy she harboured about sleeping with Danny Swift – and quite soon she was fast asleep.

The next day, Amy, Doris and Guy drove back to Newark, Aunt Harriet having insisted that she felt strong enough to manage on her own for a few days, happy in the knowledge that Amy would be returning to Greengage Hill for three nights the following Wednesday. Back in Newark, Amy went about her business as usual, including going to Sunday mass with Guy followed by roast dinner at her in-laws, doing household chores and spending time during the week with her friend, Esme. On Wednesday evening she arrived back at Aunt Harriet's house, where she was due to stay until Saturday morning. That same evening, she was sitting with her aunt, watching television, when the phone rang in the hall. She went to answer it and, upon doing so, heard the unmistakable tone of Danny Swift's voice on the other end of the line. After chatting for a while and before ringing off, they made an arrangement to have lunch together later in the week: they would meet on Friday, 18th August at 12.30 pm at the Lea Manor, a small country hotel, more or less equidistant between Greengage Hill and the Cosford airbase.

'That was Danny Swift on the phone, Auntie,' Amy said when she returned to the drawing room.

'Really, dear, that's nice. What did he want?'

'Well, he rang to suggest meeting for lunch, so that we could have a chat about old times.'

'Oh, how very thoughtful of him! I always thought Danny was such a nice young man – and it was really rather special to see him at Cyril's funeral, even though he couldn't stay long. It was so good of him to come. You'll go, of course.'

'Um, yes… well, I've agreed to meet him on Friday, if that's all right with you, Auntie? Will you be okay on your own while I'm out?'

'Yes, of course, dear, you must go out and have a bit of fun while you're here. It's so good of you to come and look after me, and keep me company, but I shall be perfectly all right on my own for a few hours. You should go into town afterwards and do some clothes shopping... buy yourself something nice to wear. It will be a nice break for you, and do you good.'

And so, two days later, Amy drove the four or five miles to the Lea Manor Hotel where she found Danny, in his RAF uniform, waiting for her in the lobby. Amy was dressed in a primrose summer frock and white slingback shoes, with her hair tied back in a ponytail. The hotel had been created around a small Georgian manor house by the erection of some rather ugly 1960s annexes and extensions. All of the letting rooms were housed in a purpose-built modern annexe, as was the ballroom. However, the reception area, bar and dining room, were all in the original Georgian building and had retained most of their period charm. Amy and Danny had a gin and tonic in the bar, after which they were shown through into the dining room where they were seated at an elegantly laid table for two, set in a large bow window at one end of the room, looking out onto the gardens. They spent a most convivial hour and a half together, eating, drinking wine, laughing and talking. Danny spoke a lot about life in Queensland and his work in the air force, and Amy told Danny about her school work and the time she had spent at college. Although she had considered telling him about her relationship with Harry, knowing he and Danny had been at boarding school together, something inside warned her against it. She recalled how sullen Harry had become, six years ago while they were out celebrating their first-year exam results, when she had told him about her brief fling with Danny, and it had occurred to her over the years, when she reflected on what had gone wrong in her grand love affair with Harry, that things must not have been quite right between the two boys during their schooldays. However, after a while Danny got onto the subject of Amy's marriage.

'So, Amy, there's something I need to know... something a tiny bit personal: how come you got married quite so young – you know, straight after leaving college?' He looked at Amy with his beguiling, quizzical grin. 'Now, I want a straight answer, young lady – no beating about the bush.'

Amy was feeling mellow and relaxed, having consumed considerably more alcohol than she was accustomed to, and she could feel her inhibitions melting away. She said, 'Well, you see, Danny, I got engaged to Guy on the rebound really – although I made him wait to get married for two years, until after I'd graduated from college – but we got engaged at the end of my first year, after a short, but very serious, love affair I'd been involved in came to an end – with someone you know, actually.'

'Someone, I know! Who on earth could that be?'

'Henry Irving... you'd know him as Harry.'

'Irving? The boy I was at school with?'

'The very same.'

'Well I never... what a coincidence; small world and all that.'

'Yes indeed.'

'Of course, Irving and I never really hit it off at school. I expect he told you that. I don't know why, but he always seemed to have it in for me. I can remember trying to make friends with him but he wouldn't have it. He was quite aggressive sometimes. I never did find out what he had against me, but there you are. Anyway, I need to know what happened to make you want to get engaged to Guy so precipitously – I must say he does seem to be a bit of a dull fish.'

Amy told Danny the story of her affair with Harry and how, without ever actually finishing with one another, they had allowed themselves to drift apart. And all the time, waiting in the wings, there was Guy desperate to get engaged. And that was how it had happened: Harry disappeared over the horizon and Amy allowed herself to become engaged to Guy. Of course, she had never told Guy about Harry.

'I see... well that explains it. Goodness, Amy, that's rather a sorry story, I must say. And how has marriage worked out for you? Something tells me – and I should warn you, my intuition on these matters is never wrong – that all is not quite as it should be in the marriage stakes, as far as the lovely Amy Anderton is concerned. I'm not wrong am I, Amy?' Danny looked searchingly and seductively into Amy's eyes, almost into her soul.

She was sufficiently in possession of herself not to reveal the secrets of her bedchamber, but otherwise she let it be known that she was unhappily married to Guy who, in private, had become cold, spiteful and unkind, and yet, in public, always put on a show of being the devoted, if over possessive, husband. All the time she was talking and unburdening herself, Danny continued to look penetratingly into her eyes. Amy knew she was more than a little tipsy and that her defences were down, but she didn't care. She could feel herself becoming mesmerised by Danny, slowly but surely falling under his spell until there seemed to be no means by which she was capable of resisting him. She loved the excitement and danger of the occasion; she was thrilled by the glamorous appeal of her handsome companion; and she yearned for the passion and romance that it seemed Danny might bring to the emotional and erotic wasteland of her life. Above all, she longed for sex.

Amy let Danny seduce her. She yielded to him, allowing him to take complete control of her. He decided that she was too tipsy to drive back to Greengage Hill, and that she couldn't possibly be allowed to go off on her own until she had sobered up somewhat: they should take a room at the hotel for a couple of hours so that she could lie down and rest. Without needing any persuasion, she agreed to Danny's proposal that they check into the hotel in the names of Mr and Mrs Swift, and then, again without demur, she went willingly with him to one of the small, purpose-built, double bedrooms in the residential annexe, where they went to bed together for the afternoon and had sex. Danny proved to be a considerate and skilful lover, with the consequence that Amy was able to experience sexual fulfilment with a man for the first time in six long years – the first time since she had last made love with Harry. She loved every minute of the experience, including falling asleep next to Danny after the coupling was done. They awoke at five-thirty. Amy got out of bed, put on those items of her clothing Danny had removed during lovemaking, made herself look presentable as quickly as she could and then hurried out of the hotel to her car for the short drive back to Wightwick, leaving Danny to check out and settle the bill – but not before making an arrangement with him for a similar encounter the following week.

When Amy arrived back at the house on Greengage Hill, she found her aunt sitting in her usual chair in the drawing room, fast asleep. Harriet stirred as Amy turned to tiptoe back out of the room, and said, 'Gracious me, Amy. I must have nodded off. Look at the time... I've been asleep for ages. When did you get home?'

'Not long since, Auntie. I was in town going round the shops for rather longer than I intended... and I still didn't buy anything.'

'Never mind, dear, perhaps you and I can go into town, one of the days when you're over here, and do some shopping together. We can choose something nice for you, as a little treat.'

'That would be lovely.'

'How was your lunch with Danny? Come and sit down and tell me all about it. Did you have a nice time?'

'Yes, I had a lovely time, thank you, Auntie. We had a very nice lunch in the hotel restaurant and spent a lot of time reminiscing about old times, particularly that week when I came to stay with you and

Uncle Cyril when I was revising for my 'A' levels, just before the Swifts emigrated.'

'Oh yes, I remember that very well. You know, Amy, Cyril thought there might be something going on between the two of you, but I could tell you were just good friends. Was Danny in his RAF suit today, dear?'

'Yes he was. He looked splendid in his uniform and he was on very good form. I do hope I shall get the chance to see him again before he goes back to Australia... and before my new term starts in September. It would be very nice.' Amy spoke the truth – but not the whole truth! The two women chatted for some time, sitting together in the spacious, elegantly furnished drawing room, until it was time for Amy to go through to the kitchen to prepare a tray supper for the two of them, which they subsequently ate together in the drawing room, watching television.

The following week Amy and Danny met twice, in two different hotels in Wolverhampton. Amy was staying with her Aunt for the usual three nights – Wednesday to Saturday – during which time the couple managed to spend Thursday afternoon together, Amy making the excuse that she was going out to meet an old college friend who lived in Wolverhampton, and most of Saturday, after Amy had left Greengage Hill in the morning, supposedly on her return journey to Newark. On both occasions they spent the afternoon in bed. They planned to see each other again the following week, probably for the last time, before Danny returned to Queensland and Amy started her new school term in the first week of September. However, Danny didn't feel able to agree a firm date and time for the tryst, since he would be busy all that week sorting things out at work in preparation for his departure for Australia on 9th September. He promised to phone Amy at Aunt Harriet's on the Wednesday evening in order to fix a time.

It was Tuesday morning, the day before she was due to receive Danny's phone call, when Amy found a mysterious looking letter amongst the morning post. Guy had gone to work and Amy was at home, busy preparing some vegetables for the evening meal, when she heard the mail drop through the letterbox in the front door. She dried her hands and went to see what the postman had delivered. It was mainly bills and official looking correspondence for Guy, but nestling amongst it all was a white foolscap envelope addressed to Mrs Boucher, the name and address hand-written in bold, ball-point capital letters. Amy was intrigued. She carried the bundle of mail into the kitchen where she opened the mystery envelope and took out a single piece of foolscap paper. There was no date, no address at the top and no signature at the bottom, just a hand written message covering most of the page, in the same large capital letters as appeared on the envelope. Amy sat down at the kitchen table and read the letter:

TO MRS BOUCHER

YOU OUGHT TO KNOW YOUR HUSBAND IS A FILTHY QUEER A PERVERT AND A CRIMINAL WHO LIKES KIDS. BOYS ANYWAY. HE LIKES INTERFEERING WITH BOYS AND HE LIKES TO ASSAULT AND RAPE THEM. HES A DIRTY PERVERT. HES TRIED IT ON WITH OUR BOY. HES DONE THE SAME WITH OTHER YOUNG BOYS TOO BUT HES ALWAYS MANAGED TO COVER IT UP OR PAY THEM OFF. HE THINKS BECAUSE HES GOT MONEY AND IS SOME SORT OF BIGWIG IN THE CATHOLICS HE CAN GET AWAY WITH IT. HE TRIED TO INTERFERE WITH OUR BOY AT THE CLUB BUT HE WASNT HAVING ANY AND TOLD US ABOUT IT AND WE WENT AND TOLD THE POLICE. THEY WOULDNT BELIEVE US. THEY JUST COVERED IT UP. THATS BECAUSE THE SUPERINTENDENTS ANOTHER CATHOLIC BIGWIG AT THE SAME CHURCH AS YOUR DISGUSTING HUSBAND. IT WAS THE SAME AT THE CLUB WHERE HE DONE IT. JUST ANOTHER COVER UP BECAUSE BOUCHERS A BIGWIG. SAME AT THE NEWSPAPER. THEY WOULDNT LISTEN TO

US COS BOUCHER SPENDS SO MUCH MONEY ADVERTISING IN THE PAPER AND THE BOSS IS ONE OF BOUCHERS BUM BOY PALS. I DONT KNOW HOW YOU CAN STAND LIVING WITH SUCH A DISGUSTING PERVERT. BUT WERE GOING TO HAVE HIM JUST WAIT AND SEE. HES NOT GETTING AWAY WITH MESSING WITH OUR KID. HE MAY THINK HES GOT AWAY WITH IT AND HES ALL RIGHT LIVING IN HIS POSH HOUSE AND DRIVING AROUND IN HIS FANCY CAR BUT WERE GOING TO GET THE FILTHY FAGGOT. THEN YOULL KNOW ALL ABOUT THE DISGUSTING HOMO YOU MARRIED

Amy read the note several times, not knowing quite what to make of the strange missive. Of course, she was taken aback to receive such an outlandish communication, and by the serious and quite dreadful allegations it contained, but somehow she was neither shocked nor outraged by it. Its main impact was to stir her from the almost dreamlike state she had inhabited since starting her affair with Danny Swift. For the past two weeks she had spent precious little time with her husband, and the time she had spent with him – sitting together occasionally in the evening; attending the odd social function; and going to church – had been rendered quite tolerable by her ability to reflect on the pleasures of her trysts with Danny and the anticipation of further afternoon delights to come. The letter brought her back down to earth.

But what should she make of it? On the one hand it was anonymous and she knew never to put much store by anonymous communications. On the other hand it wasn't really anonymous at all: it was obviously from the parents of the boy at the tennis club, Jimmy something-or-other, who had borne some sort of grudge against Guy – the couple who had kicked up such a fuss on the night of the junior tournament a few weeks earlier. Their attempt to accost Guy at the tennis club made much more sense in the light of these accusations. And was she surprised by the claim that Guy was gay? Not really: it had often occurred to her that her husband must be homosexual, such was his lack of interest in having any sort of meaningful physical relationship with her, and she was well aware that other men did find her attractive. Of course, being gay didn't mean Guy was a child abuser, a rapist or a paedophile, but he would almost certainly need some sort of outlet for his sexual desires – men usually did, it seemed – and it had occurred to her, from time to time, that he spent a disproportionate amount of his time working with the junior section at the tennis club.

And what was she to make of the allegations of a cover up? Guy had become increasingly arrogant, selfish and self-satisfied over the years, and there was no doubt that his bigotry had grown beyond measure. He had also developed a close working relationship with Chief Superintendent Carpenter, a prominent Catholic and the senior officer of the local police force, who had served with him on various church committees and was an active fellow Catenian. As for the local newspaper, Guy and Amy had known and socialised with Bill Jarvis, the newspaper proprietor, since before they were married. He was a former president of the tennis club and had been an occasional visitor to their home. She had never given any thought to Bill's sexual orientation, but it did now occur to her that he lived the life of someone who was, as he always put it, 'footloose and fancy free', having got divorced after a fairly short period of marriage with no progeny, and never having had a girlfriend since – as far as she knew anyway. It was certainly not beyond her imagining that there might have been some sort of 'bigwig' conspiracy to cover up what these men regarded as her husband's peccadilloes.

For the rest of the day, Amy's thoughts were, not surprisingly, focused entirely on the contents of the letter – she went over the issues again and again. But she did so carefully and logically. There was no sense of panic or despair, or anger even, in her deliberations: she was completely in control of her emotions. She went back to the letter several times and reread it, but it always said the same thing: it was a very simple message and there were no hidden clues or agenda to be found. At one stage, she thought she might contact her friend, Esme, so that she could perhaps go round to her flat and discuss the matter with her, but she decided against it. Tomorrow she would be going to Greengage Hill, and then she would be seeing Danny. If anybody, she would discuss it with him.

In the end she concluded that, on balance, the substance of the allegations was true, and she would act accordingly. This meant the end of her marriage – it was the final nail in the coffin of a union that was all but dead anyway. She knew she was making a critical, life-changing decision, but she had arrived at it rationally, in the clear light of day, and there would be no turning back. However, she would not act precipitously in her dealings with Guy by immediately confronting him with the letter and announcing her departure from the matrimonial home, rather she would wait until she had everything planned: where she was going to live; whether the desertion of her spouse would adversely affect her job in a Church of England primary school and, in the unlikely event that it did, how she would set about supporting herself; which of her household possessions she would claim as her own rather than his; how she would handle her mother and her mother's staunch Catholicism; what she would do about her own faith or what remained of it; how she would explain her marital breakdown to Aunt Harriet; and what she wanted to do about Danny – she was also anxious not to allow the aftermath of a confrontation with Guy to spoil what might possibly be her last afternoon of pleasure with her paramour. She knew that Guy would never agree to a divorce, whatever the circumstances, but, as far as she was concerned, the marriage was finally over. She would take matters into her own hands and do things in her own time, when she was ready and everything was planned – and after she had been to bed once more with Danny Swift.

When Guy came home from work that evening, she acted as if nothing untoward had happened. They ate dinner together, engaging in intermittent conversation in what had become their customary stilted fashion, after which they watched television in the lounge until it was time for them to retire to separate bedrooms. The next day, Amy drove to Wolverhampton for her usual three night stay with Aunt Harriet. In the evening, she sat with her aunt in the drawing room of the Greengage Hill house, expecting the phone to ring – but it didn't. The following day, she waited all day on tenterhooks, anticipating Danny's call – but it never came. There were two false alarms during the course of the day: the phone rang, her heart jumped and she raced to pick up the receiver in the hall, only to find, on both occasions, that it was someone wanting to speak to Mrs Ostime. By Friday morning, after a restless night, she determined that there was nothing for it but to drive out to the airbase at Cosford in an attempt to contact Danny herself and find out what was wrong. She had no address or phone number for him but she felt sure that, if she asked around when she got to the base, she would find someone who could point her in the right direction.

Finding Danny's quarters was easier than she anticipated. As she approached RAF Cosford, a major UK airbase just off the main Wolverhampton to Newport road, she saw that there was a barrier across the main entrance staffed by an airman on guard duty, checking vehicles as they arrived. She joined a queue of four cars, waiting to enter the base. When her turn came, she told the guard that she was looking for Flight Lieutenant Daniel Swift, and asked if someone could tell her where he might be found. The guard told her to pull over into a small parking area beside a wooden barrack hut painted in RAF colours, which served as an office for the guards, and then go into the office to have a word with the duty sergeant. She acted accordingly. Inside the hut she found a bronzed, balding flight sergeant, sitting at a desk behind a counter. He looked up from his paperwork as Amy entered, and spoke to her.

'Good morning, miss. How can I help?' he asked courteously, rising to his feet. Then, noticing Amy's wedding ring, he said 'Oh, I beg your pardon, it should be madam, shouldn't it?'

'Well, I rather liked the 'miss', actually,' Amy said, smiling flirtatiously, and the sergeant smiled back. 'I'm looking for a Flight Lieutenant Swift, Sergeant.' She continued. 'He's an Australian officer over here on secondment. Do you know where I might find him? I'm an old family friend of his.'

'I see. Well it's not customary for us to reveal the whereabouts of air force personnel to unidentified visitors, you know, but I think I can make an exception in your case. You don't look as if your about to shoot him or anything like that. As it happens, I know Mr Swift. He's got one of the officers' houses on the domestic site, the other side of the main Newport road. If you'll bear with me a moment, I'll just check his street name and number for you.' He went over to a filing cabinet and pulled out a folder which he proceeded to consult. He leafed through some sheets of paper from the file, found what he was looking for and wrote something down on a scrap of paper.

'Now, miss,' he said smilingly, emphasising the 'miss', 'I can't tell you where Mr Swift might be on the airbase at any given time, but this is where he lives, and there's a good chance he'll be at home, right now. He's been busy packing up to go back home to Australia, I believe.' He handed her the scrap of paper.

She thanked the sergeant and left the office. She had to turn her car round and go back to the main road, before crossing over onto the camp's residential sector. She easily found Danny's address among the officers' houses, and was surprised to see a substantial, double fronted, brick-built, detached house. She assumed he must be sharing the house with other officers. She parked her car outside the house, walked up the garden path to the front door, and rang the bell. She rang several times but got no response. She noticed there was a car parked on the drive of the house next door, and decided to go round and see if anyone was there who might be able to help her. She walked round and knocked on the front door, which was soon opened by an attractive red-haired woman, probably in her early thirties, dressed in slacks and a sweater. Amy assumed she must be the wife of one of the officers. The woman looked at Amy suspiciously.

'Hello,' Amy said, adopting a jovial air. 'I wonder if you might be able to help me. I'm looking for an officer who I was told lives next door.' She pointed at the house she had just come from.

'Yes, I saw you at the door. Who exactly are you looking for?'

'Flight Lieutenant Swift.'

'And who might you be?'

'I'm Mrs Boucher... Amy Boucher. I'm an old friend of Mr Swift. His family used to live next door to my aunt in Wolverhampton and we used to play together in the school holidays. Have you any idea where I might find him?'

'Oh, I see. I'm sorry... I must have seemed a little rude. I thought you were somebody else.' Her mood softened, but she didn't explain who the 'somebody else' might be. And then she said, 'I'm afraid you've missed him: Danny, Rhonda and the twins left for London two days ago. They were due to leave next week, but they wanted to spend some time in London before flying back to Australia.'

Amy was dumbstruck. She stood for a moment with her mouth open, unable to speak.

'Are you all right, Mrs Boucher? You've gone very pale, would you like to come in and sit down?'

'No... no, I'm fine thank you. I'm just rather surprised Danny's already left. I was expecting to see him this week.'

'Yes, well, it was a spur of the moment decision, I think. Danny had completed all his duties with the squadron and they were all packed up and ready to go, so they just upped and went. Rhonda wanted to show the boys some of the London sights before they went home. A bit silly, really: they're only two and a half and won't have a clue what they're looking at.'

'No, I suppose not... I've never met the twins, though.'

'Oh, they're adorable, the cutest little things you could imagine. They look just like their daddy... just like Danny.' The red-haired woman leaned against the doorframe, looking as if she was settling in for a bit of a chinwag. Amy felt sick – she needed to get away as quickly as possible and be on her own.

'Well, I'm sorry to have troubled you,' she managed to say. 'It's a shame I've missed them, but there's nothing I can do about it, so I think I'd better get on my way. Thanks for your help. Bye.'

'Oh yes, of course. You're very welcome. Goodbye.'

Amy turned and walked away.

She drove towards Wolverhampton for about a mile, until she found a lay-by where she parked the car and immediately burst into tears. She sat in the car for a long time, crying pitifully. Her emotions were confused: her tears were those of anger; of self pity; of frustration and disappointment; and of shame at having allowed herself to be so thoroughly abused by the likes of Danny Swift. She railed against the world in general and against men in particular: Danny for lying to her and treating her so shabbily; Guy for luring her into a sterile and loveless marriage; and Harry, whose failure to take her and love her when he had the chance was the root cause of all her misfortunes. Eventually she calmed down and started to regain her composure. She couldn't bear the thought of going back to Guy the next day – Danny Swift's vile behaviour hadn't changed anything as far as her attitude to Guy was concerned, but she was feeling too raw and fragile to face him so soon. So, after some thought, she decided she would phone her friend, Esme, to see if it might be possible to stay with her over the weekend, until the school term started the following Tuesday. She drove into Wolverhampton and parked near the entrance to the town's West Park, where she found a phone box from which she could make the call. Esme, who lived by herself in a two-bedroom flat, was more than happy to accommodate her friend, realising that she was in a state of some agitation, and so it was agreed that she would come to the flat at noon the following day and spend two nights there. Having made the arrangement, Amy went into the old Victorian park and spent the next hour walking the paths – through flower beds, lawns and shrubberies, and around the boating lake and the orangery – until she felt strong enough to put on a brave face when she returned to Aunt Harriet's house. That evening, while Harriet was in the drawing room, listening to music on the radio, she phoned Guy and told him that her aunt was going through a bad spell and that she needed to stay with her until the following Monday evening.

She went back to Newark the next day, stayed with Esme for two days and then returned to the matrimonial home in Balderton. She started the new term at school and quickly became engrossed in her teaching work which, as always, gave her considerable satisfaction and solace. Meanwhile, she continued to lay plans for her separation from Guy. By the end of September, her period, which was always as regular as clockwork, was three weeks overdue.

Chapter 10
August 1972: Harry

Phil was sitting by the window in The Peacock, an old pub on Maiden Lane in Covent Garden, smoking a cigarette and sipping a Scotch and soda. He was waiting for Harry whom he had arranged to meet for a lunchtime drink. Quite by chance, he had run into Harry in the same pub a week before when he was up in town on business, and Harry was in the pub with some friends celebrating the award of his external BA degree from London University. It had been the first encounter of the two friends since they had parted company after Phil's marriage to Ginger, six years earlier. They had lost touch with each other in the year following the wedding, when Harry was leading the nomadic existence of almost non-stop touring, in Britain and in Europe, with his ill-fated pop group. Phil had never known where Harry was at any particular time, and Harry had always seemed too busy and preoccupied with the band to make the necessary effort to touch base with his friend. They had spoken briefly on their fortuitous encounter and agreed to meet a week later, when Phil would again be in London on business, so that they could catch up with each other and resurrect their friendship.

The Peacock had one bar which occupied most of the ground floor of the terraced Georgian building. The pub had undergone an unfortunate 'modernisation' during the mid-sixties which had denuded it of its period charm, leaving a single bleak space with a central bar and no original features, other than the casement windows. The atmosphere was permanently smoky. Nevertheless, it seemed to attract a decent turnover of customers, and was particularly popular with local professionals as a lunchtime venue – its homemade pies and Scotch eggs were renowned locally. And so the atmosphere in the hostelry, as Phil sat waiting for Harry, was that of a busy, metropolitan, lunchtime watering hole and eatery.

Harry appeared in the doorway, dressed casually in jeans and a sweater under an old mackintosh, worn to ward off the early August drizzle. He spotted Phil at his table by the window and went over to join him, taking off his raincoat en route. Neither Phil nor Harry had changed significantly in appearance since their days together at Wessex: both men had remained slim and retained their full heads of hair, although they both now had fairly conventional and somewhat unfashionable haircuts. They shook hands and exchanged greetings, Phil saying how well Harry looked, and Harry making admiring comments about Phil's Savile Row suit. Harry went to the bar and ordered drinks – Scotch for Phil, beer for himself – before he sat down with his old friend and they started to chat.

'So how is everything, Phil?' Harry said excitedly, having lost none of his boyish charm. 'I can't say how pleased I am to see you. And how's Ginger... and the baby? Bloody hell, I don't even know what sex your child is – that's terrible – and, of course, it won't be a baby any more, more like five or six years old, I suppose?'

'One thing at a time, old sport... one thing at a time. First of all, I'm very well – in rude health, in fact – and things are pretty good in general. I must say the business is going very well: I seem to be getting richer by the minute. I'm basically running the show now, and Dad's going to retire next year, so I'll have full control then. I'll probably move into Castle Court then as well – Mum and Dad will retire to one of the estate cottages.'

'Wow, I'm most impressed, Phil. And what about Ginger?' Harry was quite keen to hear about Ginger, not least because he hoped it might lead on to some news of Amy.

'Ah... well I was about to get to that, old son. Ginger and I are divorced.'

'Divorced?' Harry murmured, after recovering from the initial shock.

'Yep. Divorced.'

'No, Phil, I don't believe it. I'm flabbergasted... totally stunned. I thought you were destined to be very happy together. You seemed so content about everything... you know: married life, fatherhood, a future together in Kent, and all that. Whatever happened? Has it been awful for you... going through the divorce, I mean?'

'Now just slow down, Harry... slow down, and I'll tell you the whole story. It's all fine, really. Ginger and I were together for nearly three years. We've got a little girl called Rebecca – Beckie for short. She's five and a half, and an absolute sweetie... the apple of my proverbial eye, in fact. Anyway, we got on fine for the first couple of years we were together: never really argued, always had lots of fun together, all that sort of thing. And then, for some reason I couldn't quite understand, the shagging side of things began to go wrong. In fact it gradually started to dry up until eventually we stopped having sex altogether. For a while I was convinced that Ginger was a lesbian: she seemed to have developed an obsession with one of her girl friends in the drama club. I don't know if anything ever happened between them but, if it did, it didn't last long because, in due course, Ginger went off with some arty-farty Dutchman she'd met on a trip to Holland – she'd gone there with a group from the local W.I. – so I suppose she isn't one... a lesbian, I mean. They've shacked up together in Amsterdam, Ginger and her Dutch geezer, where they run some sort of art gallery, or so I'm told. But the most important thing by far, old sport, is that she left Beckie with me, and now I've got custody of her. We got the decree absolute about a year ago: I got legal custody of Beckie, and Ginger declined any sort of financial settlement, even though I was prepared to make her a generous offer. She said she wanted a clean break with no strings attached and no hard feelings. So it's all worked out pretty well, as far as I'm concerned.'

'Goodness... so now you're on your own, then. How do you manage with Beckie, if you're busy with work? It must be tricky doing both things – you know, caring for a child and running a business, particularly with the business doing so well.'

'Well, I've got a nanny, of course. But I've also got a wife... a new one. We got married six months ago. Nothing fancy like the first wedding: no bridesmaids or best man or marquees at Castle Court, just my folks and her family at the registry office in Tunbridge Wells – that's where Hazel's from – and then off to an Italian restaurant to celebrate. She's a corker, my Hazel. You'll love her. Just turned twenty and as sexy as they come.'

Phil – in typical Phil style – then embarked on an enthusiastic monologue, extolling the virtues of life in Kent with his new wife and 'adorable' little daughter before getting on to the joys of running his own very successful business. This speech was only interrupted once, by his going to the bar to buy another round of drinks and a couple of chicken and ham pies for them to eat while he continued his homily. Eventually, he decided he had talked enough about himself and turned his attention to Harry.

'So, old sport, that's my news, and now I want to hear all about you and what you've been up to. I'm particularly keen to find out about what happened to your pop career. I saw you on television once, on *Ready Steady Go,* I think it was – one of those pop shows anyway – and then nothing. Harry and The Hawks faded into oblivion.'

'Well that about sums it up, really, Phil. There's not a lot more to say. Our single was released and just managed to scrape into the Top Thirty, after which sales fell away dramatically. We then started six months of constant touring, first in Britain, then in Europe, then back in Britain again. Not the posh tour, supporting The Tornados, that Jerry Somers had promised, but a seemingly endless round of second rate nightclubs in provincial towns and cities... seven nights a week with hardly a break, living out of a suitcase and travelling in a clapped out minibus. We kept pestering Jerry about making another record, but there didn't seem to be any interest from Pye Records, and then, in the February, Joe Meek committed suicide – murdered his landlady with a shotgun and then shot himself with the same weapon – in those freaky rented rooms where he had his studio... where we'd made our record. You must have read about it in the papers. He was a complete nutcase, you know. Anyway, that put the kybosh on our recording career: Jerry didn't have any other strings he could pull, and none of the recording companies seemed to want us. And then the whole thing went completely pear shaped when Dave Cant and Spud Chrisp – the group's bass player and drummer – got arrested in a drugs bust at some party they went to in Manchester... it was a Saturday night after one of our shows. They both got done for supplying drugs, and were sent to gaol for a few months. They weren't serious dealers, of course, but they always seemed to have a reasonably decent supply of pot and pills, which they would sell, or sometimes give, to people at parties. I was never interested in drugs, thankfully, and so I wasn't at the party where they got arrested. After that the band was finished, of course, although by that stage I wasn't too bothered: I'd never really got on with the other guys; they always seemed to resent me and treat me like an outsider. And then I managed to get work with a couple of other outfits, including a residency at a club in Copenhagen for a couple of months, but by summer I'd had enough and gave up. It was a pretty miserable experience, all things considered.'

'Well, Harry, old son, it certainly sounds like it. What a story! You must have made a bit of money, though... you know, from record sales and such like?'

'We didn't get a penny from the record, Phil. We'd never signed any formal contract with Pye or Joe Meek... or even Jerry Somers. I don't know where the money went but it certainly didn't come our way. But I made a bit from the touring. We were fairly well paid and we had no living expenses, and very little time to spend what we did earn. So, by the time I gave up, I had put by a tidy little sum.'

'I can remember warning you about that little bugger, Somers. I told you to nail him down with a contract.'

'Well, never mind, Phil. I'm not too bothered about the money. It's the other things I gave up in my forlorn pursuit of fame and fortune that really bug me.'

'Like what, for instance?'

'Well, there was university for a start. It didn't bother me, unduly, leaving Wessex, but it upset my old dad. He didn't try and stop me – said it was my decision and wished me good luck – but you could tell how upset he was. He'd been to Cambridge, you see, and always put a lot of store by academic achievement. I'm just glad he's still around to see me get my degree from London University. He was as pleased as Punch when I telephoned him with the results of my finals, and he'll be at the graduation ceremony.' There was a significant pause before Harry continued, 'And then, of course, there was Amy.'

'Ah yes... the lovely Amy Anderton. You know, old son, my folks were convinced you'd marry Amy. They observed how the two of you got together at my wedding, and they were quite taken with the romance of it all. It seemed to remind them of how they fell in love. They used to say they thought you were the perfect couple – made for each other, they'd say. By the way, they knew perfectly well that you'd sneaked off to Amy's room that night of the wedding.' Phil grinned mischievously; Harry smiled too, at the memory.

'You know, Phil, I really loved that girl... utterly and completely. I still do, if the truth be told. I've never met a girl like her and I doubt I ever will again. I don't half miss her... I don't suppose you know what became of her, do you?'

'Ginger was in touch with her for a couple of years. They never met up though, what with us being down in Kent and her up there in Notts. I know she got married – in 1968, I think it was – to that boring estate agent fellow Ginger used to talk about. We were invited to the wedding but we'd already booked to go away on a month's cruise at the time, so we couldn't go. I don't know what became of her after that. She's probably still living in Nottinghamshire... I can't remember the name of the town. Anyway, you must have had plenty of other girls, what with being a pop singer and all that, even if you weren't exactly a star.'

'A few, Phil, a few... but it wasn't like you might think, and it was always rather sordid and unsatisfying when it did happen. I've had a couple of regular girlfriends since my touring days, though. In fact I lived with Flic for a couple of years. You remember Flic, don't you?

'How could I forget Felicity Tustin – the most prolific tart in the history of Wessex University! How did you manage to get shacked up with her?'

'Well, after I jacked in the pop business, I got a job in a music shop in Hammersmith, where I worked for about a year. So, one day, shortly before I moved to the job I'm in now, Flic comes into the shop to buy a record. We get chatting and arrange to meet for a drink, and, hey presto, we strike up our relationship again. She was working at a nearby languages school, teaching English to foreigners. Soon after that, I started work as Latin master at a prep school in Chelsea, a job I'd got on the basis of having passed the first year of a classics degree at Wessex University! The headmaster was an old university friend of my father, so I guess Dad pulled a few strings. Anyway, on the strength of our two salaries, we managed to rent a small flat together in Acton. That's when I started my external degree – in English and History. We lived with each other for a couple of years until I got thoroughly fed up with her and her seemingly unquenchable urge to bed other men, particularly her male students from Spain and Portugal. So, when one of the masters' bedrooms became vacant at my school, I decided to leave her to it and I moved into the school... and that's where I am now – well, until the end of next week, at any rate, when I'm moving to a flat in Moseley – you know, in Birmingham.'

'Birmingham! Why are you going to Birmingham, for God's sake?'

'I've got a job there, teaching English at a very nice and quite prestigious grammar school. It's a senior school and co-educational, so I'm looking forward to it. I've enjoyed my time in a prep school, but small boys can become a bit wearing after a while, and I'm looking forward to something a bit more stimulating academically, now I've got my degree. It's better paid, as well, and I get a bit of a top up for coaching rugby.'

'Well, old sport, I never put you down as the schoolmasterly type. All you ever really seemed interested in when we were at university was pop music and shagging... and beer of course. Talking of which, it's time for another. Sup up and I'll get us a round in.' Phil started to get up.

'No, Phil, sit down, it's my shout. What are you having... same again?'

Harry went to the bar, bought his round and returned to their table with the drinks. The old friends spent most of the afternoon together, drinking and talking, and taking great pleasure in the renewal of their friendship. The landlord of The Peacock locked the doors at 3.00pm, but it was half past four before they emerged from the pub into Maiden Lane and the persistent drizzle of an English August afternoon.

A week later, Harry moved into his small studio flat in Moseley, aided by his old school friend, Jon Geary, who was a research assistant at Birmingham University – completing a PhD and doing some teaching. The apartment was the converted attic of a substantial, Victorian villa, comprising a large bedsitting room, kitchenette and small bathroom. It was self-contained, comfortably furnished and well maintained. He didn't have much in the way of personal possessions, but enough to fill the Ford van which he owned and used as his regular means of transport. Setting up home didn't take long, and so when it was more or less done, the two men went into Moseley village for the evening, firstly to a pub where a live band was playing, and then on to an Indian restaurant for a late-night curry. At the end of the evening, Jon returned to his lodgings near the university and Harry to his new home.

There were just over two weeks until Harry was due to take up his new appointment, during which time he planned to prepare his classes, make visits to the school in order to get orientated and have discussions with the other two English teachers on the staff, and generally acclimatise himself to his new environment in the sprawling city of Birmingham. The day after he moved in was a Saturday and he found himself at a loose end. Jon Geary had gone to Devon for the weekend to see his parents, and Harry had no other friends or contacts in the city. During the afternoon, he decided he would go into the city centre to see if he could get a ticket for a production of *She Stoops to Conquer* which was currently on at the Birmingham Repertory Theatre. The Rep was one of England's premier provincial theatre companies and, the previous year, it had moved into brand new premises on Broad Street. The new theatre building had just won a prize for its design, awarded by the Royal Institute of British Architects, and so he was keen to see what it was like.

He had no difficulty buying a ticket at the box office – although the only seats available were near the back of the auditorium – after which he walked into the main shopping areas of the city to have a good look round and while away the time until the evening performance was due to begin. He returned to the theatre shortly before seven o'clock, so that he could spend half an hour getting a feel of the place before the show's seven-thirty start. He liked the theatre very much: the concrete and glass façade was attractive and interesting, unlike the flat oppressive frontages of so many public buildings thrown up in the sixties and seventies; the foyer and box office area took the form of a grand atrium – a light, airy, edifice-high space extending across the full width of the building, with staircases at either end leading to the various seating levels; and there were bars and restaurants attractively set out in an adjacent area at the front of the building. But the part that impressed him most of all was the auditorium: a single democratic seating area, fanning out from the great stage, and big enough to seat the best part of a thousand theatre-goers, or so he estimated, with everyone getting a good view of the performance – no boxes or balconies or pillars. He settled down in his seat and waited for the performance to begin.

In the interval, after an enjoyable first half, he remained in the auditorium by his seat, watching as people got up to go to the bars or the toilets or to buy ice creams from the vendors standing by the various exits. It was then that he noticed a young couple standing in an ice cream queue by an exit, halfway down the theatre to his left. The man, who was tall and slim with blond hair and a blond moustache, was dressed in a blue blazer and what looked like some sort of regimental or club tie. The young woman, whose face he couldn't see, cut a slim attractive figure with shoulder-length, dark brown hair; she was wearing a sleeveless blue dress. He looked at the man and thought: I know you. It took several seconds for him to work out exactly who it was, but then it suddenly came to him – it was Danny Swift, it couldn't be anyone else. There he was, as large as life – that loathsome bastard, Swift – standing in a queue at the Birmingham Repertory Theatre of all places, when he was supposed to have returned to Australia seven years ago, and be thousands of miles away in Queensland. Harry kept the couple in his sights, confident that Danny wouldn't notice or recognise him, sitting some distance away towards the rear of the auditorium. He certainly didn't want any sort of encounter with the man.

When Danny had bought ice creams for himself and his companion, the couple turned and made their way back to their seats, about a dozen rows in front of Harry. He was then able to catch a glimpse of the woman's profile. The impact of what he saw took his breath away – for a moment he thought it was Amy. He couldn't be sure: he had only seen her profile for a few moments, but she was clearly a pretty woman with even features and a bright smile, compellingly reminiscent of Amy. She took her seat next to Danny. Throughout the second half, Harry's eyes were almost glued to what he could see of Danny's companion: her dark brown hair, just as he remembered Amy's; and the pale, uncovered flesh of her neck and shoulders, delicately framed by the straps of her blue dress. The performances on stage – the machinations of Mrs Hardcastle, Kate Hardcastle and Tony Lumpkin – might have been taking place a million miles away for all the impact they were having on Harry. Could it be Amy? Surely not: Amy was married to Guy and living in Newark. But from a distance she was the image of Amy: the same hair, the same figure, the same style, and a pretty smiling face. But what would Amy be doing with the likes of Danny Swift? Of course, she had once had a passionate fling with him before she went away to college, and maybe she was enjoying a repeat performance now that Danny was back in England. And what would Amy be doing in Birmingham on a Saturday evening? Harry remembered her telling him about an aunt she was very fond of who lived not far away in

Wolverhampton – perhaps she was staying with her for the weekend. The more he looked at the back of the woman's head and shoulders, the more convinced he became that it was Amy. He had to find out for sure and, if it was her, he would have to speak to her, Danny Swift or no Danny Swift. He decided to make a rapid exit from the auditorium as soon as the play was over, while the applause and curtain calls were still going on. He would wait discreetly near the foot of the stairway down which the couple would necessarily descend in order to exit the theatre, and, if it was Amy, he would approach the couple then and there.

He found a suitable spot in the foyer: a shaded alcove, just to the right of the approach to the staircase in question, where he could stand, hopefully unnoticed, pretending to study the contents of his programme. He watched as people began to come down the stairs. Soon the staircase was filled with theatregoers, enthusiastically discussing the evening's performance as they descended into the foyer and left the theatre. He began to panic, fearing that he would miss Danny and his companion amongst the throng but, just as the crowd was beginning to thin, he spotted the couple coming down the stairs holding hands. Danny was holding the woman's right hand, and so the first thing Harry noticed was the absence of any wedding or engagement ring on her left-hand ring finger. Then he got a clear, unobstructed view of her face – and it wasn't Amy. She was a very attractive young woman, but her features were less delicate than Amy's: her mouth too wide; her nose a little too pronounced; and her eyes smaller, with less sparkle. Harry retreated into his alcove and allowed the couple to walk by and out of the building, talking animatedly as they went. He couldn't decide if he was disappointed or glad: he would dearly have loved to have seen and maybe spoken to Amy, but he was mightily relieved that she was not Danny Swift's girlfriend. He waited for the foyer to clear before making his own way from the theatre to an adjacent car park where he had parked his van, and then drove home to his flat in Moseley.

The incident at the theatre had a profound impact on Harry and played persistently on his mind during the ensuing weeks, as he prepared for and then started his new teaching post at Harborne Grammar School. Although Amy was often in his thoughts, he had long since put aside the hope of ever seeing her again, let alone resurrecting their seemingly doomed love affair, but seeing Danny Swift escorting a pretty young woman who, from a distance and for a brief moment appeared to be the very image of Amy, had thrust the memory of his one and only love affair right back into the forefront of his consciousness. He was once again plagued by thoughts of his folly in having allowed Amy to slip through his fingers, just as he had been five years ago when his embryonic career in the pop music business had collapsed and he had found himself, at last, with time to reflect on what he had sacrificed in futile pursuit of vainglorious ambition. And now, here he was at the age of nearly twenty-six, living the lonely life of a bachelor schoolmaster in an unfamiliar city where he had but one friend. It was a difficult and unhappy time for Harry, as he strove to make something of his new career and his new life in the West Midlands. Eventually, hard work and dedication to his profession saved him from the depths of depression. He liked his new school, and he liked his pupils and colleagues. He threw himself into the life of the institution: taking great care with his classes; producing a school play; coaching the 1st XV rugby and refereeing matches on Saturdays; and assisting the music master with the school choir. By Christmas, it seemed to him as if he had been on the staff of Harborne Grammar School for years, so involved had he become with the place. He had also developed a fairly casual, but nevertheless pleasing, liaison with a young probationary French mistress on the staff called Fiona Davies, an auburn haired girl from

Swansea whose company he enjoyed, and who would sometimes stay the night with him in his Moseley apartment.

Harry would remain at Harborne Grammar School for the next four years, becoming head of the English Department in his final year there. It was only when the City of Birmingham decided to close down its municipal grammar schools, some, like Harborne, with distinguished traditions of academic and extra-curricula excellence, that he decided it was time to move on to pastures new.

Chapter 11
Autumn 1972: Amy

Esme Poppleton's home was a two-bedroom garden flat in a modern purpose-built apartment block on the outskirts of town. It was modest in size but had all the up-to-date amenities to which a single professional person might aspire, and it had been Esme's comfortable bachelor pad and refuge for the past four years. She was a tall slim divorcee in her mid-thirties, with handsome facial features and closely-cropped blonde hair. She and Amy had become friends shortly after Amy joined the staff of the Church of England primary school where they both taught. The friendship had developed and blossomed over the years until Esme had become Amy's sole confidante and support in times of trouble and distress – and it was Amy's trouble and distress that was the occasion of her impending visit to Esme's flat on a Saturday afternoon at the end of September.

Esme knew all about Amy's marital problems: the gradual deterioration of a loveless, childless union to a state where the prospect of continued cohabitation was intolerable; and her resolve to confront Guy and announce her departure from the matrimonial home just as soon as it was practicable. She was also apprised of Amy's brief affair with Danny Swift, and was aware of the impact that his outrageously callous behaviour had had on her – Esme had been Amy's first port of call after her flying visit to RAF Cosford in search of Danny at the end of August. But it now seemed that something new was afoot. Esme, who had been away from school all week on a training course, had received a phone call from Amy the evening before, asking if she could come round to her flat the next day to discuss 'something rather serious'. She was due any moment. Esme was in the kitchen, dressed casually in jeans and a sweater, preparing some afternoon tea when she heard Amy's knock at the front door. She went to greet her friend. She opened the door to find Amy standing there, clothed in a short skirt, blouse and tank top, and wearing a woeful expression on her face.

She led Amy through to the small sitting room, simply furnished with a modern three-piece suite and a teak coffee table, the plain walls adorned with a number of tastefully-arranged framed prints of modern artwork. She sat Amy down on the sofa and then went through to collect the tea things, returning with a tray a few minutes later. She placed the tray on the coffee table and settled herself on one of the armchairs.

'Now, Amy, I can see you're upset,' she began, looking at her friend's sad face. 'Is it something to do with your plans to leave Guy? Did something go wrong when you went to see Sheila after school on Monday about your job prospects?' Sheila Schofield was the head teacher of their school.

Esme started to pour cups of tea.

'Oh no, it's not that... that went pretty well, thanks Esme. Sheila was ever so nice. I didn't go into any intimate details about my domestic difficulties but I told her that I was unhappily married and planning to leave Guy in the near future and asked about how that would be viewed in a traditional church school – you know, whether deserting my husband might cost me my job. She seemed very surprised by what I had to say, and expressed her concern about my wellbeing and all that, but she was insistent that ultimately it was entirely a private matter and would make no difference to my ability to do my job, as far as she was concerned. She said I was a highly valued member of staff and that she wanted to keep me. I asked about the school governors and what they might think, and she said she was confident that any marital problems I might have wouldn't affect my position at the school; there are already two divorced teachers on the staff – you being one of them, of course. She seemed to think that the governors didn't interfere with her judgment on matters of staffing.' Amy appeared lost in thought for a moment and then continued. 'Anyway, Esme, things have moved on a bit... there's something else that'll almost certainly change everything...'

'Well, come on Amy, love. Spit it out.'

'I think I'm pregnant, Esme. In fact, if I'm honest, I know I am.'

'Pregnant! How can you be pregnant for goodness sake? Have you been to see a doctor?'

'No, but my period is four weeks overdue, and I'm always as regular as clockwork. And I just somehow feel different... you know, inside. I just know I'm pregnant. I had sex with Danny exactly five times and we never once took any precautions.'

'What! You didn't use anything? Amy, how could you be so foolish? You might have known this would happen.'

'To be honest, Esme, I was so carried away with the thrill and excitement of it all, that I never gave it a thought. I hadn't had sex for over a year, and before that I'd been having unprotected sex, after a fashion, with Guy for three years without conceiving and so I suppose I'd more or less blotted out the possibility of getting pregnant. I know it was stupid of me but I just didn't think.'

'Well what about that bastard, Danny? Why didn't he use something?'

'I don't know. In fairness, I suppose he just assumed that I'd be on the pill, being a married woman, and there was no need for him to bother. Anyway, Esme, the point is: what am I going to do? I don't give a fig about Guy and what he might think. The swine has been blaming me for being barren and not bearing him a child for ages, and refusing to have a fertility test himself... so he can go to hell. But it's my job I'm worried about, Esme. My job's just so important to me. There's no way I'll be able to keep it now, if I have a baby. And if I do have a baby, how will I afford to keep it?'

The two women sat silently for a while, Amy with her head down and her hands together on her lap, Esme looking at her pityingly. Then Esme got up from her chair and went to sit next to Amy on the sofa, taking Amy's hands in hers.

'Why didn't you tell me about this sooner, Amy? Four weeks is a long time to be late.'

'I kept thinking it would come – my period, I mean. It's really only been this past week, while you've been away on your course, that I've begun to realise that I must be pregnant and face up to reality. And it's really only been this week that I've started to feel different inside... you know, as if my body's changing in some way. And now it's four weeks and, well, here I am.'

They sat looking at each other for a while before Esme spoke.

'Well, sweetheart, it's true you won't be able to keep your baby and your job, if you're on your own. You've really only got two options: an abortion or staying with Guy and pretending the baby is his, if he'll agree to it – that is unless you've got some other way of supporting yourself while the baby's little and, even then, you'd have to give up your present job and wait to apply for another one when the child's older and you're free to go back to work. I suppose you could always go full term, have the baby, and then give it up for adoption... but that's a pretty horrid idea and not something you'd really want to contemplate. Come to think of it, it probably wouldn't solve anything, anyway – in terms of keeping your job, I mean. But then, if you were able to stay with Guy...'

'Esme, I'm not staying with Guy. It's out of the question.' Amy said this with passion.

'Okay, Amy... so what do you think about getting an abortion? It's what a lot of women in your position would do nowadays, you know, since the law was changed.'

'Yes, I know. But somehow, I can't bear the thought of it, even if the father is Danny.'

'Well, what about your mother? Surely she would be willing to take you in and help with the baby?'

'Oh, I don't know. Mum's very sweet and kind and all that, but she's also incredibly devout... a devout Catholic, I mean. I think she would find it almost impossible to cope with the idea that I was breaking my marriage vows, and that I was an adulteress who wanted to bring an illegitimate child into her home. I don't think she could handle it. And, even if she agreed, it'd be wrong of me to lay my troubles at her door. She's had a hard life and this would be too much for her to bear. Anyway, Mum doesn't earn much: she can only just about afford to support herself, let alone me and a baby... when my savings run out.'

Esme opened a bottle of wine and the two friends sat for some time, discussing Amy's options, in so far as there were any. The discussion was inevitably serious and subdued, but Esme persisted in her view that Amy should seriously consider having the pregnancy terminated. Amy was reluctant to contemplate an abortion, even though there didn't seem to be much in the way of alternatives. During their deliberations, Amy revealed that she had enough money in savings to support herself and the baby for about a year, probably longer if she was particularly thrifty – but what then? The discussion continued for the best part of two hours, returning to the same issues and going over the same ground several times. There was no ultimate decision on whether or not Amy should keep the child, but a number of resolutions were made. Firstly and most importantly, she would make an appointment the following Monday to see her doctor in order to get the pregnancy confirmed, and at the same time discuss the issues and practicalities involved in legally terminating a pregnancy. Secondly, it was agreed that she would confront Guy at the earliest opportunity and tell him she was leaving him, after which she would move into Esme's flat, where she was welcome to stay until she could find somewhere of her own. If she decided to go through with the pregnancy, she could stay with Esme at least until the baby was born, although it was accepted that Esme's small flat was not really big enough for her to stay there after that. The baby would probably be due towards the middle of May and so she would be able to continue working until the Easter holidays, all being well, which would give her time to make plans for the future. It was also agreed that she would speak to her mother and Aunt Harriet as soon as she could. She would tell them about the break up of her marriage and that she was moving in with Esme. She would also tell them that she was pregnant, if by then she had decided to keep the baby, but not that the father of the child was Danny Swift rather than Guy – at Esme's insistence, there was to be no mention of her illicit affair. The following weekend Aunt Harriet was due to stay with Doris in Newark, and so she would take the opportunity to sit down and talk with them then.

Just as Amy was putting on her coat before leaving for another bleak evening at home with Guy, Esme suddenly said, 'Amy, there's something I want you to think about.' She paused for a moment while she gathered her thoughts and then went on, 'If you decide to keep the baby, I want you to seriously consider setting up home with me. I could sell this flat, you could put up your savings, and then we could buy a little house together – with a mortgage, of course. We'd be a sort of couple. You may be entitled to some sort of social security benefit, I don't know, but anyway, I'd support you and the baby until you're able to go back to work – and we'd bring up baby together. I'm definitely not planning to get married again and I don't want to end up a lonely old spinster. It could be an ideal solution for both of us. Don't say anything now, just mull it over. There'll be plenty of time to talk about it later.' She gave Amy a quizzical smile.

'Oh, Esme... that's ever so sweet of you,' Amy said innocently. 'I don't quite know what to say, I...'

'Don't say anything now, Amy. I just wanted to plant the seed of an idea. There'll be plenty of time to talk about it when everything's settled and you've moved in here. You've got to deal with Guy first... and your mum and your aunt. You need to get all that out of the way first. But just think about it. Of course, you might decide to have an abortion, in which case it won't matter. But, from what you've been saying, I rather think you'll decide to keep your baby... so just think about it.' Esme went up to Amy, took her face in her hands and kissed her gently on the lips. Then she said softly, 'I think you'd better be getting home now. Guy will be wondering where you've got to.'

The following Monday, Amy took some time off work and went to see her doctor. He gave her an examination after which he confirmed that, as far as he was concerned, there was no doubt about her condition: she was pregnant. He arranged for her to have a sample sent for testing, but made it clear that this was really only a formality and that she should regard herself as being in the early stages of gestation and proceed accordingly. At Amy's instigation, there followed a short, terse, business-like discussion concerning the possibility and practicalities of having an abortion, the upshot of which was that the doctor reluctantly agreed that he would recommend a termination in her case, if that was what she decided she wanted, but that she should make a decision as soon as possible, preferably within the next couple of weeks. By the time Amy had climbed into her car in the surgery car park, she had already decided that she was going to keep the child.

Amy planned to confront Guy at the end of the week, when he came home from work on Friday evening. She was determined that the confrontation would be brief, after which she would leave the house for good and move in with Esme that same evening. During the course of the week, she surreptitiously moved her belongings from the matrimonial home and transported them to the flat, leaving school each day as soon as classes had finished and using the time before Guy arrived home from work, at around six o'clock, in order to accomplish the stratagem. She didn't want much, just her clothes and personal effects. She wanted nothing in the way of furnishings or household adornments, even though most of the contents of the house had been chosen by her – indeed she wanted nothing that would remind her of her disastrous marriage. She had toyed with the idea of simply writing Guy a note, telling him the marriage was over, and leaving without the unpleasantness of a confrontation, but ultimately she decided that she wanted the satisfaction of telling him face to face exactly what she thought of him and how disgracefully he had treated her.

On Friday evening at six o'clock, Amy was sitting on the sofa in the open plan living room of the Balderton house, awaiting Guy's return. She was already wearing her coat; her suitcase was in the boot of her car. She had removed her wedding and engagement rings and left them on her dressing table upstairs. As expected, Guy arrived almost on the dot of six. He came in through the front door, put down his briefcase on the table to the right of the door, took off his coat and went through to the living room. He acknowledged Amy sitting on the sofa but did not seem to notice how she was dressed.

'Hello Amy. Is there some tea?' he asked, looking at the empty coffee table in front of the sofa. 'You know I like a cup of tea ready when I get home from work, particularly on Fridays. I've had a very busy week.'

'You can make your own tea, Guy. I'm leaving.'

'I beg your pardon?' Guy looked at Amy properly for the first time, a startled look on his face. Amy rose to her feet to face him.

'I'm leaving you, Guy... leaving you for good. I just thought I'd like to tell you in person... and tell you what a thorough-going shit you are.' Amy glowered directly into Guy's eyes. He was visibly taken aback.

'Don't be ridiculous, Amy. You're my wife. You belong to me. What's all this nonsense about leaving?'

'There's nothing to discuss, Guy. I married you because I liked you and thought I might grow to love you. You were good to me when you were courting me. But I've learned that you only wanted me as some sort of trophy and as the mother of your children... and as a symbol of respectability. You've never loved me or cherished me or wanted me as a woman. I've learned that you're just a spoilt, self-centred, self-satisfied, overbearing, pompous hypocrite... and you treat me like dirt. I hate you, Guy. I loathe and detest you.'

Guy just stood there, open-mouthed and speechless.

'I suppose the fact that you're a homosexual has something to do with it. I don't know how you could have been so callous as to lure me into marriage, knowing you didn't really want me physically, but I might have been able to live with that if you'd treated me properly... AND if I hadn't discovered you were a child molester.' Amy took the anonymous note from her coat pocket and threw it at him. It landed at his feet. He ignored the note and seemed to regain his composure, glaring fiercely at his wife.

'How dare you speak to me like that after all I've done for you. I've given you everything you could possibly want: money, this house, status, a position of respect in my family and in the Church. I've taken you from that miserable, squalid little semi you lived in with that hapless mother of yours and made something of you. And what have I got back... nothing. The one thing I wanted – the only thing I asked of you – was a child, a son and heir... and you couldn't give me one. Your complete lack of respect for God and the Church has left you barren: not going to Mass, not going to confession, not supporting me in my position as a leading member of the congregation. But you're my wife and you belong to me, and you'll do what I tell you... do you understand? You swore before God to be my wife until death separates us, and that's what you'll do. There's no way you're going to leave me, Amy, and you'd better get used to the idea... and I might as well tell you now, seeing that you're behaving so strangely: I've decided that we're going to adopt a son through one of the Catholic adoption agencies, and...'

Amy had heard enough. She just wanted to go.

'You might be interested to know, Guy, that your barren wife is pregnant. That's right, Guy, PREGNANT!' she bellowed the word at him, 'and obviously not by you. So much for you and your pious claptrap about the wrath of God and my sinful ways, because it's you who's infertile, Guy, not me and, if anyone's being punished by that wonderful God of yours, it's you for being a bigot, a pervert and a molester of young boys. You're a vile, creepy, arrogant piece of shit, Guy Boucher, and I never want to see you again.'

She marched past him to the front door and walked out of the house into the twilight, leaving the door open behind her. He stood rooted to the spot watching her go, unable to speak. Just as she was getting into her car, she heard him yell after her, 'You're my wife and you always will be. I'll never give you a divorce... never!' She slammed the door of the car, started the engine and drove off the forecourt and into the road. As she drove across Newark to the other side of town and Esme's apartment, she was overcome with a feeling of elation: she was driving into an uncertain, hazardous future, but she was free at last – free for the first time in six, long years. That evening she and Esme went out together for a celebratory meal at an Italian restaurant in town. Her new life had begun.

On Saturday morning, Amy went round to her mother's house to reveal the radical changes in her domestic circumstances to Doris and Aunt Harriet. She approached this meeting with a much greater sense of trepidation than she had experienced before her confrontation with Guy the previous evening. She arrived at the semi-detached house in time for morning coffee. When the three women were seated in the small front room, a plate of biscuits and three mugs of instant coffee on the table before them, Amy began to tell her mother and her Aunt the story of her unhappy, empty, loveless marriage. Her relating of the story was done in a carefully rehearsed manner, which she hoped was both sensitive and convincing. She did not, of course, mention the matter of Guy's frustration at not becoming a father, because she was about to reveal that she was in fact pregnant. She did, however, say that she was certain that Guy was homosexual and also that there had come to her attention some fairly compelling evidence that he had an unhealthy interest in young boys. She remained silent on the matter of her relationship with Danny Swift, just as Esme had insisted she must do. She continued her tale of woe by saying that she had decided that life with her husband was so unbearable that she was going to leave him, only to discover subsequently that she was pregnant. However, the recent confirmation of her pregnancy had made no difference to her resolve: life with Guy was intolerable and so, the previous evening, she had moved out of the matrimonial home and in with her good friend, Esme, with whom she could stay at least until her baby was born the following May. What she would do thereafter was yet to be decided, although she was not intending, or indeed expecting, to move back into the family home with her mother, or to impose on her in any other way.

Throughout Amy's narration, Doris had become increasingly and visibly agitated. Aunt Harriet sat in stony silence, an inscrutably blank expression on her face. At the end of the story, Doris burst into tears. Amy went to comfort her mother, sitting by her on the sofa and putting her arm around her until she had calmed down. Then she spoke.

'I'm sorry, Mum... I'm so very sorry. I know I've let you down badly. I should never have married Guy in the first place, I know, and it's partly my fault. But I was so very young when I got engaged, and I went along with him for all the wrong reasons. But I'm going to put things right. I'm going to have my baby and look after it, just you wait and see. It will be your grandchild too, Mum – your very own little grandson or granddaughter.'

Doris sat shaking her head and said, 'It's no use, Amy my love. I know you must be very unhappy in your marriage but you're just going to have to make it work. You made those marriage vows in church, sweetheart, before God, and you'll just have to stick by them. You're a good Catholic girl, Amy, and it would be catastrophic for your mortal soul to walk out on Guy, especially now you're having his baby. No, Amy, you're just going to have to go back to him and make it work.'

'No, Mum, that's not going to happen. You've got to understand that.'

'Amy... I'm your mother and I love you more than I can say, but this isn't just a matter of what you want to do or how you feel, it's about breaking God's law and the rules of the Church. I don't think you realise just how terribly serious this is... for your soul, I mean, and what will happen to you in the hereafter. You're just going to have to go back to Guy and make it work, sweetheart. I can't believe it would be as bad as all that. Guy's such a nice, respectable, hardworking young man.'

'No he isn't, Mum, he's a monster. You can't have been listening to what I've been telling you. He's not just a hypocrite and a bully, he's a sexual deviant and predator. I couldn't allow my baby to be brought up in the same house as a man like that, even if I could put up with him myself – which I most definitely can't. I know your faith is very important to you, Mum, and that you believe in all that stuff the Church comes out with... but, you see, I don't... Oh, come on Mum, you've got to understand. I'm not asking you to do anything for me, I just want you to understand and come to terms with what

I've decided to do... and just – I don't know – just look forward to becoming a grandma.'

Doris started sobbing again and then murmured, 'How will I be able to face the priests and the people at church, if they all know that my daughter has walked out on Guy Boucher, of all people, and taken his child with her? It would be quite dreadful... absolutely dreadful...'

'That's enough of that, Doris,' interjected Aunt Harriet, who up until that point had maintained her inscrutable demeanour and uttered nary a sound. 'I don't think I can bear to listen to any more of your silly pious nonsense. This is your daughter we're talking about, and your grandchild, not some abstract person who doesn't mean anything to us. Of course Amy can't go back to Guy, if what she's told us is true... and, as far as I'm concerned, it is true.' She turned to Amy. 'Amy, my dear, I feel partly responsible for all of this. I can remember encouraging you – quite strongly, I think – to stick with Guy, shortly after you started courting him. I thought things would work out for you the way they had worked out for me and Uncle Cyril, but I was obviously very wrong, and they haven't – quite the opposite, in fact. Do you remember, dear? It was that time I told you the story of your dear father – upstairs in your little bedroom, just before you went off to college.'

Amy nodded and smiled sweetly at her aunt.

'Anyway, that was before I'd been introduced to Guy Boucher, and I disliked him from the moment I met him, although I didn't say anything at the time... or since. There was something completely artificial about him. He had an air of distant arrogance which he tried to cover up with his affected, ingratiating version of good manners. He always brought to mind that character from Dickens... you know: Uriah Heap. You've obviously had the most awful time with the man, and you've done the right thing in leaving him... well, the only thing you could have done in the circumstances. The important thing now is to plan for the future. Now, you say you want to continue working until Easter, if you can. Is that right, dear?'

'Yes, Auntie.'

'Yes... and you're quite sure you'll be able to stay with your friend, Esme, until then?'

'Yes, I'm certain of that.'

'And you'll be quite happy there?'

'Oh yes, I'm sure I will be.'

'Good. So, the most important thing by far is to make plans for when the baby is born... and afterwards, as well, of course. Now this is what I propose. I think it is a very good thing that you continue working for as long as you can. It's not just the money you'll be earning, it's a matter of keeping yourself healthy in both body and mind. So, on the assumption that you'll be staying with your friend until you resign from your school at the start of the Easter holidays, I propose that you move to Wolverhampton after that, and come and live with me at Greengage Hill. I'm living there all by myself in that great big house and I really don't want to move, even though I'm rattling around in the place. I shall look after you while you have the baby, and you'll stay with me as long as needs be after the baby is born. You can't imagine, my dear, how much I shall enjoy having you and a child in my home – a house that was meant for a family, which I was never able to give it.'

'Oh, Auntie, that's so very kind, but it would be far too much for you, having me and a child about the place all the time.'

'Nonsense, Amy. I'm still in my fifties, and I'm as fit as a fiddle. Listen, my dear: I'm all on my own in a huge house with more money than I can possibly know what to do with. It will all be yours one day – well most of it, anyway – and so you might just as well enjoy some of the benefits of it now, when you really need it. You can live with me for as long as you like... and when you're ready to go back to work, you can find a teaching post in Wolverhampton or

Staffordshire, and I shall be your childminder, looking after my own little great nephew or niece while you're out teaching. It will be like having my own grandchild. And if things get a little tough, then we'll hire a nanny, won't we?' Aunt Harriet, who was getting increasingly animated as she expounded her plan, giggled mischievously. 'Amy, it will be perfect, and we shall have such fun.'

And that was what happened. Amy did not accept her aunt's proposal there and then – she needed to speak to Esme and tell her about it first – but it didn't take long for her to make up her mind and agree to the plan. She hadn't felt comfortable with Esme's idea of buying a house together and becoming 'a sort of couple' after the birth of the baby even though at the time – and somewhat naively – she hadn't appreciated the ulterior motive implicit in Esme's proposition. It was more the fact that she didn't want the long-term commitment of buying a house with Esme – or anyone else. Also, Esme wasn't family, and Amy didn't want to impose on her kindness by exploiting their friendship for longer than she needed to. She would, of course, be paying her rent while she was living at her flat and working, which put that part of the arrangement on a more business-like footing. Esme expressed disappointment at Amy's decision to move to Wolverhampton before the baby was born, and for a short time appeared genuinely upset that her idea of setting up home together was not going to materialise, but she could understand the merits of the arrangement with Aunt Harriet from Amy's point of view, and the decision did not unduly affect the two women's continuing friendship. So Amy taught at her school and lived happily enough with Esme until the beginning of April, by which time she was heavily pregnant.

There was only one serious hiccup during this period, and that was when, early in November, Amy was called before the chairman of the Board of Governors of her school to respond to a letter he had received from Guy Boucher stating, in forthright terms, that Amy was in serious dereliction of her marital duties and breach of her marriage vows by having unjustifiably and unreasonably deserted her husband; that she was an adulteress; and that she was bearing an illegitimate child which was the fruit of her adultery. According to Guy, she was therefore not a suitable person to be employed in the capacity of a schoolteacher at a Church of England primary school. Amy, with the support of Sheila Schofield, her head teacher, was able to deal with the matter swiftly and relatively easily. She had to lie about the allegation of adultery and the legitimacy of her unborn child, but she was able to rely on the testimony of Sheila who was happy to confirm that Amy had always been completely candid about the fact that she was having serious marital problems, in consequence of which she was planning to move out of the marital home, notwithstanding the fact that she was with child. The chairman, who was well known for his antipathy towards the Roman Catholic Church, was quite content to interpret the letter as the spiteful and malicious ranting of a jilted husband, and let the matter rest. Amy heard nothing more from Guy, who never made any attempt to contact her either directly or through her mother. She feared that he might try to lay claim to her baby once it was born – after all, it had been conceived during cohabitation and would be born during lawful wedlock – but her fears were unfounded. On 18 May, 1973, she gave birth to a healthy baby girl at The Royal Hospital in Wolverhampton. She named the baby Harriet Rose.

Doris Anderton took some time to come to terms with what she regarded as her daughter's fall from grace, not to mention the connivance of her big sister in the affair. But she slowly came round, and when she was introduced to baby Harriet shortly after the birth, she simply fell in love with the child and thenceforward became a loving and devoted grandmother. But nobody, not even Amy, loved and doted on the child more than Harriet Ostime. From the moment baby Harriet was born, her great aunt adored her and, by the time she was able to walk and talk, the two Harriets had become almost inseparable.

Amy remained with her aunt on Greengage Hill for a number of years. In September, 1974, she started work again – but not as a teacher. She secured the post of personal assistant to the proprietor of Mercian News Limited, a local company which published a couple of 'free sheet' newspapers and an up-market glossy magazine, all of which were circulated in the Wolverhampton area. Amy's new boss was an old friend of Cyril and Harriet Ostime, and had known Amy since she was a teenager. Having heard from Aunt Harriet that Amy was ready to return to work and on the lookout for a job, he had invited her to come and work for him. After some initial hesitation and prevarication, she accepted the job, and very soon found that she was taking to the work like a duck to water. And while Amy was out at work, Harriet Rose was safe and sound in the loving care of her great aunt – in the big house on Greengage Hill.

Chapter 12
21 November 1974

The double-decker bus pulled up at the stop on St Martin's Circus, right outside the main entrance to New Street Station. Henry Irving and Fiona Davies alighted through the front passenger doors and started to walk, arm in arm, towards New Street and the city centre, a short distance away. It was a cold, November, Thursday evening, shortly before eight o'clock, and the couple were suitably attired in coats and scarves. They had come into the centre of Birmingham to celebrate Fiona's twenty-fifth birthday: a film show – *The Great Gatsby* – at the Gaumont cinema, followed by a curry at The Royal Adeel, their favourite Indian restaurant. They were intending to walk up High Street towards Colmore Circus where the cinema was located, when Harry suddenly stopped and turned to Fiona.

'I'm thirsty, Fiona. I fancy a pint. Let's pop into the Mulberry Bush for a quickie. We should have time.'

'Oh come off it, Harry. The film starts at eight-twenty, and it's already nearly eight. It's going to take us nearly ten minutes to walk up there, and then we might have to queue for tickets. Anyway, if you start drinking beer you'll only want to wee during the movie… and I hate it when people get up to go to the loo in the middle of a film.'

'Ah, but the film doesn't actually start at eight-twenty… it's the programme that does. You don't want to have to sit through all those tedious *Pearl & Dean* adverts and then the trailers, do you? It all goes on for ages. The film won't start until twenty to nine, I expect. Come on, Fifi… just a swift half, then?'

'Well perhaps... if you really want to. Where's the Mulberry Bush, anyway?'

'Just over there, in the Rotunda,' Harry said, pointing to the landmark, cylindrical building, about a hundred yards from where they were standing.

'Okay, but no longer than fifteen minutes... and I'm just going to have a Coke.'

The Mulberry Bush occupied the bottom two floors of the twenty-five storey Rotunda, an iconic edifice completed nine years earlier. Harry and Fiona set off towards the popular watering hole at a brisk pace. They arrived at the main entrance to the pub and were just about to enter when the doors swung open and a group of four people – two youngish couples – started to emerge from the building, talking jovially as they did so. Harry was just about to stand aside to let them pass to his right, when his eyes were drawn to the young woman on his side of the group, walking arm in arm with a broad handsome man, probably a few years older than her. She stopped in her tracks the moment she looked at Harry, letting go of her escort's arm. Harry and the woman stared at each other momentarily.

'Amy, is that you?' Harry asked cautiously.

'Harry! It is you, isn't it! I don't believe it... what on earth are you doing here?' Amy said in amazement.

The other three members of the group had now also pulled up, as had Fiona. They had all gathered round and were looking on.

'Well, I could say the same thing to you,' Harry said. 'I live here... you know, in Birmingham; in Moseley, actually. How about you?'

'I'm living in Wolverhampton at the moment... with my aunt,' she said, and then, indicating her companions, 'We're just off to a folk club in Digbeth. I'm afraid we're running a bit late. Oh... this is Roger by the way.' She touched her escort's arm. 'And these are our friends, Paul and Anna.' Harry shook hands with Roger, and exchanged greetings with Paul and Anna, before introducing Fiona to the group.

'I thought you were living in Newark, Amy,' Harry said. 'I heard from Phil, a couple of years ago, that you'd got married and were back in Nottinghamshire.'

'Oh, that's a long story, Harry. I'm separated from Guy now and living with Aunt Harriet. Anyway, how are you and what are you up to?'

The two of them exchanged trite pleasantries about their health and their jobs; Harry asked after Ginger; and Amy asked after Phil, and Mr and Mrs Semark, It was all rather frantic and superficial, although deep down they both wanted to be alone together and talk properly. But Harry could see that Amy was with Roger, and Harry and Fiona looked very much like an item to Amy, so it all seemed rather hopeless to both of them. After several minutes had elapsed, Roger touched Amy on the arm and said, 'Amy, it's gone ten past eight by my watch, we really must get going, we're already pretty late.' Amy looked at her companions and could see that Paul and Anna were looking rather agitated.

'Yes, of course,' Amy said, and then turned to look at Harry. 'I'm sorry, Harry, I've really got to be going. We've got to get down to the Civic Hall, in Digbeth.'

'Oh, yes... yes, well I suppose we'd better get going as well. We're off to the flicks at the Gaumont, the opposite way to you, I'm afraid.' He turned to Fiona. 'We'll have to pass on that drink, I suppose, Fifi?'

'Yes we will, Harry,' Fiona said. 'It wasn't a very good idea in the first place. Come on, we'd better go.'

Harry and Amy looked at each other for a moment, each one hoping the other might say something that would enable them to keep in touch, but neither, in the circumstances, feeling able to ask for the other's phone number or address. Then Roger said decisively, 'Right, we're on our way. Goodbye, Harry... nice meeting you.'

'Yes, nice meeting you too,' Harry said, and then to Amy, 'It's been great to see you again, Amy... really nice.'

'Lovely to see you too, Harry. Um... I'd better go. Bye.'

'Bye.' Harry nearly choked on the word.

Amy's group walked away towards Digbeth; Harry and Fiona set off at a brisk pace in the opposite direction towards the Gaumont cinema. They walked in silence for a couple of minutes and then Fiona said, 'So, who's Amy when she's at home? It looked like you were a bit keen on her,'

'Oh, an old friend, that's all... from university days in Wessex.'

'Seemed more like an old flame to me, the way you looked at each other... and the way you started talking to each other as if nobody else was there.'

'Yes, well I suppose we did have a relationship for a while. But it was all a long time ago, and it only lasted a couple of weeks.'

'You've never mentioned anyone called Amy before, when we've been talking about our exes.'

'Haven't I? Look, it really doesn't matter, Fiona, it was all a long time ago. Let's change the subject, shall we? Let's just enjoy your birthday.'

'Okay,' Fiona said, and she took Harry's arm as they continued on their way together in silence.

Five or six minutes after the couple had left the Rotunda, as they were nearing Colmore Circus towards the top end of Bull Street, they were startled by what sounded like an explosion, coming from the part of the city centre they had just left. They came to a halt and looked round, but there was nothing to be seen from where they now were. The explosion was followed by the distant wail of emergency vehicle sirens coming from the same direction. They both expressed concern at what they had just heard, and dallied for a while, debating whether or not they ought to double back and find out what had happened. But they didn't want to miss the film and there was probably nothing they could do if they did go back, so they decided to press on. A few minutes later they were approaching the grand façade of the art deco cinema. The sound of sirens was still persisting in the distance, and again they stood for a while on the pavement outside the building, weighing up whether or not they should join the queue for tickets inside. Harry looked at his wristwatch – it was just after twenty-five past eight, and so they decided to go in. Just as they were entering the cinema there was the sound of another explosion, more muffled this time, but coming from the same direction as the first. That was enough for both of them – and for several others who were queuing for tickets. They decided to head back towards New Street and The Rotunda.

As they neared New Street, it soon became apparent that something very serious had happened: people were hurrying away from the area in large numbers; sirens continued to wail; ambulances were approaching from different directions; and police were busy erecting barriers and cordoning off the disaster zone. Harry stopped a couple who were hurrying towards them, part of the crowd apparently vacating the district, and asked them what had happened. He was told that there had been two big explosions in city centre pubs – they weren't sure which ones – and that the whole area was being evacuated. It seemed to Harry and Fiona very unlikely that they were going to be able to find their way to a bus stop where they could catch a bus home, and so they decided to turn back and head for Snow Hill Station where they hoped to pick up a cab. They made the short walk to Snow Hill, only to discover that quite a number of other people had had the same idea – they had to join a queue. Eventually they were able to share a taxi back to Moseley with an elderly couple who were going the same way, and they arrived home safe and sound about nine-thirty. It was not until they saw the late-evening, television news that they learned that the two explosions had been caused by bomb blasts, the first of which had been in the Mulberry Bush.

Amy and her companions also heard the distant blast of the first bomb, shortly before arriving at Digbeth Civic Hall, but missed the second blast because, by the time that bomb detonated, they were settled inside the crowded folk club listening to the music. When the club closed at about eleven o'clock, they only had to walk a short distance to where Roger had parked his car earlier in the evening, before they had walked up to the city centre to meet Paul and Anna in the Mulberry Bush, and so they were able to drive home to Wolverhampton without encountering any difficulty. They only learnt about the bombings and the full extent of the disaster – and how close they had come to being victims of the first blast – the next day.

The Birmingham pub bombings – almost certainly the responsibility of Irish republican dissidents, as part of their mainland terror campaign during 'the Troubles' – took place on the evening of 21 November 1974. The first bomb exploded at seventeen minutes past eight in the Mulberry Bush and the second, ten minutes later, in the Tavern in the Town, a basement pub some fifty meters along New Street from the Mulberry Bush. Nineteen people were killed – ten at the Mulberry Bush and nine in the Tavern in the Town – and two more victims would die subsequently as a result of their injuries. One hundred and eighty-two people were wounded, many of them seriously. A substantial number of the victims were permanently maimed as a result of the wounds they had suffered. At the time, the bombings were the deadliest act of terrorism in mainland Britain since the end of the Second World War.

Harry and Fiona had avoided possible death by a few minutes. Indeed, if they had not fortuitously run into Amy and her party at the entrance to the Mulberry Bush, they would inevitably have become victims of the first bomb blast. Harry was neither religious nor superstitious, and he certainly had never been a believer in destiny, but he could not help but feel that fate or a guardian angel – or God even – had somehow intervened by contriving this unlikely encounter with Amy – the only girl he had ever loved – on the night of the Birmingham bombings.

Seeing Amy again outside the Mulberry Bush that night had the same effect on Harry as his sighting of Danny Swift's girlfriend at The Rep had done two years earlier, although the sense of loss and personal folly was even more intense, having this time actually seen and spoken to his lost love. Over the following days he carried an almost constant picture in his mind of Amy, walking arm in arm with her handsome escort, and he knew in his heart of hearts that all was lost. Then he suddenly remembered that Roger was the name of her brother, and it occurred to him, for the first time, that the Roger he had seen her with that evening bore an undoubted facial resemblance to Amy. The realisation that she had almost certainly been out with her brother seemed to lift the cloud of doom that had been hanging over him. Again he became absorbed by the notion of fate: not just that fate had saved him from disaster through his encounter with Amy, but that fate had decreed that he and Amy were made for each other, and that they were one day destined to be together.

Amy had also been profoundly affected by her encounter with Harry. Ever since their love affair, eight years earlier, there had hardly been a day that passed without her thinking about him, but she had long since come to terms with the idea that their love was not to be, and that their time together was nothing more than a fond and increasingly distant memory. But seeing him again and knowing that he was alive and well, and living in Moseley, little more than sixteen or seventeen miles away from where she now lived – and knowing that their encounter had almost certainly saved him from becoming the victim of a terrorist bomb – opened up the possibility that something just might be about to happen to bring them together again. She had known as soon as she saw him standing outside the Mulberry Bush that nothing had changed: she was still in love with him, just as she had been ever since the day they had first met. But as the weeks went by, the idea of getting together with him, which at first had seemed such a tantalisingly plausible prospect, became less and less likely: they had no means by which they might contact each other; she chided herself for not having introduced Roger as her brother, almost certainly leaving Harry with the impression that she and Roger were a courting couple; Harry was with an attractive girl called Fiona and was probably firmly committed to his relationship with her; and, in any event, what would Harry want with a separated woman with an eighteen-month-old child. Hope gradually turned to despair, as Amy came to realise that she must, once again, condition herself to a life without the one she loved.

It was Harry who was determined to keep the torch burning brightly. He knew that they would meet again sooner or later – fate had ordained it – and, when that day came, he would be ready.

Part Two

PROVIDENCE

Chapter 13
June 1976

It was Saturday morning. Mary Irving was busy cooking lunch in her sparsely equipped rectory kitchen, a cigarette between her lips as she mashed the potatoes and a glass of whisky and water, for sipping purposes, on the kitchen shelf above the cooker. She was a small, slim, erect woman in her mid-sixties, with a gentle, rather careworn face surrounded by a mass of untamed, wiry, grey hair. Harry was visiting his parents at their home near Swindon. St Bartholomew's – better known as St Bart's – rectory, the Irvings' family home, was no longer the rambling, six-bedroom, somewhat threadbare, Edwardian parsonage where he had grown up but an unassuming little box of a house, built some five years earlier in the orchard of the old rectory which had then been sold by the Church to a wealthy Swindon scrap merchant, and converted into a rich man's luxury residence, complete with a cinema, gymnasium and sauna. He tried to visit his parents as often as possible – their house was less than a two hour drive from Moseley – but on this occasion it was his father, the Reverend Lyndon Irving, who had asked him to come home for the weekend, because there was something of importance he wanted to discuss with his son.

Harry also had some news he wanted to share with his parents: a new teaching post to which he had recently been appointed. Harborne Grammar School, where he had spent four happy years as an English master and rugby coach was due to be merged, along with its five hundred scholars, with a nearby secondary modern school in order to create a vast comprehensive school of some fourteen hundred pupils, with little in the way of planning, preparation or the investment needed to make a success of such a radical academic enterprise. The teaching staff of both existing schools had been told that they would not automatically be transferred to the new institution but would need to reapply for posts and go through a competitive selection process before having an appointment confirmed. Harry, who regarded the whole business as a shambolic nightmare, had decided to decline the opportunity to apply for what he regarded as his own job, and to move on. Quite by chance, he had been offered a well-paid job as a resident master and senior teacher of English at Castlecroft College, an independent boarding school on the outskirts of Wolverhampton. The location of the school was, of course, highly significant in his decision to accept the position, which he would be taking up the following September.

Harry walked into his parents' kitchen, put his arm around his mother, who had finished with the potatoes, and asked, 'Is there anything I can do to help, Mum?'

'Yes, would you just set the table for me, darling? Then we can sit down and eat. Your father will be home any minute and we both want to hear all about your new job, and then there's another matter that we want to discuss with you.'

'I know,' Harry said, making his way to the kitchen table. 'Dad wouldn't say what it was on the phone. He made it seem very mysterious. What's it all about, Mum?'

'I'm afraid I can't tell you, dear. Lyndon asked me specifically not to say anything until he was here and we could all sit down and discuss the matter as a family.'

'Okay... but I can't imagine what it's about.'

At that moment, Harry's father arrived home from his morning's pastoral duties: taking communion to the homes of parishioners too ill or infirm to attend church services in order to receive the sacrament. He entered the house through the kitchen's external back door, and immediately went to greet his much loved son. A rotund, jolly, bespectacled man with a florid complexion and balding head, the Reverend Lyndon Irving wore a dog-collar and cassock, as was his custom when engaged on parish business. The little family, when assembled, presented a curious spectacle to the world: Harry – very tall, slim and handsome, with a full head of thick, straight, brown hair; his mother – small, pinched, careworn and not exactly pretty; and the Reverend Irving – short, round, ruddy and bald, with bulbous features which were only made appealing by his indefatigable jollity. Harry had brown eyes whereas his parents both had hazel blue eyes. If ever there was a family with an adopted child, this was it.

The members of the little family busied themselves getting ready for lunch, chatting happily as they did so. When they were seated, and after Lyndon had said grace, Harry's parents asked him to tell them about his new teaching post. He told them about the school and its attractive surroundings – an eclectic mixture of ancient and modern buildings set in thirty acres of grounds and playing fields – and then went on to explain what the job entailed, including his pastoral duties as a resident master in a boys' boarding school – with girls recently admitted to the sixth form. He would be giving up his flat in Moseley and moving into an apartment in one of the school's boarding houses. He also related the story of the unusual circumstances under which he had come to be appointed to the post:

He had taken an under-fifteen cricket team from Harborne Grammar to play a fixture at Castlecroft College and, during the match while umpiring at square leg, he had been approached by a white haired gentleman, dressed in a black academic gown, who proceeded to engage him in conversation. At the end of each alternate over, when Harry came back from umpiring behind the wicket at the bowler's end to umpire at square leg, this same gentleman would return from the boundary to where Harry was standing and continue the conversation. It transpired, in due course, that the gentleman in question was the headmaster of Castlecroft and that he had, in effect, been carrying out an informal and surreptitious job interview with Harry. After the game had finished and the boys were having tea in the pavilion, he had asked Harry if he would consider taking a job at the college. Harry had revealed, during the course of the afternoon conversations with the headmaster, that he would be relinquishing his current position at Harborne at the end of term, and that he was looking for a new challenge. It just so happened that the post of senior English teacher at Castlecroft had recently and unexpectedly become available for the forthcoming academic year, and the headmaster was keen to make a suitable appointment as soon as possible. Harry had been taken aback at being offered a relatively senior teaching post in a prestigious, independent school in such unlikely circumstances. The one thing that had put him off was the fact that the post was residential. He had prevaricated at first, and so the headmaster had invited him to visit the school the following Saturday in order to have a look round and ask any questions he might have before making a decision. In the end he had had no difficulty in accepting the job: it was a well paid post at a prestigious school in delightful surroundings; the teaching would be very similar to what he was currently doing – very successfully – and which he enjoyed; the post was sufficiently senior to be regarded as a step up in his teaching career; and the burdens of a residential post were more than offset by the prospect of rent-free and bills-free accommodation.

What Harry did not reveal to his parents, while he was telling the story, was that the one thing which really tipped the balance in favour of accepting the job was the school's location. He would be getting closer – very close, in fact – to Amy. It was providence that had presented him with such an opportunity – an opportunity he could not possibly eschew.

After he had finished telling his story, Mary Irving said, 'Now, Harry, I want to know if you're doing any courting at the moment. Your father and I were quite upset when you told us that you and Fiona had split up, weren't we, Lyndon?'

'Yes, Harry, we thought she was a very nice young woman ... just the right sort of girl for you, dear boy,' agreed Lyndon Irving.

'Oh, come on, Mum... Dad, it's a year since Fiona and I parted company. We've been through all of this before. You know very well that it was Fifi who finished with me... you remember: because I refused to make the commitment she wanted. I've told you this before... more than once.'

'Yes, dear, I know... such a shame,' continued Mary Irving,' but you need to find yourself a nice girl, you know. You'll be thirty soon and it's time you were thinking of getting married and settling down. Isn't there some nice young woman you know, who might do?'

Harry thought for a moment. He had never told his parents about Amy, and the depth of his feelings for her. He decided he would mention her, just briefly, if only to keep his mother happy. 'Well, there is somebody, actually, Mum. A very beautiful girl I met when I was at Wessex. She lives in Wolverhampton now, and that's where I shall be next term. I can't say much, because we're not actually in touch at the moment, but it is my firm intention that we will be... and that we will eventually be together.'

'Oh, Harry, how very romantic and exciting,' enthused Mary. 'Do please tell us more.'

'No, Mum, there's nothing more I can say at the moment, but there will be... just you wait and see.'

'My word, dear boy,' Lyndon said. 'What an enigma! You've never mentioned this before. Aren't you going to tell us just a wee bit more about your mystery girl?'

'Not now, Dad. I will, in due course, when things start to happen... which they will, you can be sure of it.'

'Well, at least tell us her name, darling,' pleaded Mary.

'It's Amy, Mum... her name is Amy.'

When the meal was over and everything had been cleared away, the three Irvings reconvened at the kitchen table to discuss the main item on the agenda for the family gathering. The Reverend Irving took the chair.

'Harry, my very dear boy, I think you know how much your mother and I love you, and how, as far as we're concerned, you are our son and that's the end of the matter. But we have also always been completely candid about the fact that we adopted you as a newborn baby, because God, in His wisdom, had chosen not to bless us with the ability to procreate. Of course, in having had you as our child we feel blessed many times over.'

'Dad, you don't have to say all this. You've been wonderful parents. I couldn't have wished for anything better than having you and Mum as my parents. We haven't talked about this for many years and it's something I hardly ever think about. You two are my Mum and Dad and there's really nothing more to be said.'

'That is a great comfort to us, Harry, a very great comfort indeed. But I feel I have perhaps been rather remiss in not having discussed this matter with you more often ... and certainly when you got to be twenty-one and came of age...'

'Not having discussed what, Dad?'

'Well... whether you might have some secret desire, or at least curiosity, to know a little more about your natural heritage... you know, to find out more about your birth parents. It seems to be increasingly the trend these days for adopted children to want to trace their blood relatives, particularly when they get older. I feel that I might have been rather complacent in assuming that you weren't interested in doing so.'

'No Dad, you haven't... and neither have you, Mum. I promise you, it has never occurred to me to want to go ferreting around after... well, after what? I've got all the heritage I need in this family. I'm Henry Irving and very proud to be Henry Irving. I don't need anything else.'

'Oh, Harry, you're such a darling,' Mary said, with tears in her eyes.

'Thank you, Harry, my dear boy. But you must excuse me if I persist a little further. The law, as it stands, makes it virtually impossible for birth parents to search official records with a view to contacting children they have given up for adoption, and it is still difficult for an adopted child who is trying to seek out his or her natural parents, because adoption agency records remain confidential, and children have no legal rights to access them. They do, however, now have the legal right to apply for a copy of their original birth certificate. But that would be of no use in your case because, as you know, your adoption was a fairly informal affair and it was I who registered your birth as our child. So there is no other certificate with your birth mother's name on it. However, what I want you to know is that Mum and I adopted you through a parish priest in Yorkshire, who was a very good friend of mine from theological college. He only dealt with babies that had been given up at birth, but his parish was quite well known at the time for handling this kind of work, which it ultimately had to stop because of new adoption laws which were brought in after the war. Now, dear boy, Mum and I have never known for sure who the person was who gave you up for adoption and, for obvious reasons, we would prefer not to know, but... well, if it was the case that you wanted to know the name of your birth mother, I daresay I could pull a few strings, break a few rules and get access to the parish records... and probably find out for you. My friend is still the incumbent there. It would be breaking the rules and possibly the law but, in my judgment, it would be the right thing to do, if that's what you wanted... and I feel I owe it to you, my dear son, to give you the option. I feel guilty that I did not do this in 1967, when you were twenty-one.'

'Very well, Dad. I understand why you have summoned this meeting, and I appreciate the fact that it is your wish to be open and frank with me about what could be a very delicate matter. However, I just want to say that I find this discussion really quite difficult and rather upsetting. I know you're only seeking to do what you believe to be the right thing but I want to make it clear, once and for all, that I have no interest in my so-called birth parents. I only need two parents, my Dad and my Mum, that's all. I am Henry Irving and proud of it, and that's all that needs to be said. So can I just say, Dad... and Mum, that it would make me very happy never to have to discuss this matter again... with you, or anyone else for that matter.'

There was a long pause while the three Irvings sat quietly, slightly slumped on their chairs, reflecting on what had been said. And then the Reverend Irving suddenly sat up straight and said, 'Right... that's agreed then. Now, Harry, my boy, it's a most pleasant afternoon, so let's all go for a nice walk in the sunshine. I'll go and take this ridiculous cassock off and get changed into something more suitable. Then we can all stretch our legs over the Common. And tonight I've got tickets for the Wyvern Theatre in town. They're doing *The Importance of Being Earnest*.'

* * * *

That same Saturday, Amy was at Wolverhampton Race Course, reporting on the Ladies' Day race meeting for *Elite Magazine*, the glossy, monthly journal, produced by Mercian News Limited. Leslie Young, Amy's boss, had recently started asking her to go out on reporting assignments for the magazine, an aspect of her work which she particularly enjoyed. She was with the firm's photographer, Mike Dyke, a slim, bald, pleasant-looking divorcee in his early forties. Mike accompanied Amy on all of her assignments for *Elite,* their combined efforts ultimately being edited into magazine articles reporting on local 'society' events. The pair had finished their work for the afternoon – the race meeting was drawing to a close – and they were returning to the car park where Mike had parked his company car. He had picked Amy up from Greengage Hill at midday, and was now due to drive her home. The two colleagues had become quite good friends since they had started working together, and they would often go to a pub for a drink after completing an assignment. Amy liked Mike and enjoyed his company, but she was becoming concerned that he was developing a crush on her, and so she always made sure that she stood her round. She liked him but she didn't want to start a relationship with him – he was too old, for a start.

When they arrived at Mike's car, he said, 'Amy... I haven't got time to go for a drink with you right now. I've got to go and pick my son up from a party he's gone to at a friend's house over in Sedgley. I don't suppose you're free later on are you? I thought we might go out for some food together... I quite fancy a curry. What do you think?'

'Oh, I'm sorry, Mike. My mum's come over from Newark this afternoon... she's going to stay the night. I'll be spending the evening with her and my aunt. And, anyway, I wouldn't feel right about leaving them to babysit Rosie this evening, when they've been looking after her all afternoon.' Harriet Rose was always called 'Rosie'.

'Oh well, never mind; another time maybe?'

'Yes, Mike, perhaps another time.'

They got into the car and drove off.

When Mike dropped Amy off at the house on Greengage Hill, Harriet and Doris were taking tea in the drawing room. Rosie, who had been playing with her model farmyard on the rug in front of the fireplace, jumped to her feet when she heard her mother coming in through the front door and rushed to greet her. She was a remarkably pretty little three-year-old, dressed in a floral pinafore dress, with startlingly blonde, almost white, hair and bright blue eyes. She was, in many ways, the image of her father, Danny Swift. She ran to Amy who scooped her up and gave her a big hug and a kiss, and then carried her back to where she had been playing before welcoming her mother with a kiss and saying hello to her aunt. Rosie was anxious to show her mother the new toy farm animals her grandma had bought for her to add to her collection. When that was done, Amy sat down in one of the comfortable armchairs and relaxed with a cup of tea, chatting contentedly with her two senior relatives.

Later that evening, when Rosie was in bed and the three women were sitting round the dinner table, having just eaten, Doris turned to her daughter and said, 'Amy, my love, there have been some things going on in Newark which I haven't mentioned to you before but which I think you ought to know about…'

'Yes, Mum. Go on.' Amy was intrigued.

'Well, you know, of course, that Guy's father passed away six months ago…'

'Yes, Mum, you sent me the cutting from the local newspaper. It must have come as a bit of a shock. He always seemed to be so very fit and active, although I was surprised to see that he was actually seventy-three, according to the cutting you sent.'

'Yes, I think that's right, and I suppose that's not a bad age after all. But the thing is some very strange things have happened since. I'm not sure quite what's true and what isn't, there have been so many different rumours going around, but there are two things I do know: the estate agent business has been sold… and so has your old house.'

'What! That ugly modern box in Balderton that the Bouchers had built for us?'

'Well, you didn't think that at the time, Amy, when you first got married. You were rather proud of it, if I remember rightly.'

'Okay, Mum, I suppose I was. Anyway, tell me more ... what else do you know?'

'Well, the business was sold very soon after Mr Boucher died. A Nottingham businessman bought it apparently, and immediately changed the name. It's just called Bulstrodes now – no mention of the Bouchers at all, and they say he's brought in all new managers. And then the next thing we learnt was that your old house was on the market... for nearly £20,000! Just think of it... all that money.'

'And shouldn't half of it be yours, dear?' enquired Aunt Harriet. 'Most married couples have their houses in joint names.'

'Not Guy Boucher. He always wanted complete control. The purchase was all signed, sealed and delivered before we got married. I wasn't party to it in any way. If I had been, he wouldn't have been able to sell the place now without my signature.'

'No, I suppose not,' Aunt Harriet said. 'Nevertheless, I think you should be entitled to something. Do you want me to fix up a meeting with one of the partners from Cyril's old firm. I'm sure they could help you get some sort of settlement.'

'Not really, thanks all the same, Auntie. I don't really want anything at all that's connected with my marriage... or from the Bouchers. And I couldn't bear some sort of legal dispute or court case with them. It'd be too painful. I just want to put all that behind me.'

'Yes, dear, I quite understand.'

'So, what's happened to Guy then, if they've brought in new managers and changed the name of the business?' Amy asked her mother.

'Well, I was just getting on to that,' Doris continued. 'Guy hasn't been seen at church since the business was sold, or about town generally, so they say. It's said that there was some sort of scandal involving him and that he's gone off to live in Spain... with a man friend. There have been some very scurrilous rumours going around which I couldn't possibly repeat... horrible things which I can't believe to be true.'

'Well, if they're anything to do with Guy sexually abusing boys, they probably are true.'

'Oh dear ... please don't start that again, Amy. I really don't like to think about it.'

'Well, I can believe it,' chimed in Aunt Harriet. 'That young man is a loathsome creature. He very nearly ruined our Amy's life. Thank goodness she's safely here with me... and dear little Rosie.'

'Yes, Auntie, thank goodness. Anyway, Mum, I'm glad you've told me what's been going on. I ought to know these things, I suppose. I am still officially married to Guy, after all, so I ought to know what's happening.'

'Yes, dear,' Aunt Harriet said. 'You're legally his next of kin. But in a year's time, it will be five years since you left him and you'll be able to get a divorce, whether he likes it or not. Then you can forget about him for good.'

For a moment, Doris looked as if she wanted to challenge her sister's suggestion that Amy might be thinking of seeking a divorce, but she managed to check herself and allow the matter to drop, fully aware of what Harriet might have to say about her religious objections to divorce. And so Harriet's observation had the effect of putting the topic of Guy Boucher to bed, and the conversation moved on to other things.

Later that evening, the three women settled down in the drawing room to watch a variety show on television. Amy wasn't particularly interested in the programme, and couldn't concentrate on it anyway – her mind was preoccupied with Guy's apparent disappearance from Newark, leaving behind all that he had ever strived for. Business reputation and success, social standing and a position of influence and esteem within the Catholic Church had always been the very essence of life as far as he was concerned, particularly in his native town. So she could only assume that some very serious scandal involving Guy had come to light for him to have given up everything he cherished. His flight to Spain – with or without a boyfriend – must have been part of the price he had had to pay to avoid not just a scandal but a possible criminal prosecution. It would be part of an elaborate cover up engineered by his influential Catholic cronies. She realised that she was not totally indifferent to the whereabouts of her estranged husband, and was, in fact, very relieved to learn that he had almost certainly gone to live abroad: it would be one more step – and a very big one – in putting her life with Guy and her catastrophic marriage behind her. And, as far as Aunt Harriet's observation about divorce was concerned, Amy knew she would one day have her marriage dissolved, but she felt no sense of urgency in this regard. Physical distance between her and Guy was of much greater significance than the question of her marital status, because she had no pressing need or desire to be free to marry again – she was content as she was, with her aunt and her career and her beautiful child. However, if by some unimaginable twist of fate, Harry should come back into her life…

Chapter 14
September 1976

The long, dry, sun-baked summer of 1976 had come to an abrupt and dramatic end on August Bank Holiday when the nation was hit by thunder storms and deluged by torrential rain. Denis Howell MP, who had been named by the government as 'Minister for Drought' in August, had proved to be so successful as a rainmaker that he had been forced rapidly to change his role to that of 'Minister for Floods' as two months of almost constant rain ensued. It was teeming with rain the Friday in late September when Amy and Ginger met for lunch in Birmingham city centre. Ginger had telephoned her old college friend from her parents' house in Coventry, saying that she was in England visiting firstly Phil and Beckie in Kent, and now her parents in the Midlands. She had suggested that they meet up half way between Wolverhampton and Coventry, somewhere in Birmingham being the obvious choice of venue. Although the two young women had not seen each other since the day of Ginger's wedding, they had kept loosely in touch over the years through the exchange of annual Christmas cards and the occasional letter.

They were sitting at a table in the restaurant at Rackhams department store on Corporation Street. Amy was dressed in one of the black, tailored skirts she wore for work together with a floral blouse in autumnal shades – her favoured colours. Even though she was approaching her thirtieth birthday, she had changed little since her student days and had retained her perennially youthful beauty – Ginger would have known her anywhere. Ginger, on the other hand, had not worn quite so well. Amy recognised her immediately because of her bohemian mode of dress, her unchanged figure and the same urchin hairstyle she had worn as a student – before being temporarily 'glammed up' for her marriage to Phil – but upon closer inspection she had undoubtedly aged: there were streaks of grey in her dark brown hair; her face was lined; and the absence of any make-up made her appear somewhat tired and worn. There had been so much for the two old friends to catch up on during their convivial encounter that the conversation never lagged. However, throughout their time together, Amy had been itching to find out if Ginger had any information about Harry, given that, just the previous week, she had visited Phil at his home in Kent. So when Amy had finished telling her friend the story of how she had come to be living with her aunt in Wolverhampton, she decided to steer the conversation away from herself and round to Phil, hoping that it might lead on to news of Harry.

'You know, Ginger, you've never mentioned in your letters exactly how and why it was that you came to split up with Phil. I can remember you being so happy and positive about everything when you got married. Are you going to tell me what happened?'

'Yes, of course, Amy, there's no great secret, really. There were two things that finished it for me: boredom and sex.' Ginger looked at Amy mischievously, waiting for a request for further and better particulars.

'Yes… well, go on,' demanded Amy.

'Okay then. Firstly boredom: I was living the life of Riley down there in Kent with Phil, and I had absolutely everything I could wish for in material terms, but eventually I came to realise that I had nothing of any significance to do. There was Beckie, of course, but we had a nanny to do most of the work, and, if I'm honest, I wasn't really able to warm to motherhood. I'm just not maternal by nature, and I find babies just… well, just boring – and smelly, of course. Anyway, after a couple of years, filling my time with local drama clubs and choirs, joining the Women's Institute, of all things, and gardening, I had almost reached screaming point. I just had to escape... you know, regain my independence and find a few challenges in life.'

'Yes, I know the feeling. What about the sex, though?'

'Ah, well that was what really finished things off. I should never have married Phil, you know. He's such a nice guy, but I didn't love him and I never really fancied him. He always wanted a lot of sex, and I went along with it for a couple of years but I never particularly enjoyed it, and it got to the point where I simply couldn't face it any more. So I put a stop to it. I told Phil I'd had enough, I couldn't do it any more. Of course, I like sex really... I just wasn't getting anything out of it with Phil.'

'And how did Phil react to that?'

'Well, ultimately the decision to separate was mutual, but at first he just shrugged and then started to ignore me. I think he must have found some place else where he could get his oats. He did accuse me of being a lesbian a couple of times though.'

'No... that was a bit unkind and unfair of him wasn't it?'

'Not really... I did try a bit of girl-girl sex with an attractive woman from the drama club, but it didn't amount to much.'

'Ginger, how could you?' Amy said, quite taken aback. 'I remember you telling me that you weren't of "the sapphic persuasion". I remember it very well because I didn't know what sapphic meant and I had to go and look it up in the college library the next day.' They both laughed. 'Did you enjoy it?' Amy asked.

'Well it was okay, and I wanted to see what it was like, but basically I like men, and that's that. Have you ever tried it with a girl, Amy?'

Amy was silent for a moment, and then said, 'My friend Esme tried it on with me. It was shortly after I got pregnant and, as I told you earlier, I was living with her in her flat in Newark. It was only a bit of kissing and cuddling in bed one night after we'd polished off a bottle of wine together, and I didn't let it happen again. She'd been such a good friend to me and I didn't want to upset her, but after I told her it was not for me, she never tried again. She'd been married and divorced and I'm not sure she knew quite how to go about it herself. But she is a real lesbian: she treated it almost like a divorce when I moved out of her flat to go and live with Aunt Harriet, and since then she's set up home with another woman – "a proper lover" as she says in her letters.'

'And did you like it… dipping your toes in the sapphic sea?'

'I can't really remember much about it, to be honest: I was quite squiffy at the time. I can't say I disliked it but it's not something I particularly want to do again. I'm like you… I like men.' They both laughed.

'Any man in particular, at the moment?' Ginger enquired.

'Not really, there's an older man, a photographer at work called Mike, who keeps asking me out to dinner. I like him, he's a good friend and colleague, but I don't really want to start a relationship with him… you know, make the same mistake I did with Guy. Anyway, he's been very persistent, and I've finally given in and agreed to go out with him next Saturday evening – a week tomorrow. So we'll see what happens.'

'You'll let me know how you get on, won't you Amy? You're still a real peach you know. You really mustn't let yourself go to waste… Talking of men, when I saw Phil last week, he told me he had recently seen Henry Irving, your long lost Romeo.' Ginger said this without the need for any prompting from Amy, whose heart skipped a beat at the mention of Harry's name. 'But I'm sure you're not interested in hearing about him any more,' Ginger continued. 'It was all such a long time ago.'

'Don't tease, Ginger. Tell me what Phil said… please!'

'Well, Phil said that Henry Irving went down to Kent to stay with him for the weekend at Castle Court... in mid-August, I think. It was at the height of the drought and apparently they spent most of the time keeping cool in Phil's new swimming pool.'

'Was he with anyone?'

Ginger paused, and looked quizzically at her old friend, her head tilted slightly to one side. She said, 'You're still crazy about him, aren't you, sweetie? After all this time, and after all that's happened to you.'

Amy looked solemnly at Ginger and just said, 'Yes.'

'He was on his own, Amy. Apparently he isn't attached to anyone at the moment. He split up with a long-term girlfriend about a year ago and hasn't had another one since.'

Amy just smiled. It was the answer she wanted, however tantalizing it might be.

'There's something else you might be interested to hear. He was due to start a new job in September, teaching at some posh boarding school... I can't remember its name. Apparently he's got quite a good job there.'

'Does that mean he's left Birmingham?' Amy asked tentatively, hoping the answer would be 'no'.

'Yes... but I can tell you where his new school is.'

'Where?'

'In Wolverhampton.'

The following Monday, at work, Amy did some background research into the two major independent schools in her adopted town: The Royal School and Castlecroft College. Like most town residents, she was well aware of their existence, both institutions occupying landmark buildings and extensive grounds in their respective districts of the town – Castlecroft College was only about a mile from where she lived. However, Amy was eager to find out more about them in the hope that she might find some clue concerning which of the two schools Harry might have chosen to work at. At the offices of Mercian News, where Amy worked, there was a room which contained the firm's archives and a small library. She spent her lunch hour there going through old magazine and newspaper stories featuring the schools. She found little to help her, other than the fact that Castlecroft College was a rugby-playing school whereas The Royal played association football, and she knew enough about Harry to appreciate that it was more likely he would go to a rugby school. She also discovered that Castlecroft College was founded in 1876 and that it was therefore in its centenary year. Founders' Day always took place on the second Saturday in October, and there were sure to be some major events this year in celebration of the hundredth anniversary of the founding of the school – surely *Elite* magazine would be doing a story about the centenary.

During the course of the afternoon, when Amy was sitting at her desk in the corner of the office which she shared with Leslie Young, the firm's proprietor, she asked him, 'Are we going to run a story on the centenary of Castlecroft College? I hear there are going to be some big celebrations at the school on Founders' Day in a couple of weeks' time.'

'Yes,' replied Leslie, looking up and peering at Amy over the top of his spectacles. 'Why do you ask?' He was a plump balding man in his late fifties.

'Well, you haven't mentioned it to me. I thought you might have wanted me to cover the story, with Mike.'

'No.'

'Why not, Leslie: it's just the sort of thing we usually cover?'

'Because, young lady, I happen to be a Castlecroft old boy, and I shall be covering the story myself. I know all about what's happening on Founders' Day, because I happen to be on the school's Board of Governors.'

'Oh, I see, what a pity! Yes, well I suppose that's that… only I was hoping I might go up to the school with Mike before Founders' Day to take a few photographs and perhaps interview some of the staff and pupils, and… you know, give the story a bit more human interest.'

Leslie thought for a minute and then he said, 'Yes, okay, that sounds like quite a good idea. It would be good publicity for the school if we made a bit more of a spread. Okay, Amy, you haven't got any other assignments coming up in the immediate future, so why don't you ring up Mrs Appleby, the headmaster's secretary, and arrange to go up to the school at the end of the week. I'm sure the headmaster will approve.'

And that's just what Amy did. The following Saturday at about twelve-thirty, when morning classes at the school were about to finish, she and Mike Dyke found themselves arriving outside the main entrance to the original college building. It was a stone-built, symmetrical, Tudor-Gothic edifice, constructed in the Victorian era with a central clock tower, crenellated parapets, leaded windows and tall gabled wings at either end. They entered the building through the main double doors and made their way to Mrs Appleby's office, located along a corridor on the ground floor. She had arranged for Amy to interview a group of specially selected senior pupils and a couple of members of academic staff over lunch in the school's lofty wood-panelled dining hall. Amy harboured the remotest of hopes that Harry just might be one of the staff members chosen for this exercise – of course, she wasn't even sure that he worked at Castlecroft and, even if he did, it was unlikely that a new teacher would be chosen to be interviewed about the school's centenary; but this did not stop her fantasising that he might be there.

He wasn't there, but Amy was still disappointed, despite knowing full well that there was hardly any probability, or even possibility, that he would be. However the interviews went well and Mike Dyke took individual photographs of the pupils and a group shot of everybody present. Amy then took down the names and details of the staff and students involved so that they could be mentioned in her report, before concluding the session. At the end of the meeting, Amy asked one of the teachers whether, by any chance, an old friend of hers called Henry Irving was on the teaching staff of the school. Before the teacher could answer, one of the senior girls she had interviewed butted in: 'Mr Irving? Oh yes, Mr Irving's here. He started this term. I'm in his 'A' level English class. He's a great teacher… and dead dishy. Everybody loves Mr Irving… all the girls, anyway.'

Me too, thought Amy, almost overcome with emotion.

'Yes,' said the teacher, 'I've heard that Mr Irving's got a bit of a following among the sixth-form girls. Anyway, he's probably refereeing a rugby match this afternoon, or will be soon. So it's unlikely you'll be able to speak to him, unless you hang around until the match is over. Come to think of it, he may have gone off with one of the away teams, in which case he won't be here at all.'

Amy did not pursue the matter. She was overjoyed to learn that Harry was working little more than a mile from where she lived. Much as she yearned to see him, she could bide her time and find a way of contriving a meeting with him, one way or another – hopefully sooner rather than later.

Mrs Appleby had told Amy and Mike that, once their interview session with the staff and students was over, they were free to walk around the school in order to take photographs. So Mike suggested that they spend half an hour or so taking shots of the school grounds and buildings, and any interesting activities that might be going on. They exited the main building into a quadrangle at the rear of the school, which in turn led onto the school playing fields. They marched across the quadrangle and through an archway onto a tarmac terrace adjacent to the fields. Pupils were wandering around the terrace and fields but Amy was disappointed to note that no competitive rugby matches had yet begun. Mike decided to set off to take some pictures, but Amy, who had dolled herself up a little bit in the hope of encountering Harry, was wearing high heels, unsuitable footwear for traversing muddy games fields, and so she decided to wait on the terrace until he had finished.

Harry had emerged from the staff changing room into the quadrangle just in time to spot Mike and Amy disappearing through the archway at the far end. He was wearing his blue and white rugby kit in readiness for the match he was shortly due to referee. At first, he didn't take much notice of the pair of strangers. However, when he passed through the archway himself and could clearly see the back of an attractive woman dressed in a green raincoat and high-heeled shoes, standing by herself on the terrace as her companion wandered off across the field, camera in hand, he had to do a double take. He could hardly believe what he was seeing, because he knew instinctively, and almost at once, that it was Amy – even though he couldn't see her face. He approached her stealthily from behind, and when he was just a few feet away from her, simply said, 'Amy?'

She spun round, immediately recognising his voice, and when her eyes confirmed what her ears had heard, she gasped and dropped her workbag. Harry stepped forward and picked it up for her.

'Harry, it's you,' is all she could say.

'Yes, it's me. How wonderful to see you, Amy... but what on earth are you doing here?'

It took Amy several seconds to collect herself and then she said, 'Um... I'm working actually. I work for the local newspaper company and we're doing a piece about the school's centenary. That's my colleague over there, taking photos.' Amy pointed out Mike Dyke across the fields.

'Yes, I see... but how fantastic that you're here, and that I actually spotted you!'

'Yes.' There was a long pause while Amy just looked at him, and a tear rolled down her cheek. 'Oh Harry, it is fantastic... absolutely fantastic. And it's truly wonderful to see you. I can't tell you how happy I am.'

'Me too, Amy.'

'You know, Harry, I only live about a mile away. Where are you living? Are you still in Moseley?'

'No, I live right here in college... which means I live a mile away from you.' They beamed at each other.

'Can we meet, Amy? Are you free to meet me any time? I don't want to let you slip away from me again, only I've got to go off and referee in a minute, so now is not a good time to talk... and there's so much to say. Can I please see you, Amy?'

'Yes, of course. I'm free as a bird, and I must see you again, as soon as possible... just as soon as we can arrange something.'

'How about tonight? I'm not on duty tonight, so we could meet somewhere: a local pub perhaps or somewhere in town?'

'Yes...' Amy suddenly remembered that she had promised to go out for dinner with Mike Dyke that evening: the date had been arranged two weeks earlier, the table was booked, and she knew how much he was looking forward to it.

At that moment, the two senior rugby teams and their coaches emerged from the boys' changing rooms in the sports pavilion, twenty yards or so from where Harry and Amy were standing, and started to jog onto the adjacent pitch. Harry took a stop watch from the pocket of his shorts and looked at the time.

'...Oh, Harry, I've just remembered I've arranged to go out tonight. What about tomorrow?'

'Well, I'm supposed to be on house duty all day tomorrow. I'm a resident master, you see. I might be able to rearrange it... you know, swap with someone.' He looked across at the boys, warming up on the field. 'Look, Amy, I've got to go... the teams are out. Can you write down your phone number and address for me, and I'll ring you later.'

'Okay.' Amy rummaged in her bag for a notepad and pen. She quickly scribbled down her address and number, tore off the sheet of paper and handed it to him. 'Ring before seven-thirty... and don't let me down. I'll be devastated if you don't call.'

'Amy, there's no way on earth I won't call. You're not getting away from me this time.' He gave her one of his wonderful, youthful smiles. She felt as if she would melt. Then he said, 'Bye for now, Amy. See you very soon,' and started to jog off onto the field. When he was halfway to the centre spot, he turned, smiling as he ran, and waved. Amy thought he looked so wonderful: tall, athletic and handsome, and so boyish in his rugby outfit. She watched as he took control of the two teams and started the match; and then Mike Dyke returned from his labours.

'Right, Amy, I've got all I need... time to go,' he said, and the two of them made their way back to his car. As they walked, Amy turned her head for one last glimpse of Harry, and knew how much she was in love.

It was just after quarter to three when Mike dropped Amy off on Greengage Hill, promising to pick her up at seven-thirty for their evening out together. During the short drive from Castlecroft College to Aunt Harriet's house, Amy, overwhelmed with emotion by her encounter with Harry, had decided that she just had to see him that very evening, and she would have to find a way of excusing herself from her date with Mike. Before she parted company with Mike, she told him that she had developed a splitting headache during the course of their time at the school and was going to lie down for the rest of the afternoon. This was, of course, untrue. At five-thirty she telephoned Mike and said that she was feeling very unwell and running a temperature. She was very apologetic, but insisted that she was too ill to go out that evening. Mike said that he quite understood, but she could tell from his tone of voice that he was more than just disappointed – he was choked.

Of course, Amy felt bad about letting Mike down in this way, and about having to lie to him. He was a good friend and colleague, and she liked him a lot, but she had only agreed to go out to dinner with him because of his persistence: his stubborn refusal to take no for an answer. There was no possibility, from her standpoint, of any sort of romantic relationship blossoming between them, which is clearly what he wanted, and so it was just as well that Harry had suddenly appeared on the scene to thwart Mike's ambitions: Amy had once before given in to an over-persistent suitor, namely Guy Boucher, and look where that had got her. In any event, being within touching distance of being able to regenerate her love affair with Harry made it an irresistible and overriding necessity to see him again as soon as was humanly possible – nothing must be left to chance this time.

The phone rang at six o'clock, and Amy rushed to answer it. It was Harry. She told him straight away that she had cancelled her engagement and that she was now free to see him that evening. She had already arranged for Aunt Harriet to babysit for her date with Mike, insofar as any formal arrangement was necessary, and so there was no need to organise childcare. They agreed that Harry would come to Greengage Hill and pick her up at seven-thirty. They wouldn't go far, just to the Plough Inn, an old semi-rural pub about half a mile away. Amy spent the next hour and a half getting ready for her date with Harry. She could scarcely contain her excitement.

Harry had to catch his breath when Amy told him she was free for the evening. He wanted to punch the air and shout out, 'YES!' Try as he might, he had not been able to rearrange his Sunday residential duty, and he was beginning to fear that his endeavours to engineer an early encounter with Amy were going to be foiled. By the time he picked up the telephone to call her, he had worked himself up into a state of unwarranted anxiety. So the relief was tangible when he knew he was to be with her that very evening. They made the arrangement to go to the Plough, where they would be able to talk.

As soon as the phone call was over, he too went straight away to his bedroom to start getting ready for their night out together – it was over ten years since the last one. He felt relieved that he had just recently offloaded his ancient Ford van – with its rusted dented coachwork and scruffy faded interior – and replaced it with a sort-of-smart second-hand Citroen saloon, which he felt was just about okay for picking up a beautiful woman from one of the posh houses up on Greengage Hill – Amy wouldn't have minded what he turned up in, just so long as he came. At twenty-five past seven, dressed in his best new trousers and his favourite summer jacket, his face clean shaven and his locks carefully combed, he climbed into the Citroen and set off for his date with Amy.

Chapter 15
Saturday Evening and Afterwards

They sat closely together on an upholstered window seat, built into one of the bay windows of the lounge bar, where they could converse intimately and hold hands. Once a country pub, surrounded on all sides by farmers' fields, the oak-beamed, half-timbered Plough Inn had been gradually engulfed by early twentieth century urban sprawl and the smart suburban homes of local well-to-do residents. However, it had retained its rustic ambience on the inside, and its setting, amidst big houses in spacious plots on what had once been a country lane, remained leafy and bucolic. The pub was quiet on Saturday evenings, unlike the raucous city-centre pubs of downtown Wolverhampton, and so the two lovebirds could relax and talk quietly and freely.

None of the magic had gone – it was almost as if they were nineteen again. They were totally at ease with one another, and they had so much to tell. Amy sat enthralled while Harry told her the sorry tale of his unhappy career as a pop singer, and Harry did likewise as Amy related the story of her disastrous marriage. There were many other things to tell: Amy's time at college in Southwell and her career as a teacher; Harry's period in London, including his time with Flic; his part-time study for an external degree from London University; and how it was that he went on to become a schoolmaster. They both expressed wonder at their fateful encounter outside the Mulberry Bush pub on the night of the Birmingham bombings, and how that meeting had not only sown the seeds of their ultimate reunion but undoubtedly saved Harry – and Fiona – from the catastrophic consequences of that night of terror. And they both expressed deep sadness and regret at their youthful folly in having let immature ambition rob them of something so precious as their unyielding love for each other. It was towards the end of this part of the conversation that Harry raised the vexed issue of Danny Swift.

'Do you remember, Amy, the evening we went out to celebrate our exam results?' he asked her. 'It was our penultimate night together in Wessex. We went into the city centre for steaks and a bottle of wine at the Berni Inn.'

'Yes, of course I remember,' Amy replied, a note of caution in her voice.'

'Well something happened that evening, something that's hard to explain. It was something you said to me. I don't know... it sounds a bit childish now, but you told me something that really affected me and affected my decision to go off with the band. It was when you told me about your little fling with Danny Swift... you know, the boy I was at school with.'

A chill of trepidation ran through Amy at the mention of Danny Swift, and the colour drained from her cheeks. 'Yes I remember very well... almost as if it was yesterday,' Amy murmured. 'You went very quiet on me for the rest of the day.'

'Yes, I know. It was wrong of me. But the thing is – and I never told you this at the time – Danny Swift was never a school friend of mine. In fact, he was the only person I'd ever really hated... still is, for that matter. He was a bully, a coward and a sadist at school, and yet he had this smarmy urbane manner that seemed to impress adults and helped him to get on. Girls always seemed to like him too... I can't think why. When I first went to Regis, he bullied me remorselessly. He was bigger and older than me. I was small for my age and a new boy, on my own at a boarding school in a class of boys a year older than me. He nearly broke me. If it hadn't been for the fact that I was befriended by Jon Geary, the form's boxing champ, he would have done.' There was a pause while they both looked at each other. Amy was ashen by now, and on the verge of tears. 'He's also the only person I've ever hit in earnest. I knocked him out... stone cold, with a single punch. I was older and much bigger by then.' Harry didn't seem to be aware of Amy's growing distress and went on to tell the story of the incident in the dormitory washroom, when he had discovered Danny beating one of the junior boys, and intervened.

At the end of the story, he said. 'You see, Amy, I loved you so much – and I still do – but I couldn't bear the thought of your having any sort of physical relationship with the one person in life I loathed and detested. It was very wrong of me, I know, but I allowed it to taint our relationship, and I'm so very, very sorry.' Harry took both of Amy's hands in his as he noticed the tears rolling down her lovely face. 'Please don't cry, my darling. I didn't mean to upset you. I'm so sorry if I have... I just had to tell you about it, that's all.'

'Oh Harry, I know, I know... and I'm glad you have. It explains so much. But there's something very important I need to tell you too... something I haven't been brave enough to mention so far.' She looked around her. 'I can't tell you here, in public, with people looking at me: I shall only start crying. It's really important, Harry. Is there somewhere we can go and talk in private?'

Harry thought for a moment. 'There's my small flat at college. We could go there, I suppose. It's not particularly comfortable, I'm afraid, but at least we'd have some privacy.'

'Yes... let's go there, if it's all right with you, Harry?'

They left the pub and made the short drive to Castlecroft College, travelling in silence. The moment Amy had been dreading all evening was fast approaching: the moment she would tell Harry about her own, more recent, experience with Danny Swift and his silver-tongued perfidy – and the existence of Harriet Rose, the fruit of their brief illicit union.

They parked the car outside Cotlake House, where Harry was assistant housemaster. It stood in the college grounds, an extended Edwardian gentleman's residence, now a boarding house for forty-five schoolboys. They entered through the front door and climbed a rather grand oak staircase to the first floor where Harry's flat was located, at the end of a corridor towards the rear of the building. It was half past nine and many of the younger boys were making their way to the dormitories to get ready for bed and lights out. The flat was small: a cluttered study-cum-sitting room, furnished with, amongst other things, a couple of ancient armchairs and a sturdy writing desk; a small and equally cluttered bedroom, with a single bed, washbasin and shower cubicle; and a tiny kitchenette. Harry apologised to Amy for the state of the flat and the absence of any toilet facilities, the nearest staff lavatory being located at the other end of the corridor. He sat Amy down in one of the armchairs, and poured them each a large Scotch – the only liquid refreshment available, other than water. Then he sat down in the other chair next to Amy's, and gently asked her to tell him what it was that she had to say.

'This is very difficult for me, my darling, but I'll try not to beat about the bush. I thought you might have heard about it somehow from Phil, but you obviously haven't.' She stopped and tried to compose herself, again feeling herself on the verge of tears. 'I don't know quite how to say this, Harry. I couldn't bear to lose you again…'

'It doesn't matter what it is, Amy, you're not going to lose me,' Harry said, leaning across and taking her hand in his. 'Don't worry, sweetheart, just tell me… whatever it is.'

'All right, but you must promise not to interrupt until I've finished. Whatever you're thinking, whatever you want to say, just wait till I'm done. Promise me.'

'Okay, Amy, I promise. Go ahead.'

'Harry, I've got a child… a three and a half year old daughter called Rosie… Harriet Rose to be precise. She's a little angel, and I love her more than I can say…' Harry's eyes opened wide. He sat up and was about to speak but Amy looked at him plaintively and placed her index finger on his lips. 'Harry, you promised,' she said and he quickly subsided, smiling gently at her. 'There's more, I'm afraid. Rosie's father isn't Guy, he's someone else, someone I had an affair with.'

'Go on,' Harry said cautiously, breaking his promise not to speak.

'Well, it's only now, this evening, that you've explained how finding out about me and Danny Swift, and the brief holiday romance we had all those years ago had such a profound effect on you, and how it played a part in our drifting apart. And that he had bullied you at boarding school and was the one person in life who you really hated… and then you found out from me that he was the only boy, before you, I had ever allowed to touch me… you know, sexually. I didn't know any of this until tonight.' She started to sob quietly. 'Harry, I've got to tell you… you have to know: I had a very brief affair with Danny Swift four years ago. It started at Uncle Cyril's funeral. I was in the depths of depression about my marriage to Guy, and along came Danny, looking dashing and handsome in his RAF uniform, and he deliberately set about seducing me. I was so very vulnerable at the time and I gave in to him. I let him seduce me. Harry… Danny is the father of my child.'

Harry was stunned. He went momentarily numb. He looked straight at Amy, so lovely despite her tears and bloodshot eyes, and thought: oh no, not again! He was dumbstruck, unable to speak for several seconds – although it seemed like an eternity to Amy. She saw the look of horror on his face and burst into tears. Her distress snapped Harry out of his state of shock, although it still took some time, and all of his mental strength and concentration, to regain his composure. But he got there. For there was one thing he knew for certain, deep down in his heart of hearts, and it was that he loved Amy – loved her more than anyone could imagine – and he was not going to lose her this time, come hell, high water or anything else for that matter. He rose from his chair, knelt down in front of her, put his hands on her shoulders and drew her to him. He kissed her forehead and her cheeks and tenderly wiped away her tears with his finger tips. He told her he loved her and that he would never let her go. He stood up, took her hand and led her gently to his little bedroom where they lay down together on the single bed, locked in a firm embrace. They held each other tightly for some time, almost afraid to let go. But they didn't make love – this was neither the right time nor the right place to consummate their reunion.

Later on, when they were back in the study, sipping their whiskies, she told him the full story of her affair with Danny Swift, from his surprise appearance at Uncle Cyril's funeral right through to her forlorn flying visit to the Cosford air base, three weeks later, in search of her perfidious paramour. The telling of this tale stirred in Harry the memory of his own sighting of Danny, at the theatre in Birmingham back in 1972.

'You won't believe this, Amy, but I saw Swift myself... it was at the Rep, shortly after I arrived in Birmingham. That would have been towards the end of August, four years ago, just at the time when you were seeing him. I spotted him in the ice cream queue during the interval. He was with an attractive girl, who I mistook for you at first. I didn't make myself known to him, but it was Swift all right. I made sure I could get a closer look at them after the show, and that's when I knew the girl wasn't you, although she was like you in many ways... not as beautiful, of course.'

'That would have been Rhonda, his wife,' Amy said. 'I shan't forget that name in a hurry... but what a strange coincidence!'

'I doubt it was his wife, Amy. She wasn't wearing a wedding ring, or an engagement ring for that matter.'

'The bastard!' Amy spat out the word – and then after some thought said, 'It must have been the woman his neighbour mistook me for when I called at his house that day. She was quite rude to me until she realised I was somebody else. The bastard was screwing both of us.'

'So it would seem,' Harry said, and then deliberately changed the subject. 'Look, enough of Swift; when am I going to meet Harriet Rose?'

'Oh Harry, just as soon as possible. I want you to get to know each other, and love each other. She's a sweetheart really, even though she can be a little madam at times.' She leant across and put her hand on his shoulder. 'But how will you feel about little Rosie, knowing who her father is... and I have to say, she does look very like him?'

'Rosie hasn't got a father at the moment, as far as I'm concerned.'

'What do you mean?'

'Listen, darling, there's something else I haven't told you about myself...' He sensed Amy starting to stiffen. '... No, don't get alarmed, it's nothing serious. It's just that my parents aren't my natural parents. They adopted me at birth.'

'Harry! Why didn't you tell me? I can't believe you never told me something as important as this?'

'Well, that's just the point: it's not that important. It's something I've always known but hardly ever thought about. It's never been an issue for me. I never told you because I never even thought about it. You see, as far as I'm concerned, I couldn't have had better parents than Mum and Dad. I'm proud of them, and proud to be their only son... proud to be Henry Irving. My mother and father are Mum and Dad, and it's as simple as that.'

'But haven't you ever wondered who your birth mother was?' Amy asked, surprised by the apparent strength of Harry's feelings.

'No... never! A few months ago, Dad told me he might be able to find out the name of my birth mother for me, if I wanted to know. He thought I might want to do some sort of research into my natural lineage. It got me quite upset really, so I told him no, and that I didn't want to hear any more about it. I mean, why would I want to go rummaging around uncovering all sorts of sordid secrets... you know, opening up cans of worms and upsetting people unnecessarily? For all I know, the geezer who sired me might have been some sort of serial rapist – probably was, in fact – or my so-called birth mother some sort of promiscuous tart... or both of these things might be true.' He realised he was becoming rather too animated, and so he calmed himself before continuing. 'Look, sweetheart, what I'm trying to say is that, as far as I'm concerned, your parents are the people who nurture you and love you and work hard at bringing you up, not the people who just happened to be responsible for your procreation; usually they're the same but not always. I know this from my own life: I'm Mum and Dad's child, not the child of a couple of people I know nothing about, who did a bit of humping one night which resulted in an unwanted child.'

Harry took hold of Amy's hand and drew her towards him. She moved across to him from her chair and sat on his knee. Then Harry said, 'You see, darling, Rosie isn't Danny Swift's child, and she never will be... and I will never think of her as his. Rosie is your child, and I hope very much that one day soon she'll be mine too.'

'Oh Harry, I love you so much.' She put her arms around his neck, kissed him on the lips and hugged him tightly.

It was gone midnight when he dropped her off on Greengage Hill. He saw her to the door but did not cross the threshold. They kissed each other goodnight, Amy went inside and Harry drove back to his lonely little flat in Cotlake House – he was due to be on duty at seven-thirty the next morning.

The following Wednesday evening, Harry returned to Greengage Hill, this time crossing the threshold in order to meet Aunt Harriet and little Harriet Rose. Amy was filled with pure happiness at the prospect of presenting to her nearest and dearest the man whom she loved and with whom she intended to spend the rest of her life – of course, she did not introduce him as such. She had lived with her aunt for three and a half years and, although from time to time the occasional male had called at the house to collect her for one reason or another, including Mike Dyke who would collect her from home to go on work assignments, she had never once brought home someone who might remotely have been referred to as a boyfriend. The evening went well, but Aunt Harriet, although perfectly hospitable and pleasant, appeared somewhat reserved and ill at ease. This was not because she had taken a dislike to Harry, quite the reverse in fact, but she could see immediately how Amy was with him, and understood intuitively that her niece was deeply in love with the tall handsome newcomer. She had always been alive to the inevitability that one day some man would come along and claim Amy for his own, and knew she should be happy for her sake, but she couldn't help succumbing to an overwhelming sense of sadness that the arrival of Henry Irving on the scene signalled the beginning of the end for the life she cherished so much, sharing her home with her beloved Amy and adorable little Rosie.

Rosie took to Harry at once. Amy had feared that, because the little girl was unused to men, having spent practically all of her short life in the company of women, she would not care for him at all or, at least, be very shy of such a tall, imposing male presence. But she was wrong: Rosie was fascinated by Harry from the start and, because of his broad smile and naturally charming way with her, soon captivated by him. He played with her, teased her, helped Amy to bath her, and then read her a bedtime story before kissing her goodnight on the forehead. It was the beginning of a profound, loving relationship that would last for ever.

At the weekend, Harry and Amy made love for the first time in over ten years; not just once but several times. They were spending

Saturday night alone together at a hotel in Stratford-on-Avon, thanks to Aunt Harriet's willingness to look after Rosie overnight. It was there that they agreed to get married. It happened as they were dining in the cosy restaurant of their small Victorian hotel, and Harry had just spilt a little salt on the tablecloth.

'That's bad luck,' Amy said, pointing at the salt. 'You know, spilling salt. But if you pick some up with your right hand and throw it over your left shoulder, that'll bring good luck... and you can make a wish too.'

'Is that so?' Harry said. 'Well, as you know, I was brought up in a rectory, where I was supposed to believe in the will of God rather than luck, so I'm not very good at this sort of thing. Anyway, you do it... go on, show me how it's done.'

'All right, then'. She picked up a pinch of salt and threw it over her left shoulder, closed her eyes and tipped her head back slightly for a few seconds while she made her wish, and then opened her eyes again, smiling coyly at him but saying nothing. He looked at her for a few moments, while she continued to smile silently.

'Well... go on then. Tell me what you wished.'

'I can't do that, Harry. If I do that, my wish won't come true.'

'I wonder what it is you want, Amy?' he said, with a knowing smile. 'What was it that George Bailey said to Mary in *It's a Wonderful Life*? It was something like: "Tell me what you want, Mary. You want the moon? I'll throw a lasso around it and catch it for you".' His James Stewart impersonation was far from convincing.

Amy laughed and said, 'I don't want the moon, Harry, or the sun. I just want you.'

'Then you shall have me, my darling, and I will have you. Amy, let's agree to get married... just as soon as we can. I know that's not a very romantic proposal, and I haven't got a ring to give you to seal the deal, and I know you're not free at the moment anyway. But let's agree to get married. What do you say?'

'I say yes, Harry. Yes, yes, yes!'

'Then that's agreed. We're engaged to be married.' They chinked their wine glasses, toasting the agreement, and then looked happily into each other's eyes as they sipped their wine.

Two weeks later, Harry, Amy and Rosie drove down to St Bart's Rectory to spend Saturday night with Lyndon and Mary Irving so that Harry's parents could meet their son's new girlfriend, and her little daughter, and be apprised of his engagement. Harry had telephoned them a week before in order to arrange the visit but had said very little about Amy, other than that she had a daughter aged three and a half – and he had said nothing about their betrothal. In the meantime, the couple had visited a second-hand jewellery shop in town to buy Amy an engagement ring. She had insisted that she did not want a flashy, expensive, diamond ring like the one Guy had foisted upon her, but something modest, antique and elegant. In the end they had settled upon a simple, delicate, semiprecious jade stone set in an art nouveau, sterling silver band. Amy adored it.

Harry's parents could not have been more pleased with their son's choice of fiancée: they both found Amy quite enchanting. Mary Irving was particularly delighted that there was a wedding on the horizon, although Harry had made it clear that they would not be getting married until Amy's divorce was finalised, which would probably not be for at least another eighteen months. It was, however, quite apparent that Harry's father was disappointed that he would not be able to officiate at his son's wedding because, as a Church of England priest, he was not free to marry a divorcee. He was not making any moral judgment about his son's choice of bride, it was purely a matter of sadness that his church prevented him, in the circumstances, from being able to administer the sacrament of marriage for Harry and Amy. But he did make it clear that there was nothing to prevent him from performing a blessing ceremony, after the civil marriage had taken place, and that this was something he would very much like to do, provided that both Amy and Harry were willing. Amy, who found the Reverend Irving's almost Pickwickian air totally endearing, said that nothing could please her more – and Harry agreed.

Unfortunately, Rosie was not on her best behaviour during the early part of the stay: she was bored and fractious, and came across as being rather spoilt. Lyndon and Mary didn't seem to mind the occasional tantrum from the child: they were good Christian souls and, in any event, quite understood that there was little to amuse a small child in their somewhat spartan dwelling. And so on Sunday morning, before going off to matins, Mary went up into the loft where she rummaged around and subsequently came down with a boxful of Harry's old toys, which had never been discarded. Among them were some wooden jigsaw puzzles, just right for Rosie's age, and a toy farmyard complete with animals, all of which kept the little girl amused for the rest of the visit.

That afternoon, Amy happened to mention, during the course of a conversation she was having with her prospective parents-in-law, that since separating from her husband she had reverted to using her maiden name, and that she liked to be known as Amy Anderton rather than Amy Boucher, even though she was still officially married. Up to that point, the Irvings had not been aware of her surname, as Harry had introduced her simply as Amy, no other name having been mentioned.

'So you're an Anderton are you, Amy?' enquired Lyndon Irving, sounding cautiously intrigued.

'Yes, my father was Arthur Anderton. Why… is there something unusual about the name?'

'No, not really, my dear, it's just that I knew a family of Andertons during the war, when I was in the army. It's an old Anglo-Saxon name apparently, deriving from people who once inhabited one of the two English villages called Anderton: one is in Cheshire and one in Lancashire. That's going back to the sixth century though.'

'How interesting! I've never heard that before.'

'Of course, if you were an Anderson, you would be a Viking, but Andertons are Saxons, I'm pleased to say.'

'Thank goodness for that!' Amy smiled and then, turning to Harry, said, 'Did you realise you were finally going to join The Saxons, Harry?'

'No, I didn't. I'm sure it's a good omen, though. After all, I spent months trying to become a Saxon when I was at university.'

Amy and Harry smiled at their little private joke.

'You're from Nottinghamshire, aren't you, my dear?' Lyndon continued.

'Yes, but I found out some years ago that my father was originally from Yorkshire… Bradford, I think.'

'Really!' Lyndon peered over the rim of his spectacles, obviously surprised by this piece of information.

'Yes. My Aunt Harriet told me once that Daddy had originally come from some well-to-do family in Bradford, but his father disowned him when he dropped out of university.'

'Well I never, Bradford! That's where the Andertons I used to know lived. They too were a very wealthy family, in fact they were the leading family in the parish where Oliver Foreman, a very good friend of mine, became the incumbent – he and I had been at theological college together. He's still at the same church, in fact… well just about. He's even older than I am, and really ought to be thinking about retiring. Anyway, my dear, I was an army chaplain during the war, stationed at some barracks nearby when he was first installed as vicar, and I became a regular visitor to the vicarage. I got to know Mrs Anderton really quite well: she was a leading light in the church community and did a great deal of voluntary work for the parish. I never met Mr Anderton though. He was much older than his wife and seldom attended church services. I remember they had a very pretty daughter who would have been in her early teens – I can't remember her name – but I don't remember Mrs A ever mentioning a son. They're long gone now though, the Andertons, or so I'm told. The dye works closed down many years ago.'

The mention of 'dye works' didn't register with Amy. She had forgotten that her aunt had once told her that the source of her paternal grandfather's great wealth had been a successful Bradford dye works.

'The Mrs Anderton you knew could have been my father's stepmother,' Amy said. 'His own mother died in childbirth, so I'm told... So, do you think they could be the same family as mine, Mr Irving?'

'Oh, do please call me Lyndon, my dear. I don't think I can cope with Mr Irving,' Lyndon said, smiling kindly at his prospective daughter-in-law. 'Yes, I think it very likely they were, which is really quite a remarkable coincidence, isn't it?'

'Yes it certainly is.'

'Yes, it is,' Harry agreed, joining in the conversation. 'It's very strange to think that you might once have known Amy's grandparents, Dad, very strange indeed. Anyway, changing the subject for a moment, I wanted to tell you and Mum about the centenary celebrations at school last weekend.'

Harry was desperate to steer the conversation away from anything to do with the Reverend Oliver Foreman, his father's old theological college friend in Bradford, lest Lyndon should be tempted to start talking about his friend's role in arranging Harry's adoption. So he persisted in talking in great detail about the preceding weekend's events at Castlecroft College until the conversation eventually moved on to other things. The Andertons of Bradford were not mentioned again until Harry and Amy were in the car, driving back to Wolverhampton.

'I know you didn't seem to want to talk about it earlier, Harry,' Amy said when they had been on the road for about twenty minutes, and Rosie had fallen asleep on the back seat, 'but it was very strange what your dad had to say about the Anderton family he used to know in Bradford. I've been thinking about it quite a lot, and it is pretty weird that he should have known people during the war who might well have been my close relatives.'

'Yes it is, sweetie, and I'm sorry I butted in rather rudely and changed the subject, but I didn't want Dad getting onto the question of my adoption. You know how much I hate talking about it.'

'Yes I do, Harry,' Amy said, looking at him quizzically. 'But I don't understand what this has got to do with your adoption?'

'Well, the Reverend Foreman – you know, Dad's friend in Bradford who was the Andertons' vicar – well, he used to run some sort of dodgy adoption service, before the laws were tightened up after the war, and he was the guy who found me, as a baby, for Mum and Dad when they decided to adopt a child. I just had this horrible feeling that Dad would start going on about it.'

'Oh I'm sorry, darling, I had no idea. No wonder you were starting to get a bit twitchy.'

'Well, I'm very sorry, Amy. I shouldn't be so sensitive, I suppose. It's just that, well, as you know, I've never really thought of myself as being any different from anybody else when it comes to who my parents are, and I don't want the fact that I was adopted to start becoming an issue now, at my age... Oh, I'll shut up about it, you know all this already.' They were silent for a while and then he said, 'Do you think you would like to find out more about your long lost Bradford relatives, Amy? You know, try to make contact with them and all that? I'm sure Dad could help, if you did.'

'No, not really, darling... in fact, not at all, actually. The Andertons disowned my father very cruelly, all those years ago, and he went off into the world and made a life of his own. It may not have amounted to much but he did it by himself, without much help from them. I'm like you, Harry: I don't want to go ferreting around looking for people I know nothing about and who have never done anything for me, just because I happen to be related to them by blood. They can go to blazes, for all I care.' She leant across and kissed him on the cheek.

Harry and Amy hardly ever spoke about The Andertons of Bradford again.

Chapter 16
Happy Ever After

They shared a life of profound happiness, if ever that could be said of a union between man and woman; they not only loved each other, they remained emotionally and physically in love until death separated them. Harry often reasserted to Amy his belief that their union was not a matter of chance but of providence: that it was destiny which had caused them to meet all those years ago at Wessex University, in the autumn of 1965; and destiny which had reunited them for ever, against all odds and despite their own youthful folly. The child of the rectory, who normally professed to having no belief in things supernatural, remained convinced that something far beyond his knowledge and understanding, something more than simple good fortune or human design, had conferred on him – on them both – the precious gift of pure, romantic and lasting love. That is not to say that there were never differences of opinion or arguments, or rows even, between them, but such occurrences were rare, and there was never once a prolonged falling-out. And in all their years together, neither of them was ever once seriously tempted to stray from the nest, even though they were both attractive human beings who were not infrequently the object of other people's covetous advances. They remained lovers in every respect, and had neither need nor desire nor time for paramours.

Their love for each other was, without question, exceptional but otherwise their lives were unexceptional. There was the usual variety of incidents, items and individuals that make up the mundane lives of most of us who negotiate, and often muddle, our way through the obstacle course of imperfect human existence: careers and the raising of children; homemaking and hobbies; Christmases and birthdays; holidays and outings; and friends and relations. There were successes and failures; times of great joy and times of deep sadness; prolonged periods of good health and fortune, and occasional times of illness and anguish; and always the unfailing comfort of devoted companionship, marred only by the acute pain and suffering of ultimate bereavement. Harry and Amy lived an ordinary life together, sustained throughout by their extraordinary love.

They married in July, 1978. It was a simple civil ceremony at the registry office in town, with only the bride and groom and half a dozen close relatives present, but this was followed by a blessing service conducted by the Reverend Lyndon Irving in the Castlecroft College chapel, attended by over a hundred guests, after which everyone adjourned to Aunt Harriet's's grand house on Greengage Hill. Amy and Harry, with Harriet's blessing, had decided to have a marquee erected in the large grounds of the house for the wedding breakfast, a reminder – on a somewhat less grand scale – of Phil and Ginger's wedding twelve years earlier, where they had first truly found each other. It was the happiest of occasions, celebrated with gusto by everyone there. Even Doris Anderton had come to terms with the idea of Amy's remarriage, and was able to rejoice in her daughter's newfound and patent happiness. All of their old friends were in attendance: Phil and his family; Ginger and her Dutchman; Jim and Sylvia Semark; Esme Poppleton and girlfriend; Jon Geary and boyfriend; Mike Dyke and Leslie Young; and even Flic and her husband, the original 'proper boyfriend' from Knotty Ash, were there. Amy didn't wear a wedding dress – she had done that once before and it had brought her nothing but unhappiness. Instead she wore an elegant cream-coloured suit which had been tailor-made for the occasion. Harry and Phil, the nominal best man, were attired in new, light grey, tailored suits, similar to the ones they had worn for

Phil's marriage. The wedding reception was the grand finale for Aunt Harriet's occupancy of the Greengage Hill house – a month later she was to move out for good.

After the wedding – and a four night honeymoon in Paris – Harry, Amy and Rosie moved into their new home: a three-bedroom, 1930s, detached house in the nearby suburb of Compton. The couple had not cohabited before the wedding – although they had spent many nights together – because Harry was under an obligation to maintain his status as a residential master at Castlecroft College, where his small apartment was hardly big enough for a couple, let alone a family of three – even in the unlikely event of the college authorities' countenancing his extramarital cohabitation on the school's premises. And there was also the problem of Aunt Harriet, to whom Amy owed so much and whom she felt unable to abandon to the solitude of living alone in her rambling homestead. However, Harry had eventually managed to renegotiate his position at the college, with the result that, from the ensuing September, he would be replaced as assistant housemaster at Cotlake House by a newly appointed member of staff, while retaining his position as senior English teacher on a non-residential basis. The problem of Aunt Harriet was solved by her decision to sell the Greengage Hill house and use the proceeds of sale to buy a modest house for Amy and her little family, and a bungalow for herself. The bungalow she had chosen and into which she was shortly to move was a few doors away from Amy's new home, on the same road. The two Harriets would not be far apart.

Eighteen months later Harriet Rose had a little sister, Eleanor May, or Ellie, as she soon became known. Amy gave birth to her new baby in the same ward at the Royal Hospital where Rosie had been born six and a half years earlier. This time she was not alone – Harry was in attendance at the birth. The new arrival was the cause of great rejoicing in the Irving, Ostime and Anderton households. With the addition of a second child, Harry and Amy felt that their little family was complete: Rosie had long since adopted Harry as her daddy; all the bedrooms in their modest home were now accounted for; and, in any event, they both felt that two children were enough for any couple. Furthermore, Amy wanted, and needed, to go back to work as soon as she could. She had given up her job at Mercian News three months before giving birth to Eleanor, and there was no likelihood of her going back to work in the immediate future, even though Leslie Young had promised that there would always be a job for her at Mercian. There was no maternity leave and little in the way of affordable childcare, and so a third child would put an end to any realistic prospects of Amy restarting her career. The days of relying on an ageing Aunt Harriet for free childminding were now in the past. As things turned out, it was events that determined the course of Amy's future working life.

In 1982 the United Kingdom went to war with Argentina, following that nation's invasion of the Falkland Islands. The conflict did not last long – just seventy-four days – but long enough to cost the lives of two hundred and fifty-five British military personnel, including eighty-six Royal Navy seamen. Among these was Amy's brother, Roger Anderton. Doris was, inevitably, devastated by the loss of her only son, a tragedy from which she would never be able fully to recover. Amy too grieved for the loss of her older brother, and would always miss him, even though she had seen relatively little of him in the years immediately preceding his untimely death. A year later, Aunt Harriet also passed away, the day after her seventieth birthday. Her death had been expected as she had been seriously ill for several months, but it was, nevertheless, another heart-rending loss for Amy – and for ten-year-old Rosie also, who adored her great aunt and would miss her greatly. It had been a year of bereavement and great sadness for Amy, during which time she had been succoured and sustained in every way by Harry, her loving husband and steadfast rock.

The demise of Harriet Ostime changed the material circumstances of Amy and Harry quite dramatically, and for good. As a result of Roger Anderton's death, Amy had become her aunt's sole beneficiary – she was heiress to a substantial fortune. The value of Aunt Harriet's estate was such that, barring profligacy on a prodigious scale, the little Irving family need never want for anything again. All the material wealth which Amy had so coveted as a teenager, and the pursuit of which had led to her disastrous first marriage, was now hers. There would be no need for her to return to work or for Harry to remain in his teaching job, if either or both of them decided to do other things. As it turned out, Harry wanted to continue with his work at Castlecroft College, an institution of which he had grown very fond and to which he had become almost unaccountably attached. Amy, freed from the need to work for an employer and earn a regular salary, decided that she wanted to devote her future professional life to freelance writing. She had developed a great interest and significant skill in writing journalistic prose, as a result of several years of writing articles and reports for Mercian's *Elite Magazine*, and wanted to try her hand at writing pieces for other publications and for a wider audience. She consulted Leslie Young, who had wide experience of the world of periodical publishing, and an extensive network of contacts. He was extremely supportive of her enterprise and was able to put her in touch with a number of magazine editors who might be interested in her work. He also commissioned her to write a monthly feature for *Elite Magazine* – usually an interview with a local or visiting minor celebrity. The plan worked well and Amy was gradually able to build up her reputation to a point where she was being offered more work than she could handle. In due course, she moved on to writing short stories which, after a shaky start, eventually proved equally successful.

Harry stayed on at Castlecroft College, where he was to build a career spanning nearly twenty-nine years. He became deputy head in 1986 and was appointed headmaster in 1991.

Fifteen months after Aunt Harriet's death, Harry, Amy and the girls moved house. Newfound wealth allowed them to buy an imposing, double-fronted, Victorian 'gentleman's residence' in large gardens, not far from their first home in Compton – it was called The Grange. The house became their much loved, family home, where they would remain for many years, and the setting for numerous, joyful, family occasions. It was here that Harry and Amy hosted Rosie's wedding reception in the millennium year of 2000, and their own silver wedding celebrations in 2003.

Lyndon Irving died in late March, 1988, at the age of eighty-two. He and Mary, who was seven years his junior, had moved from St Bart's rectory some years earlier – Lyndon having relinquished his parish incumbency– and they had been enjoying a happy retirement in a village near Cirencester, where they had been able to acquire a small cottage. When the funeral was over and the dust had settled, Harry and Amy tried to persuade Mary to come and live with them at The Grange – they had plenty of bedrooms – but she insisted that she was still fit and well, could afford the upkeep of the cottage and wanted to maintain her independence for as long as possible. She remained in Gloucestershire, and busied herself in the Women's Institute and with parish affairs at her local church.

In September, 1988, six months after her husband's death, Mary experienced a strange and rather unsettling episode. One Friday morning in September, when she was at home in her cottage, doing some chores, there was a knock at the front door. When she opened the door, she found a stranger standing there – an attractive, statuesque woman in her late fifties, who announced herself as Mrs

Bessie Kitson. She asked Mary if the Reverend Lyndon Irving was at home.

'I'm afraid not,' Mary said. 'Mr Irving passed away six months ago.'

'Oh dear, I'm sorry,' Mrs Kitson said. 'I hope I haven't called at an awkward time, but I've come quite a long way to see him. Are you his widow, by any chance?'

'Yes I am. Is there something I can do for you?'

'I don't know... probably not, I suppose. But I've come all the way from Yorkshire – Harrogate actually – and... well, um, do you think I could come in for a minute and have a quick word? I know I should have telephoned before I made the journey, but I only had the address... no telephone number, you see.'

'Yes, I see... we're ex-directory, I'm afraid. But, of course... of course you must come in. You've come all this way. Please come in, my dear.' The front door of the little terraced cottage opened straight into the modest parlour where Mary invited her visitor to sit down on the sofa. She offered her a cup of instant coffee which she declined. Mary sat down in an adjacent armchair

Bessie Kitson was a handsome, dark-haired woman, expensively dressed and immaculately groomed. She had a most pleasant demeanour and manner of speaking, which Mary found quite disarming. After a few pleasantries, she got straight to the point: 'The purpose of my visit, Mrs Irving, was to try and obtain some information from the Reverend Irving about the adoption service which his colleague, Father Foreman, used to operate in Bradford, during and just after the war.'

'I see,' Mary said, a note of caution in her voice.

'Yes. Father Foreman passed away several years ago, so I've been unable to speak with him, but I was told that your husband may have been involved to some extent with the work, and so I was hoping to speak to him. Apparently he helped quite a lot with the work in Father Foreman's parish during the war.'

'Well, Mrs Kitson, my husband knew Oliver Foreman well... they were very good friends, in fact, and they were particularly close during the war. Lyndon helped out in the parish, as you've said, when his duties as an army chaplain allowed. But, as far as I know, it was always pastoral or liturgical work that Lyndon did in the parish. I don't think he was ever involved in the adoption service. That was very much Oliver's sideline.'

'Did he not have any connection at all with Father Foreman's adoption work?' Mrs Kitson persisted.

Mary felt that the conversation was getting dangerously close to home. She did not want to lie to Mrs Kitson, who she could tell was a good person trying to resolve something personal and pressing – and probably very distressing – from her intimate past, but she was not prepared to reveal to her visitor her own transaction with Oliver Foreman, namely the adoption of her son, Harry.

'My dear, you must understand, I was living in officers' quarters at the army barracks in Leeds at the time, where my husband was stationed during the war. I was not aware of everything Lyndon did when he went over to help out in Oliver's parish, only what he told me. I was aware of the adoption work, but Lyndon never mentioned helping with it. I really can't tell you any more.'

'No, of course not, I'm very sorry for pressing you on the matter. Please forgive me. It's just that I was so sure Reverend Irving would be able to help me. I suppose I shall just have to leave it at that.'

Mary should also have left it at that, but she could not resist trying to find out what it was Mrs Kitson was searching for so desperately. 'I'm sorry I can't be of more help,' she said, '... I wonder, are you able to tell me what it is you wanted Lyndon to help you with?'

'I suppose I owe it to you to explain myself, having bothered you like this... and while you're still probably grieving for your husband.

I'd prefer not to go into the details, but I'll tell you basically what it's about:

'I gave birth to an illegitimate child shortly after the war. I was only fifteen at the time and I'd been sexually assaulted by an older man... a so-called family friend. There was no possibility of my family allowing me to keep the baby, so they contacted Father Foreman, who was their vicar, as well as being quite well known in the area for his adoption work, and arranged for the baby to be taken away after the birth and placed with an adoptive family. The baby was taken from me by the nurses almost immediately after it was born, and that was the last I saw of him. I only got to hold him for a matter of minutes. A few years later, I got married – when I was nineteen – and had two other fine children, but I have never stopped wondering what happened to the little boy I had to give away. It has bothered me all my life. Shortly before my mother died, about a year ago, she told me that it was Father Foreman who had taken the child and arranged the adoption – I had never been told this before – and that he might be able to tell me who had adopted the child, and maybe help me to find him. Failing that I should try to contact the Reverend Irving, who used to be quite active in the parish, about the time my baby was born. As you know, Father Foreman died some years ago. The current parish priest, who still holds all the adoption records, was sympathetic when I spoke to him, but refused to give me any information – quite properly, I suppose, because all the records are strictly confidential – and so I set about tracking down your husband. And that's what has brought me here today.'

Mary was moved by Bessie Kitson's story and felt she could not allow her to set off on her journey back to Yorkshire without resting and having some refreshment, and so she persuaded her to stay for a while and have an early lunch. After the simple meal was over and Mary had seen Bessie on her way, she poured herself a whisky and water, and sat down in the parlour to reflect on what had just transpired. While they had been eating, she had become increasingly uneasy about her visitor and who she might be. She could detect very little physical resemblance between Bessie and Harry, and there was no other evidence to suggest that there might be a connection between the two – after all, Oliver Foreman had arranged a fair number of adoptions over the years, and Bessie had given no indication of the date, or even the month, of her baby's birth – but there was something about her demeanour and her manner of talking that reminded Mary of Harry. And, although Mary tried to dismiss the idea as purely fanciful, somehow, deep in her heart, she felt sure that she had just been speaking with her son's natural mother. She never told Harry or Amy, or anyone else, about Bessie Kitson's visit to her little cottage in Gloucestershire that warm September morning, and so the story went with her to her grave. Mary Irving died peacefully, at home in her bed, in the spring of 2001.

When Harriet Rose was sixteen, in May 1989, the whole family went to London for the weekend to celebrate her birthday. She wanted to see *Les Miserables* at the Palace Theatre on Cambridge Circus for her birthday treat, having been encouraged and inspired by her singing teacher to take an interest in musical theatre. The whole family had tickets for the Saturday evening performance. During the afternoon, Harry took Rosie to the National Gallery to look at the Turners and Constables, and other great paintings that Rosie wanted to see. Nine-year-old Ellie didn't fancy going to look at fine art in a 'boring old gallery' and so Amy decided to take her to Madame Tussauds for the afternoon to see the waxworks. At about five o'clock, after they had finished at the National Gallery, Harry and Rosie were walking along St Martin's Lane on their way back to their hotel, where they were due to meet Amy and Ellie and have something to eat before going to the theatre. Harry, dressed in a blue mackintosh, was still tall and slim with a full head of hair, greying at the temples, and Rosie was wearing a black leather jerkin over a pretty, green frock, her pale blonde hair tied back in a ponytail. They were talking enthusiastically about some of the paintings they had just seen. As they passed the Salisbury pub – the hostelry where Harry had gone to meet Jon Geary all those years ago, the day after he had first met Amy – Harry suddenly felt himself being grasped on the right arm by someone approaching him from behind. He swung round and was alarmed to see a somewhat dishevelled, disreputable looking man, grinning at him though nicotine-stained teeth. The man had a wasted look about him, with his grey complexion, hollow cheeks and pinched nose; and his perfectly bald pate, surrounded by unkempt, straw-like hair gave him the sinister appearance of a circus clown. He was wearing a stained fawn raincoat and looked, for all the world, like a tramp or some other type of vagrant. He smelled of alcohol. Harry tried to shake his arm free but the man's grip was firm.

'Get your hands off me, will you!' Harry said through gritted teeth. 'What is it you want?' He put his free arm firmly round his daughter's shoulders to protect her.

'Don't you recognise me, Irving?' said the man in a gravelly, educated voice, letting go of Harry's arm. 'It is Irving, isn't it... Harry Irving?'

'Yes, it is, as a matter of fact,' Harry said, unnerved that the man should recognise him. 'Who are you?'

'I'm surprised you don't know me, Irving. I thought you'd never forget me...even after all these years. I'm Daniel Swift, your old school chum.'

'What... Swift! Danny Swift! I don't believe it.' Harry studied the man's face carefully and could just about make out in his features a semblance of the Swift he used to know.

'Well, you'd better believe it, because that's who I am.'

'Well, if that's who you are, Swift, I have no wish to talk to you, now or ever. You're no friend of mine and never were, so please leave us alone and we'll be on our way. Come along, Rosie.' He started to turn in an attempt to make his escape.

'Hold on, Irving. Don't be like that,' Danny said, putting his hand on Harry's shoulder in order to stop him. 'We haven't seen each other in years and this is such an unlikely, chance meeting. Let's let bygones be bygones. How about popping into the Salisbury for a drink, eh? Have a chat about old times, over a couple of bevvies. What do you say? I'm sure your pretty little companion won't mind, will you, sweetheart?'

Rosie remained silent and nestled closer to her dad.

'I don't think so, Swift. Look, I don't know what's happened to you, and if I'm honest, I don't really care. All I know is, I don't want to talk to you, and we're in a hurry anyway…'

'…and who is your little friend then, Harry?' Danny said, looking at Rosie and ignoring Harry's attempt to get away.

'She's my daughter, if you must know… my daughter, Rosie.'

'Really?' Danny said, peering at her. 'Yes, I can see now. Yes, I see. She looks like you, Irving, just like you. She's very lovely. I've got children you know, Irving: twin boys. I don't see them though. They're in Australia with their mother, and I'm divorced. I'm afraid I've fallen on hard times since…'

Just at that moment, an elderly gentleman, dressed in a smart overcoat, polished brogues and trilby hat, approached Harry from Danny's rear and said in a clipped voice, 'Excuse me, sir, is my nephew bothering you… I do hope he isn't. He hasn't been badgering you to buy him drinks, has he? You haven't, have you, Daniel? You know I've forbidden you to go into pubs while you're staying with me.'

'No, Uncle Stanley… um, I just happened to run into Irving here, and his daughter… quite by chance, you know. We were at school together. You know, at Regis.'

'Well,' Harry said to Uncle Stanley, 'he did suggest that we might go into the Salisbury for a drink, although, to be fair, he didn't ask me to pay. We hadn't got that far.'

'I see,' Uncle Stanley said. 'Well, he hasn't got any money of his own, so you would have ended up paying.' He turned to his nephew, 'Really, Daniel, I can't leave you alone for a minute, can I?'

'Look, I don't want to appear rude,' Harry said, 'but we really must be going, we're late as it is. Come on, Rosie. Goodbye, sir… goodbye, Swift.'

'Goodbye, Mr Irving, and goodbye to you too, miss.' Uncle Stanley said, giving Rosie a slightly quizzical smile. 'I apologise for my nephew's behaviour. I just left him alone to amuse himself for an hour while I went off to sort out one or two matters of business, and I find him up to his old tricks again. He hasn't been the same since his wife left him, you know, and that's several years ago now. Anyway, I hope you'll forgive us… good day.'

Harry and Rosie left Danny and his uncle standing on the pavement outside the Salisbury. After they were well clear of the two men, Rosie said to her father, 'Who was that horrid man, Dad? He was very scary.'

'Oh, nobody really, just a fellow I knew when I was at boarding school. He wasn't like that then though, he was good looking and clever. He even got a place at Cambridge University. But I hated him… he was a sadist and a bully. Nobody really liked him.'

'It looks like he's hit rock bottom now, though.' Rosie said. 'I expect he deserves it… he's horrid!'

'Yes, you're probably right, darling.'

Later that evening, when Danny and his uncle were sitting next to each other on the tube, travelling back to Uncle Stanley's mansion flat in Swiss Cottage, Uncle Stanley said, 'It's very strange you know, Daniel: that girl we met outside the Salisbury, Mr Irving's daughter, she reminded me very much of Vera, your mother, when she was in her teens. Your mother was a very pretty blonde girl too... I was always very proud of her, as her big brother.' He mused for a while and then said, 'It's quite uncanny, really: that girl was almost the spitting image of Vera.'

Danny grunted an acknowledgement, but all he could think about was when and where he was going to get his next drink.

As soon as Rosie got back to the hotel, she told her mother the story of the horrible man who had accosted her and her father outside the pub on St Martin's Lane. She didn't mention the man's name – it hadn't registered properly with her at the time or, if it had, she had forgotten. It was only later that evening, after the two girls were in bed in their own room, that Harry revealed to Amy the identity of their assailant.

'I can't believe that it was actually Danny.' Amy said, after Harry had elaborated on Rosie's account of the incident. 'It's just... well it's just incredible... and he's a down-and-out to boot.'

'Yes, and I would very much like to have booted him,' Harry said with feeling.

'Me too. Although you know what they say, darling: you shouldn't kick a man when he's down.'

'Perhaps not. Anyway, I don't think we shall have cause to run into him again. He looked on his last legs to me.'

'I hope we never do. But I still can't get over the fact that he came face to face with Rosie like that – his own flesh and blood – and he couldn't see it.'

'Don't start that sort of talk, please, Amy. You know what I think about the whole idea of birth parents.'

'Yes... I'm sorry, Harry.'

'Anyway, there's absolutely no reason why he should have suspected anything, even if he had been his old, fully compos mentis self. Rosie was there with me, her father, and Swift has no idea who her mother is.'

'Of course, of course… but it still seems almost spooky that Rosie should come across the man who sired her like that... you know, a chance meeting in a huge anonymous city like London.'

'I suppose so. But, if the truth be told, all Swift was interested in was getting hold of some booze at my expense… or anybody else's for that matter.'

'Dear me… just think of it: Danny Swift the dashing, handsome, smooth-talking air force officer – a down-and-out drunk, scavenging for alcohol on the streets of London.'

'Yes, I reckon he's a goner, and I can't say I'm the least bit sorry for him, whatever Dad would have to say about the need for Christian charity and forgiveness. I doubt Swift will make fifty.'

Neither of them saw or heard of Danny Swift again. Rosie was never told who her birth father was, other than that he was something of a scoundrel who had deserted her mother and gone off to live in Australia before she was born, and she was able to live a happy life without knowing or wanting to know who it was that had sired her. But what Amy and Harry would never know is that Danny, with the help of his Uncle Stanley, managed to pull himself back from the brink, and slowly but surely get his life back on track. In due course, he returned to Australia, started a business with the money he had inherited when his father died, and eventually married again and had two more children. He eschewed alcohol for the rest of his life and lived to an undeserved ripe old age!

Chapter 17
Revelations

---

36   Wednesday 23 November 2005, *West Midlands Gazette*

Obituary

Henry Irving
Public School Headmaster who had a hit record with Harry and The Hawks in the 1960s.

Henry Irving, who died last Saturday, aged fifty-nine, was unique among the ranks of independent school headmasters, in having once been the lead singer and guitarist on a 1960s' top thirty hit record. *Everyone But Me* by Harry and The Hawks briefly reached number 27 in the charts in August 1966.

   Mr Irving was better known in the Midlands as headmaster of Castlecroft College, one of the region's leading independent schools. He was appointed to the headship in September, 1991, but had been on the teaching staff of the school since 1976, having originally joined as Head of English and assistant housemaster of one of the school's boarding houses. He gave a total of twenty-nine years service to Castlecroft, a period which would have been longer if his tenure as head had not been cut short in August this year when he resigned his position, having been diagnosed with pancreatic cancer.

   The fourteen years of Mr Irving's headship were a period of substantial growth and notable improvement in the fortunes and reputation of Castlecroft College. Under his leadership, there was a significant improvement in the school's performance in external examinations which, in turn, led to a marked increase in the number of sixth-formers gaining admission to leading universities. The consequent improvement in the school's reputation led to a growing demand for places, in spite of the decision to increase fees in order to improve the school's facilities. Enrolments rose by over fifty percent during his time as head. However, he was not just interested in improving examination results, he was also particularly active in enhancing the range and quality of extra-curricular activities available to pupils. He strongly believed that education was not simply about academic performance but about developing all aspects of the individual child. He was held in high regard by pupils and colleagues alike.

Henry William Irving, better known to his friends as Harry, was born in November, 1946, the son of the Reverend Lyndon and Mrs Mary Irving. His father was rector of St Bartholomew's Church in Wiltshire. At thirteen he won a scholarship to Regis College, a boarding school near Gloucester, where he excelled at rugby union and music. It was while at Regis that he discovered his interest in rock and roll, and where he formed his first pop group. After leaving school he went to Wessex University to read classics, but dropped out, after passing his first year exams, when the university pop group, which he had joined half way through the academic year and which came to be known as Harry and The Hawks, was given a recording deal by the legendary Joe Meek. The group only made one record – *Everyone But Me* – and then faded into obscurity, partly owing to Meek's suicide in February, 1967. When Henry Irving's brief pop career collapsed, he enrolled on an external degree at London University, obtaining his BA in 1972, and took up teaching. He taught at a preparatory school in Chelsea, Harbourn Grammar School in Birmingham, and Castlecroft College in Wolverhampton.

As well as having a strong commitment to his professional life, he was also a devoted husband and family man. He enjoyed opera, theatre visits, watching cricket, reading, and playing the piano. He was an enthusiastic supporter of Wolverhampton Wanderers. He has been described as 'a genial, generous gentleman with a dry sense of humour and incisive wit'. In later years, after his two daughters had grown up, he and his wife, Amy, took great pleasure in overseas travel, using their summer vacations to visit distant parts of the world. He was diagnosed with cancer in June this year, and his health subsequently deteriorated rapidly. He died in Merridale Hospice, with his beloved wife and two daughters at his bedside. He will be

> sadly missed by his wide circle of friends and colleagues. His passing will also be mourned by the many hundreds of pupils and former pupils of Castlecroft College, upon whose lives he exerted such a powerful and beneficial influence.
>
> He is survived by his wife, Amelia, and his two daughters, Harriet, 32, and Eleanor, 25.
>
> **Henry Irving, headmaster and pop singer, was born on November 9, 1946. He died of cancer on November 19, 2005.**

Harry's illness and subsequent rapid decline came as a complete shock to Amy – and everyone else who knew him. He had hardly had a day's illness throughout his adult life, and had never missed a single working day during his twenty-nine years at Castlecroft College. He was still slim and physically active, and at fifty-eight retained his good looks and much of his boyish charm. Just over two years earlier, Harry and Amy had celebrated their silver wedding with a lavish garden party at The Grange. It took place on a fine Saturday afternoon in late July, with a great gathering of friends, relatives and colleagues enjoying the sunshine in Harry and Amy's extensive gardens. Many of their old friends who came, and whom they had not seen for some years, such as Phil, Ginger, Jon and Flic, remarked on how well – and youthful – Harry looked. And he remained fit and well and youthful until the pains in his abdomen and back, which had begun in the April of 2005, became so debilitating that, at Amy's insistence, he went to see his doctor, something he hadn't done since going to have his ears syringed twenty years earlier. By this time he was beginning to lose weight and suffer from excessive tiredness. His doctor warned him to expect the worst before referring him to an oncologist and sending him for various tests. Private medical insurance, provided as part of his remuneration package as headmaster, meant that his diagnosis of pancreatic cancer was not long in coming. His condition was too advanced to warrant either risky surgery or the unpleasantness of chemotherapy, and so his treatment became a matter of purely palliative care. The need to monitor carefully the drugs used to control the pain he was suffering led to his being admitted to the local hospice for the last four weeks of his life. Throughout it all, Harry maintained a stoical good humour, which was only dampened when he was rendered excessively drowsy or semiconscious by the effects of his drugs.

Amy was aware that his condition was hopeless, and so she did her best to prepare herself for the worst. She knew she must remain strong in supporting both Harry and her daughters, and endeavoured to be the stalwart mainstay of her little family. She busied herself in looking after her husband and doing all the things that he would normally have done in keeping hearth and home together. When the end finally came, she was both exhausted and devastated. She had lost her husband, her lover and her best friend – the person she loved and liked way beyond all others, and who was completely irreplaceable. The idea that she would never see him again and that they would not now grow old together was almost more than she could bear. Harry died on November 19th, ten days after his fifty-ninth birthday, and forty years to the day after he and Amy had first met. She would never truly recover from the loss of her one true love.

As time went by, her pain and anguish were replaced by a dull ache. She tried to do some writing – she had not put pen to paper, or digit to keyboard, for over eighteen months – but initially found the process difficult, if not impossible. But eventually words and ideas started to come and she was able to complete a short piece that she felt was worthy of publication. In due course, it would be her writing that was the one thing, other than her love for her daughters, and in due course her grandchildren, that sustained her through a long life.

Of course, there were friends who rallied round and gave her support, not least her old colleague, and would-be suitor, Mike Dyke. Mike, now turned seventy and not long since retired, still lived alone in his semi-detached house in nearby Penn. He became a regular caller at The Grange to check on how Amy was coping and to ask if there was anything he could do to help. He would run errands and do various DIY jobs about the house for her. Everybody could see that he was devoted to her, if not a little besotted. Amy was aware of this and tried hard not to take advantage of the generosity and best intentions of such a good kind man, but he was always insistent that he wanted to help her as much as he could, and expected nothing in return. Occasionally they would go out to a pub or to the cinema together, and sometimes he would call for her on Sunday at midday and take her out for lunch. Mike was aware that there was almost certainly no hope of ever marrying Amy or securing her as his permanent partner, and anyway he was no longer sure that he wanted to marry again – whether cohabitation would suit him, having lived for so long on his own – and so he avoided ever doing or saying anything that might be interpreted as some sort of proposition or proposal, lest it might spoil their friendship.

Amy grew to appreciate Mike in no small measure, because of all the things he did for her: she realised just how important his company and fellowship were – not to mention all the practical help he gave in keeping things running smoothly at The Grange. In due course they would spend more time with each other; they would even go away on holiday together a couple of times, though purely for companionship. He was a true friend to her in all respects, and without him she would have found rebuilding some sort of life for herself, following the devastating blow of losing Harry in such an untimely and unforeseen way, even harder than it was.

She counted her blessings, which helped her to manage her grief. She was eternally grateful for having been granted thirty years with

Harry and for having experienced a deep, lasting love affair with him, the like of which so few of her fellow humans seemed lucky enough to encounter and sustain, even though she rued the lost ten years between their first brief affair and their eventual reunion. She was thankful for her loving daughters, both of whom seemed to be happily married and well established in the world. They cared for her and did everything they could to ease the burden of her unexpected and premature widowhood. Her work as a wordsmith was a constant source of fulfilment, and she knew how fortunate she had been to discover her flair for writing under the tutelage of Leslie Young. And when she had grandchildren – a granddaughter via Rosie and, two years later, twin grandsons via Ellie – she experienced a little of the profound happiness she had known before her desolating bereavement. As well as all of this, she was, in most people's estimation, a wealthy widow who would want for nothing as she grew old – as far as material things were concerned, at any rate.

She had long since lost her faith, but from time to time, when she went into the city centre, she would go into St Peter's Collegiate Church, an imposing fifteenth century minster, built on the site of Wolverhampton's original Saxon hilltop settlement, where she would sit quietly and alone on one of the pews, gazing at the fine stained glass window behind the high altar at the far end of the chancel, and reflect on her life and fate. And despite her grief and crushing sense of loss, she would always give thanks – to whom or what she did not know – for all the many blessings she had received in life.

* * * *

On a Friday morning in late August 2006, the year following Harry's death, Amy received an unexpected letter in the morning post. She examined the envelope, turning it over in her hands. It was obviously from a business of some sort but didn't appear to be just another item of junk mail, like the unsolicited letters she was used to receiving. It was marked *Private and Confidential*, and on the reverse, near the top of the envelope, were the words: *If undelivered, please return to DTS, Nelson House, 9, Doncaster Road, LS31 7DS.* She took the letter into the kitchen and sat down at the table to read it. She was both alarmed and intrigued by the contents of the envelope, a letter which read as follows:

22 August, 2006

Private and Confidential

Dear Mrs Irving

DTS is an organisation which specialises in tracing lost relatives for its clients, in particular children given up for adoption in infancy by their birth mothers. We endeavour to provide this service in as sensitive and discreet a manner as possible.

I am writing to you, in strictest confidence, on behalf of one of our clients who wishes to make contact with you. We have been instructed by our client to trace a child she gave up for adoption in 1946. Our research has revealed that her child was Henry William Irving, who was adopted by the Reverend and Mrs Lyndon Irving the same year. We understand that Henry Irving passed away in November, 2005, and we have advised our client accordingly. However, she has expressed a strong wish to make contact with you as Mr Irving's widow. She hopes that you will be willing to meet with her and talk to her about her lost son. She also believes that she has some pertinent information which would be of great interest to you. Our client wishes to remain anonymous at present, but we will be happy to reveal her identity in the event of your agreeing to a meeting.

I would be most grateful if you would contact me, as soon as is convenient, either by letter or telephone, to let me know whether or not you are willing to agree to a meeting with our client.

I appreciate that you may still be in mourning over the loss of your husband and I do hope my contacting you at this time has not caused you any undue distress.

I look forward to hearing from you in due course.

Yours sincerely

Lynda Swales
Executive Director, DTS

Amy's immediate reaction was to screw the letter up and throw it in the bin. This was something she could well do without: a stranger arriving on the scene, claiming some sort of emotional connection to Harry, at this stage in her bereavement. And, of course, she knew exactly how Harry would have reacted if he had still been alive, given his dogmatic, almost fanatical, views on adoption and birth parents. But something stopped her, and she put the letter back in its envelope and placed it on the mantelpiece over the cooking range, where she could see it. She couldn't help being curious, despite the upsetting nature of such a communication arriving out of the blue while she was still grieving. She was particularly intrigued by the letter's claim that the birth mother might have information about Harry of which she was not aware.

The letter remained in its place on the mantelpiece for the next two days, while Amy reflected on how she should respond. She gradually warmed to the idea of the proposed meeting. Lyndon and Mary Irving were both dead, and she and the girls had no other contacts on Harry's side of the family. There might be some comfort in developing a relationship with the woman who had carried an embryonic Harry, without now causing any hurt to his adoptive parents; and a woman who had conceived and given birth to her beloved husband could hardly be a bad person. Also, she continued to be intrigued by the 'pertinent information' which the birth mother claimed to have; the more she thought about it, the more she wanted to discover exactly what it was. However, in the end, what made Amy decide to go ahead with the proposed meeting was a growing empathy with and sympathy for another woman – a woman who had almost certainly been forced to give up her child at birth. She herself had given birth to an illegitimate child who, if circumstances had been different, might well have been taken for adoption. How would she have felt if, after decades of searching and at the very last hurdle, she had been denied access to her lost child, or her child's family, on the selfish whim of one insensitive and uncharitable individual? So she picked up the telephone and rang DTS to arrange the meeting. She was told that the name of Harry's birth mother was Mrs Eliza Kitson.

Although Lynda Swales recommended that the initial meeting take place on neutral ground, such as a hotel or restaurant, Amy felt that they should meet in private – a place where their conversation would not be inhibited by the proximity of other people, and any spilling over of emotions not exposed to public view – and so it was agreed that Mrs Kitson would come to The Grange the following Saturday afternoon at two o'clock, and stay as long – or as short – as circumstances dictated. She arrived on the dot of two o'clock.

When Amy opened the front door to greet her visitor, she beheld a handsome woman – tall, erect and elegantly dressed – almost certainly in her mid-seventies, although looking much younger: she was carefully groomed; had retained a slim, attractive figure for an older woman; and had thick, wavy hair, dyed dark brown and expensively cut in a short, youthful style. Amy, who at fifty-nine had herself remained a most attractive, slender woman, despite having allowed her hair to go grey, showed Mrs Kitson through to the main reception room: a rather grand, high-ceilinged chamber with elaborate plasterwork, a wide bay window with French doors leading onto the back garden, and an imposing marble fireplace. She invited her to sit down on one of the two sofas which faced each other either side of the fireplace. Amy sat down opposite her. She could detect very little of Harry in his birth mother's appearance, other than the fact that she was tall and slim. It was when she started to talk that the likeness instantly struck Amy. There was an uncanny similarity in her intonation and the modulation of her speech: a sort of rhythmical, almost musical cadence. And her mannerisms and facial expressions as she spoke bore a striking resemblance to Harry's. At first, Amy found listening to Mrs Kitson quite eerie and not a little unsettling but, as the meeting progressed and she found herself beginning to take a liking to her visitor, her voice began to sooth Amy and had an almost hypnotic effect upon her.

They sat and exchanged pleasantries for a little while, until Amy decided it was time to stop the prevarication and get down to business.

'So, Mrs Kitson,' she said, trying not to sound too abrupt, 'let's not beat about the bush any longer. You've come a long way from Harrogate to see me, and I think we ought to get started on the real agenda… you know: say what needs to be said and ask what needs to be asked.'

'Yes, you're quite right, we should. But do please call me Bessie; that's what everybody calls me. And is it all right if I call you Amy?'

'Yes, of course… Bessie and Amy it shall be. Now, who's going to start? Do you want me to talk about Harry, or would you prefer to begin by telling me your side of the story?' Amy had considered kicking things off by warning Bessie about Harry's strongly held views on adoption, particularly his negative estimation of 'so-called birth parents', but she had decided it would be better, and kinder, to allow Bessie to lead off.

'I think I should start, if you don't mind, Amy. I think, before anything else is said, you should know why and how it was that my child came to be given away, nearly sixty years ago.' There was a sadness of expression and a slight catch in Bessie's voice.

'I agree, Bessie. Please tell me the story... and please take your time. I can see this might be a little distressing for you. Um... can I get you a cup of tea, or perhaps something stronger, before you start?'

'That's kind of you, Amy... perhaps later. I'd prefer to get on with it right now.'

'Okay. Go ahead,'

'I'll try and keep it short, but please stop me if I start going into unnecessary detail... Right then,' Bessie took a deep breath and began her story. 'When I was fifteen, in 1946, I was raped. It was at our family home – my parents' big house in Bradford. The man was called Leonard Greene and he was a so-called family friend. He was staying for the weekend, having just been demobbed from the air force. I liked him. He played the piano beautifully and I could listen to him for ages. He was also very charming: he would tease me, in a nice way, and make me laugh. He was, of course, a lot older than me, probably in his late thirties. I never thought about him in any sort of romantic or sexual way – I was quite immature and unworldly in that respect – I just liked him as a friend of my parents... and I'm sure I never gave him any encouragement to try anything on with me. Anyway, on the second night of his visit, he came into my bedroom during the night, took of his dressing gown and got into bed with me, in his pyjamas. As I've said, I was a very naïve fifteen-year-old, and, at first, I didn't really understand what was going on. I won't go into details, suffice it to say that he started to touch me intimately, and it was then that I understood what was happening and told him to stop. But he persisted, and I found it impossible to stop him. He had his way with me and left the room.

'The next morning, after a sleepless night, I told my mother what had happened. She was a very sweet-natured woman, much younger than my distant and sometimes rather stern, but loving, father, and I was always able to confide in her. She was naturally shocked by my story but I could tell she was having difficulty believing me. So I took her upstairs to my room and showed her Leonard's dressing gown which he had left there, thrown on the floor. From then on, things happened very quickly. My mother told my father what had happened and Leonard was summoned to the library where he was challenged by both my parents. He denied everything at first, but when confronted with the dressing gown, claimed that I had invited him into my room to make love to me. That was enough for my father, who knew quite well how implausible – fanciful even – such a claim was. Leonard Greene was sent packing and was never seen or heard of again.'

'Didn't you go to the police and press charges?' Amy interjected.

'No, we didn't. It was extremely difficult to prove rape in those days, a lot more difficult than it is today. It would have been his word against mine: there was no corroboration or other evidence. And, anyway, my parents were anxious to avoid any sort of unpleasant publicity or scandal – my identity would not have been protected, as it would be nowadays.

'So, as you will have guessed, I ended up pregnant. I was removed from school and spent the duration of my pregnancy pretty well confined to barracks. I knew from the start that I would not be allowed to keep the child.' Bessie started to sob quietly. There was a lull, while she gathered her thoughts and regained her composure. 'When the baby was born, I held him for a few minutes, and then the nurses came and took him away, and I never saw him again.'

'And you had no idea what happened to him?'

'None at all, other than that he had been adopted by "a respectable couple".'

'So what happened then?'

'I got on with my life. I got married when I was nineteen to a good man, who was ten years old than me, had two fine children, both boys, and then five grandchildren. My husband died in 1987, so I've been a widow a long time. But you know, Amy, I never stopped thinking about my lost child. I've had a good life, a happy life even, but there has always been a feeling of sadness inside me, a yearning for my lost baby. It's almost like a permanent, dull ache. Shortly before my mother died, she told me that the adoption of my child had been arranged by our vicar, Father Foreman.'

'Father Foreman!' Amy said. 'I've heard that name before somewhere.'

'Yes, you will have done. He was a good friend and colleague of the Reverend Lyndon Irving, Harry's adoptive father.'

'Yes, that's right. I can remember Lyndon talking about him.'

'Anyway, after my mother died, I started trying to trace my lost baby. Father Foreman had long since died, so I couldn't consult him, and I was unable to gain access to the parish records. So I then tried to find Lyndon Irving, who used to help in Father Foreman's parish round about the time of the birth, but he too had passed away. I discovered this when I went to his cottage in Gloucestershire and met his widow.'

'What! You went to see Mary Irving?'

'Yes, I did, in 1988. Of course, at the time I had no idea she was my baby's adoptive mother, and she would have had no reason to think that I was her son's birth mother: Father Foreman had arranged a number of adoptions during and immediately after the war. Of course, she was unable to help me, but she was very kind to me. When I eventually found out who had adopted my baby, I was amazed to learn that it was the Irvings. But I was also very thankful to have met Mary, quite fortuitously, and been able to find out for myself what a good woman Harry's adoptive mother was.'

'Well, Bessie, Mary never told Harry, or me for that matter, about her meeting with you. I wonder why. I wonder if she suspected that you were Harry's natural mother, and didn't want to talk about it with us.'

'She may have done but, if she did, she certainly didn't show it.'

'So, how did you eventually find out who Harry's parents were?' Amy had become both moved and enthralled by Bessie's story.

'The law changed last year, allowing birth mothers to have access to adoption records, and then approach their lost children with a view to making contact. So from then on it was quite straightforward. I instructed DTS to do the research for me and they did the rest.'

'And that's what brings you here today.'

'Yes.'

Amy rose to her feet and went across to sit next to Bessie. She took Bessie's hands in hers and said, 'Well, I'm so glad you're here, Bessie. I have to say that I was very apprehensive about our meeting, not least because Harry had very strong views about adoption. He was devoted to Lyndon and Mary Irving, you know, and never really thought of himself as an adopted son. But now I'm truly glad you've come.'

'I'm so glad to hear that Harry had a happy upbringing and loved his parents. It's an enormous comfort to me.'

'Good. Now what can I tell you about Harry? What would you like to know?'

'Everything, Amy, absolutely everything you can tell me. But before we get on to that, there's something else you need to know... something that might come as rather a shock to you.'

There was a long pause while Bessie looked searchingly into Amy's eyes, waiting for Amy to give the signal for her to proceed. Amy nodded and said, 'Go on.'

'Well, Amy, you know me as Bessie Kitson… Eliza Kitson, if you like. That's all you've been told about me. But Kitson is my married name. I was born Eliza Anderton… in Bradford in 1930, the daughter of a wealthy industrialist, owner of the city's biggest dye works. So you see, Amy, if you haven't already guessed, I'm Eliza Anderton, your father's half-sister. I'm not just your mother-in-law, I'm your aunt too… well, half-aunt, if there is such a thing.'

'What!' Amy released Bessie's hands and sat back on the sofa, completely stunned – her mouth ajar, her eyes wide open, staring amazedly at Bessie.

'I only found out, recently. It was all unearthed by DTS, after they discovered that my son had married someone called Amelia Anderton in 1978. It seemed too much of a coincidence – the name, Anderton – so I asked them to look into it. Of course, I never really knew my big brother, Arthur… your father. I was only three when Pa disowned him. It was a terrible thing, of course… unforgiveable really. Apparently Mum did all she could to stop it, but Pa was insistent. He could be very harsh, your grandfather, although he was always kind and gentle towards me. But it means that now I've found a long lost niece, as well as my son's wife.'

'Yes, I see. But this is quite something to take in… quite something. After all, it means that Harry was my cousin. It means I fell in love with – and married – my cousin.'

'Well, your half-cousin really: you only share one grandparent with Harry, and that's my father; full cousins share two.'

'But it's incredible,' Amy said quietly, almost whispering. 'I can hardly believe it: Harry, my cousin… my lovely Harry. No wonder… no wonder!'

Bessie stayed until the evening. The two women talked for several hours and shared an early supper. They parted company as good friends, having made arrangements for a future meeting. Later on, after Bessie had gone, Amy sat quietly on her own in her grand lounge, trying to grasp fully all the implications of her newfound relative's revelations. She had always been sceptical when Harry had waxed eloquent about destiny and the role it had played in bringing them both together, back in 1965; then reuniting them, ten years later; and then determining their future happiness together. For her it had always been simply a matter of good fortune, although good fortune which she never took for granted, and for which she was eternally thankful. But now she knew that Harry had been right all along. She sat with tears in her eyes and knew for sure that theirs was a love affair made in the stars – decreed by destiny, prescribed by providence.

Chapter 18
Friday, 19 November 1965

Breakfast had been cleared away at Mrs Scrutton's boarding house. Hedley Stevens and Harry, two of Mrs Scrutton's four lodgers, were sitting at the breakfast room table, finishing cups of tea before setting off to the Wessex University campus for their respective nine o'clock lectures. It was a modest room, just big enough to accommodate a small dining table and four chairs, a sideboard and an occasional table in the corner upon which rested a birdcage, home to Joey the budgerigar – Hedley, when he was bored, took great delight in either taunting Joey or trying to teach him swear words. There was a coal fire in the hearth of the tiled fireplace, which heated not only the room but also the boiler that provided hot water for the house. The breakfast room was the only warm room in the house that Friday morning, there being no other source of heating.

'So, Irving,' Hedley began, 'you know what the arrangement is for this evening, don't you... that is if you still want a lift to London with my parents?'

'Yes, I'm still up for it,' Harry said. 'I'll meet you and your folks after you've been to the theatre, hop in the car and off we'll go.'

'And where are we going to meet?'

'Good point, Hedley. Where shall I meet you?'

'God, Harry, you're completely hopeless, aren't you? We're going to meet you outside the main entrance to the Students' Union building. Okay... got that?'

'Yes, of course. I would have remembered anyway, you needn't have worried.'

'And what time are we meeting, then?'

'Ten?'

'Eleven, Harry, eleven... Christ, get it right! The play finishes at about ten-thirty, but it'll take us half an hour or so to get clear of the theatre, collect the car from the car park and come round to pick you up.'

'Right... got it. Eleven o'clock outside the Union building. I'll be there. And thanks, Hedley... it's very good of your parents to give me a ride up to town and a bed for the night.'

'Yes, well just make sure you're there on time. My dad is a stickler for punctuality, so don't do anything to get him in one of his foul moods.'

'I'll be there Hedley, don't you worry. I'm not doing anything this evening.'

Just then Mrs Scrutton appeared through the door that led from the kitchen, wiping her hands on a tea towel. She was a short, round woman in her late fifties, with a ruddy complexion and blue-rinse permed hair. She wore an old-fashioned print dress under a stained pinafore.

'Isn't Philip down yet?' she demanded.

'Not yet, Mrs Scrutton,' Hedley said.

'That wretched boy... he's hopeless in the mornings. This is the second time this week I've had to throw away his breakfast; such a waste.' She walked through to the hallway, and yelled up the stairs, 'PHILIP! PHILIP! Get down here. You can't lie around in bed all day... PHILIP, can you hear me? You've already missed your breakfast. Now get down here this minute!' She walked back through the breakfast room and into the kitchen, watched by Harry and Hedley, tut-tutting as she went.

'Come on, Hedley. We'd better go and catch a bus if we're going to get to our classes on time,' Harry said. 'There's no chance of a lift from Phil now. He's probably still flat out.'

'Damn!' Hedley snarled. 'I hate using the buses. Why can't that lazy bugger shift his arse and get up in the morning like the rest of us?'

The two students rose from the table, went to collect their things, put on their donkey jackets and set off to catch the bus.

When Harry's lecture finished at ten o'clock, he made his way from the Humanities building to the student refectory in order to spend the next hour reading the newspaper and drinking coffee, before going off to the library to do some work on an essay he was writing. The refectory was relatively quiet as he queued up at the cafeteria counter to buy a cup of coffee and a Kit Kat. He took his purchases to an empty table by one of the floor-to-ceiling windows that ran along one side of the room, overlooking a broad sweep of tree-studded lawns, and sat down. While he was sitting there, absorbed in an article about the war in Vietnam, he suddenly felt two small, soft hands close across his eyes from someone who had approached him furtively from behind, accompanied by a female voice saying, 'Guess who?' Even though only two syllables had been uttered, Harry could tell immediately whose voice it was from the owner's Liverpool accent.

'Cilla Black?'

'Don't be daft,' Flic said, taking her hands away. 'You know it's me.'

'Hi, Flic. How's it going?' Harry said, as she sat down on the chair beside him.

'All the better for seeing my favourite, little, posh boy. What are you up to?'

'Nothing much… can I get you a coffee?'

'No thanks, handsome, I'm not stopping. I've got to go and see my personal tutor. He wants to see me about my dissertation.'

'That sounds a bit heavy.'

'Oh, it's not so bad; I don't mind seeing him. I quite fancy him really. If he'd shave that horrible bushy beard off, he'd be really quite dishy... I might even make a play for him. But he's not as dishy as pretty-boy Harry, eh?' Flic pinched Harry's left cheek gently with her right hand. 'What are you doing this evening, Harry? Me and some friends are going ten-pin bowling at the Top Rank in town; why don't you come along? It should be fun. Yeah, come with us... I'll look after you.' She looked at him coquettishly.

'Sorry, Flic, I can't tonight. I'm going to London. I've got a lift from one of my housemates. Otherwise, I'd love to.'

'That's a shame. Oh well, never mind; another time, maybe. Anyway, chuck, I'd better be going. Don't want to be late for Professor Walton,' she said, getting up to go.

'Okay Flic... see you around.'

'See you around, handsome,' she said, and then sashayed off towards the doorway on the other side of the refectory, her hips swaying in a skirt that was rather too tight for her ample posterior. As she went, she passed Phil coming in the other direction. He had spotted Harry sitting at his table and was walking over to join him.

'Who was that tart you were talking to, then?' Phil said without any preliminary greeting, sitting down next to Harry.

'Hi, Phil. That's Flic... the Scouse girl I've told you about.'

'Have you? I don't remember. Anyway, she looks like a complete scrubber to me.'

'Oh, she's all right. I quite like her, actually. She seems to like flirting with me. Anyway, Phil, you managed to get out of bed then? Did Mrs Scrutton give you a hard time?'

'Oh, just the usual stuff about having to be out of the house by nine-thirty in the morning, and wasting her precious, bloody food, which I happen to have paid for in my rent... oh, and wartime rationing and food shortages, of course, and the profligate ways of spoilt young people today. Anyway, how long are you here for? Shall I get myself a coffee?'

'Yes, Phil, go ahead. I'm here for another twenty minutes or so.'

The two friends chatted over coffee, simultaneously making a lukewarm stab at solving *The Times* cryptic crossword puzzle. Shortly before it was time for Harry to go to the library, Phil said, 'By the way, old sport, there's a dance on in here tonight. They're starting to put up the stage for the band at the far end of the refectory. I think I'm going to go... it's about time I found myself a nice girl for a little bit of the old how's-your-father. You know, I haven't had any serious contact with a bit of skirt since I've been here, so tonight's got to be the night. Do you fancy going? We can have a bit of a laugh together, and you can lend me some moral support in my search for a filly?'

'Well actually I can't, Phil. I'm going to London tonight with Hedley Stevens and his folks. I'd like to help you out but I can't. Sorry.'

'Yes, yes... I know all about your trip to The Smoke with horrible Hedley, but that won't be till later, will it? What time are you going?'

'Come to think of it, I'm not due to meet Hedley and his parents until eleven o'clock, but...'

'...well there you are then,' Phil interrupted. 'The dance starts at seven-thirty. You can spend two or three hours here with me and then bugger off to London with Hedley at eleven: QED. Come on, old son, you know girls always go dancing in pairs, which makes it almost impossible for a chap to operate on his own. And anyway, you might find a nice girl of your own, someone a bit classier than that Scouse bint you were talking to just now.'

'Look, Phil, you know perfectly well I'm not actually on the lookout for a regular girlfriend at the moment... and, anyway, stop being rude about Flic; she's all right, I tell you. But I suppose...'

Harry paused and thought for a moment, and then said, 'Okay then, I don't see why not, if it'll help you out. Anyway, The Saxons will probably be playing, so it will give me another chance to check them over.'

'Good man, Harry, good man. That's settled then. We'll go together in my car, get there reasonably early, have a bit of a bop with some nice pretty girls, and then you can push off at eleven... excellent.'

Just after half past seven, Harry was in the hall of Mrs Scrutton's boarding house dressed in his best Friday-night-out clothes, waiting for Phil to come down the stairs so that they could head off to the university together in Phil's old Morris. After a few minutes, Phil appeared on the staircase, dressed in a stylish Carnaby Street jacket and tie, and reeking of Old Spice aftershave.

'How do I look, Harry? Pretty sharp, eh?'

'Pretty sharp, Phil, pretty damn sharp; you'll knock 'em dead.'

'Good! Come on then, old sport, let's go... let's get at 'em.'

They set off in Phil's car, arriving at the Students' Union building fifteen minutes later. The Saxons were belting out their crude pop covers at an alarming volume, as Phil and Harry walked down the long corridor leading to the refectory entrance. There they bought their half-crown entry tickets from the two student volunteers who were manning a desk by the door, before entering the hall. The dance was already in full swing, the cavernous room crowded with young people: some dancing; some standing around in groups or pairs, drinking and trying to talk above the blare of the music; some just observing proceedings. The young women were dressed, almost without exception, in skirts or dresses, fashionably cut just above or on the knee; the boys in jackets and trousers, many of them wearing ties. There was not a pair of jeans to be seen.

Harry and Phil walked around the perimeter of the dance floor, on the lookout for a likely looking pair of girls who might be approached for a dance. They had agreed that Phil would decide who to ask – after all, he was the one on a girl quest. The two friends continued their perambulation for a while until Harry spotted a couple of attractive looking girls, dancing together some way off on the other side of the dance floor, and pointed them out to Phil. Phil took a look at them and nodded his approval; so they set off across the floor to where the two girls were dancing. As they came near, one of the girls glanced in their direction and saw Phil approaching. She looked aghast and, turning to her friend, quickly whispered something in her ear before taking her by the hand and briskly leading her off the dance floor in the direction of the bar.

'Bugger!' Phil exclaimed, though he could barely be heard above the noise of the band.

'Never mind, Phil. There're lots more girls here,' Harry said, consoling his friend.

'What about those two?' observed Phil, pointing out a pair of girls who had appeared on the dance floor about thirty feet from where they were standing. 'Yes, they'll do.'

It was then that Harry saw Amy for the first time. He was immediately struck – almost mesmerised – by her: she looked so very lovely, she literally took his breath away. Just for an instant – the briefest of moments – his whole consciousness, his entire field of vision, was taken up by her: he stood, frozen to the spot, unaware of the girl she was dancing with, or anyone else in the room. But then he saw Phil, already on his way, and it was clear to him that Phil was making a bee-line for Amy. He sprang into action. Completely forgetting that it was Phil, not himself, who was girl hunting and entitled to first pick, he charged past his friend, virtually barging him out of the way, and arrived at Amy's side. She turned to look at him, frowning at first – a frown which quickly morphed into the sweetest of smiles. Harry mimed a sort of dancing motion with his arms and shoulders, a questioning grin on his face, and Amy smiled back a 'yes'.

They danced together for a few minutes, the whole time looking into each other's eyes and smiling, and then Harry leaned forward and said, as loudly as he could without appearing to yell, 'I'm Henry... Henry Irving; people call me Harry. What's your name?'

ACKNOWLEDGEMENTS

Catherine Clark
Brian Stringer
Catherine Howe
Robert Clark
William Clark